MW01136028

WAR MERCHANT

Patrick Parker

This book is a work of fiction. With the exception of well-known historical events, the names used herein and the characters and incidents portrayed are fictitious and any resemblance to the names, character, or history of any person, incident, or technology is coincidental and unintentional.

Cover by Stefanie Stevenson

Part One

1

April 4, 1994
Kigali, Rwanda

L'Oiseau Blanc was a dangerous place to be—especially for a white woman at night. Although a fragile peace currently existed between the Tutsis and Hutus, tension filled the warm evening air like the calm before a thunderstorm. On a night like this every dubious character for miles would be out.

The woman entered the bar, which was located in a seedy part of Kigali. Her boots thumped the bare wood floor as she crossed the room with confidence, and sat in an out-of-the-way booth in the corner with her back to the wall. A zebra hide draped over the back concealed a large split in the well-worn leather of the booth. Dim lights suspended from the ceiling struggled to penetrate the dense haze from cigarettes, cigars, and everything else that was being smoked. Old ceiling fans hummed, but did little to move the humid tropical air. Music blared from an antiquated jukebox, but no one seemed to pay any attention to it, just as long as it played. A large corkboard covered with notes, advertisements, and business cards was nailed to the wall by the entrance. Numerous crossed spears and shields, animal hides, and skulls decorated the walls. A dust-covered wooden statue of a gorilla, sporting a sweat-stained bush hat and a sign around its neck that read Save the Gorillas, stood guard by the bar. A spear leaned between the giant beast's body and right arm, while a shield leaned on its left side.

Wooden tables filled the room, providing a place for customers to sit and drink, eat, or pass the time playing cards. For those who desired more privacy, booths were available. A number of patrons on this particular evening already exhibited various stages of inebriation. Occasionally, the gambling and booze led to a fistfight outside, which provided onlookers another opportunity to bet.

On the far side of the room, a small railing separated the main floor from the shadowy, subdued area reserved for things that happen in those kinds of places. The bar served warm beer, cheap whiskey, and a limited variety of local food not found on any healthy menu. The available meat dishes sizzled on an open grill behind the bar. It was best not to ask what kind of animal it was from. Most patrons were just glad to have something hot to eat.

Several of the men had consumed enough alcohol to obscure their otherwise discriminating judgment of the women available for the evening. Anything one wanted could be found here—anything. The bar's reputation attracted all sorts of mercenaries, thugs, criminals, and other unsavory types.

The woman in the booth looked to be in her midthirties. She was a plain woman with a full round face and wide nose—not really attractive but most certainly intriguing. She sat quietly and smoked a cheroot. Her wavy hair was long and brown, the kind a man could get lost in. Her soft-yellow cotton shirt, partially unbuttoned, showed just enough to be enticing. A delicate gold chain encircled her neck, and large round gold hoops dangled from her ears. Her makeup erred on the heavy side while her perfume, neither strong nor sweet, left in its wake a scent that was light, fresh, and captivating. She was mzungu—white, out of place, and mysterious. That in itself lent her a certain charm to those around her, especially those in the bar that night.

She was there to meet with a man. Not for pleasure, sex, or for money. She was meeting a special kind of man. A man she didn't particularly trust or like, but needed. The kind of man who didn't ask a lot of questions and was very good at what he did. This man called himself David McNair—Mac to those who knew him. Mac was a soldier of fortune and part-time safari guide. Although likely an American, he could produce passports from New Zealand, Canada, and South Africa as well as the United States. He gave his age as forty-two but his weathered skin made him look much older. Most people thought he was ex-Special Forces. No one knew whether he had retired and moved to Africa or left the Special Forces under questionable circumstances. Mac had two ex-wives and no children that he spoke of. An expert in small unit tactics, arms, hand-to-hand combat, explosives, and communications, he was also proficient in other military skills, most of which didn't need explanation. Mac didn't have an address. Anyone who wanted to see him needed only to ask around and wait for him to make contact.

The Hutu barmaid, in her shabby, faded floral dress and flopping sandals, approached the woman's booth. She scrutinized her customer.

"This dangerous place for mzungu woman like you. Sure you in right place?"

"I can handle myself."

"What you drinkin'?"

"Whisky," she replied.

The barmaid scoffed. She knew this woman meant trouble. She put her hands into the frayed pockets of her apron and went to the bar to get the whisky. Within minutes she returned with a short, round glass of cheap liquor. She set the glass in front of the woman, stood motionless and glared at her, a signal payment was due. The woman pitched an RF 500 note on the table. The barmaid scooped it up and walked away.

The mzungu woman watched a white man two tables from her set his glass down with a clack on the tabletop, and

5

stand. He adjusted his faded and worn fatigue pants and began a slow approach to her table, his scuffed jungle boots heavy on the floor. A bush hat sat on the back of his head and his black T-shirt hugged his well-defined arms. A large hunting knife hung from the right side of his belt. He telegraphed his intentions clearly as he approached. At least he thought so.

Not interested, you scum, she thought. She took a drag on the cheroot and blew the smoke upward. *Just walk on by. You've had too much booze and you're pathetic.* She continued her discreet and cautious observation of him as he advanced.

"Hey, sweet thing," he said as he slid up next to her and placed his arm around her. "You look like you could use another."

She looked deep into his eyes and replied with a cold, calm voice, "No thanks."

"The nights are long and hot around here. Drinking is about all there is to keep the shadows away."

Shadows weren't the only thing she wanted to keep away. She maintained her stare into his bloodshot eyes. Silently, she pressed the button on the handle of the stiletto she had palmed as he approached. The razor sharp blade locked into position and she thrust her right hand forward, stopping as the blade pricked the left side of his abdomen.

Even though the alcohol had already begun its numbing effects, he knew instantly he was too close and could not win this round. He froze, desire drained from his body. Expressionless, he waited for her next move.

"I said no thanks. You have fifteen seconds to unass that chair or your guts will be all over the floor," she said, her voice frosty and assured, her brown eyes motionless.

He paused to analyze his options, his eyes open wide. He slowly rose and lifted his arms. The thin, sharp blade remained in contact with his side until he stood. Conceding defeat, he shuffled away without looking back.

She took another drag from the cheroot and slowly exhaled. *Scumbag!* she thought. After he had taken a couple of steps, she collapsed the blade and returned it to the pocket of her khaki pants. She took another sip of what she suspected was watered-down Old Crow. Against the heel of her boot, she rolled the ashes off the end of the cigar and they fell onto the floor. Across the room she saw a man, wearing a khaki shirt with the sleeves rolled up, stand and grasp a rucksack by one shoulder strap. He strode toward her with a half-consumed bottle of Mützig beer in his right hand. His halfway unbuttoned shirt exposed a tight olive T-shirt beneath. He was attractive and rugged looking, with broad shoulders and a narrow waist. She took another drag from the cheroot and locked her gaze on him. When he reached her booth, he dropped the rucksack on the floor in front of him and sat. Placing both hands around the bottle, he rested his forearms on his thighs.

"Hello, Mac," she said.

"Hello, Gretchen. You handled that well."

"If you had come over sooner, I wouldn't have had to deal with that scumbag."

"I just wanted to see what you'd do," he said, before adjusting his jungle hat, exposing more of his short, sun-bleached hair. "That was the best entertainment in here all night, maybe all week."

Mac knew her only as Gretchen. He didn't really care much if that was her real name, nor did it matter whether she gave him a surname to go along with it. He was interested only in her money. And, after business of course, maybe a little sex. He hadn't been with a white woman in a while. "Nice perfume. It's exotic," he said softly.

"I thought I was going to have to cut him." She smiled as she lifted the glass to her lips.

"So did I," he replied. He paused to take a mouthful of warm beer. "People are pleased with the results. They're saying good things about you."

Gretchen made an imperceptible nod of her head as she flicked the ashes to the floor.

Mac's cryptic comment gave her feedback without revealing any information to eavesdroppers. In June of 1993 Mac arranged for Gretchen to meet with warlord Mohamed Farrah Aidid. Suspecting the US was about to go beyond just posting a bounty on his head, Aidid purchased arms and, most importantly, intelligence from her. In October, US Army Rangers and Delta Force landed in Mogadishu on orders from the president of the United States to capture Aidid and his henchmen. The intelligence Gretchen provided, however, helped deal the US forces a humiliating defeat and Aidid remained in control. The president, reluctant to risk further losses, ordered the US forces out of Somalia.

From October 1993 until March 1994, Gretchen had contracted with Dzhokhar Dudayev, president of the Chechen Republic of Ichkeria, for weapons and explosives as well as military trainers to Dudayev's forces. Mac, who was one of the trainers, led a small team that trained Dudayev's forces in guerrilla warfare. His success in training the fighters was born out in Russia's inability to quickly and decisively crush the Chechen fighters. Much praise and accolades were bestowed on his team, and Gretchen received the rewards.

She had become acquainted with Mac the year before in the Bosnia and Herzegovina war, which had been raging since March 1992. During that conflict it was suspected that he offered his services to one side then the other. Gretchen didn't bother with the details as long as he was straight with her.

"Did you bring my money?"

She pulled the envelope from beneath her shirt and held it in front of him. "Half now, half when you finish."

He turned to face her and took the envelope with his left hand. Counting it would be an insult, so he placed it in his shirt pocket. If the amount wasn't right, she wouldn't get results and she knew it. Then, with the back of the first two fingers of his right hand, he reached up and gently stroked the freckled skin of her partly exposed breast. "Ready to leave?" he asked, his brow raised as if in anticipation.

Without flinching, she took another drag on the cheroot. "Mac, I'm not one of your black whores." She lightly stroked his shoulder down to his exposed bulging muscle. "You'll have to earn it."

He grabbed her shoulder and pulled her close.

She felt his taut muscles. "I'll rattle your bones like you've never been rattled as soon as the job is finished," she said.

Although his desires were powerful, he knew not to push it with her. He released her and took another sip of beer. It took everything he had to wrestle his desires to a calm. "All right, your way. Give me the details."

She handed him a piece of folded tissue paper. "Day after tomorrow, be at these grid coordinates. Don't drive—go on foot, alone. The second set of grid coordinates is where you'll meet me. I'll bring you back." She handed him a second piece of paper. "Contact this man. He'll meet you across the border in Kabale, Uganda. He'll provide you with an SA-16 and two spent launchers. Just before you go to the firing position, put the spent tubes at these coordinates. After you fire the SA-16, bring that spent tube back to me."

"SA-16...," Mac began. "Soviet pieces of shit! A US Stinger is better."

"No, it must be the Soviet surface-to-air missile system," she said.

"That means a low-flying aircraft is the target. They're supposed to home in on airframe radiation and differentiate between flares and the aircraft. My experience with them is not that good. I suggest a backup one, just in case."

"Okay, two," she replied.

"What's the deal with the two spent launcher tubes?"

"Mac, not that you need to know, but I'll tell you. I may need you for something else." She paused and looked him in the eyes. "The two tubes you are going to plant will be found and the Hutu extremists will be blamed for shooting down the plane."

"Must be someone important on the plane."

"Important enough, but don't worry. I have ensured the missile tubes can't be linked back to you or me."

"I understand you want a fall guy for this, but this seems kind of an elaborate scheme to assassinate someone."

"My boss wants something dramatic and thinks this will be good for business. He believes the Tutsis and Hutus will get in a little skirmish and need to replenish their arms. I want you on my side on this, Mac. I'll make it worth your while."

"It'll be dramatic. Okay. Evening of 6 April, one aircraft," he confirmed.

Gretchen had agreed to pay his asking price without negotiation, and although Mac was curious about the target, he always figured some questions were better left unanswered. He looked at the grid coordinates and then at her. "Shit, that's about three and a half kilometers away."

He slid his rucksack closer to him with his foot, then opened the top and inserted his hand. A well-worn map appeared in his weather-beaten hand when he withdrew it. Using the tissue paper as a reference, he located the grid coordinates with his index finger on the map, then folded the map in about a foot square with Gretchen's desired launch location in the center, and placed it on the table. He double-checked the location with those on the tissue paper. She watched him lean over to study it, and observed his face as it slowly registered disapproval. When he looked up, he whispered, "Damn, Gretchen! That's not where I'd like to do this. Too many buildings."

"I know. Just shoot. Don't wait to see if you hit it. I'll do the watching. You just beat feet over to my location without being seen and we'll go from there." She took another drag on the cheroot and flipped the ashes on the floor again. Holding the cheroot between her thumb and first finger of her left hand, she took the tissue paper with the grid coordinates and touched the paper to the glowing embers of the cigar. When the coordinates on the paper disappeared, she ground the remainder into powder with her boot. "We'll settle up at my location," she said softly as she touched his broad chest and lowered her hand to his crotch. "Just remember what is waiting for you." She was as sultry as a summer night in Venice.

2

April 6, 1994

Gretchen sat inside the dark-green Land Rover, camouflaged by the thick, green growth so prevalent during the rainy season. She left just enough space in the cover to see where Mac was supposed to be in the savanna grassland below and the sky overhead without giving away her position to a casual observer. Her location was in the Masaka sector of the Kanombe commune on the outskirts of Kigali, where aircraft make their final approach before landing, more than five kilometers from the airport. The late afternoon rain had tapered off, and the sun was breaking through the dark clouds. Beneath the vegetation, it was already getting steamy.

Beside her, a radio tuned to the air traffic control frequency was switched off. She would only switch it on to confirm whether an approaching flight was the designated target. The jet she looked for was not due to arrive until approximately 8:15 p.m. But from 6:00 p.m. on, Gretchen switched on the radio when any flight approached in case the target arrived early. As soon as the flight identified itself and she determined it was not the target, she switched the radio off.

A small two-way radio also lay in the seat next to her. It, too, remained switched off until 6:00 p.m. She would use this radio to confirm to Mac that the approaching jet was his target. Neither would use this radio other than to confirm the target and acknowledge.

She constantly listened and searched the terrain for humans. She became a part of the forest, taking a disciplined approach to her movements, slow and deliberate, to make sure her presence did not frighten the inhabitants. Startled animals could reveal her position.

Gretchen lifted the binoculars to verify Mac was in place. She steadied the glasses and searched the field of view, section by section, looking for any unusual movement in the surrounding vegetation. *Come on, Mac,* she thought. *Where are you? I know you're there.*

She continued to search the terrain and thick grass in the area of the grid coordinates—a location in the vicinity of the road between the nearby Masaka Hill and the main Kigali-Rwamagana-Kibungo road. The location was approximately two kilometers from the Kanombe military base, where the presidential guard was based. She knew Mac preferred a more remote location with better cover and concealment for his escape and evasion to rendezvous with her, but she had chosen this location for a specific reason and paid Mac well to follow her instructions.

For the third time since 6:00 p.m., a jet approached the airport. Gretchen checked her watch, *Seven thirty.* She switched on both radios. As she put the binoculars to her eyes, she located the inbound aircraft. *It's close to the time. Mac, be awake.* She listened intently as air traffic control contacted the plane. The landing lights of the westbound jet glistened like diamonds on a necklace in the evening sky as it made its final approach. When the pilot acknowledged the tower, she relaxed and lowered the binoculars. The response was not the identification she was looking for. She switched the radios off and turned her attention to the location where Mac was supposed to be. As she scanned the area, a slight movement caught her attention. She studied that spot. "There you are," she mumbled as she watched him lower his binoculars.

Gretchen settled back to wait for the next plane and, on the slope across from her, she saw two monkeys playing. Farther down she spotted a leopard lounging in a tree and looking for its next meal. Once again she surveyed the terrain for evidence of anyone who might see her or what was about to happen. *No one in sight. Good.* As she panned the binoculars, she saw two wild dogs eating the carcass of an animal that only a few minutes before had been eating its dinner. Half a dozen vultures waited in a nearby tree for their turn. Gretchen placed the binoculars on the seat beside her. Resting her head on the seat back, she observed an Egyptian cobra as it digested a small rodent ten feet in front of her Land Rover. Satisfied the environment functioned as usual, she relaxed.

The lights of another jet appeared in the night sky and Gretchen sat upright. She switched on the radios and peered through the binoculars. *This has got to be it.* The jet approached from the east, still quite a distance from the airport but on its final approach. The landing lights of this plane—reaching out with a long arm of illumination—shined much brighter than those of the previous aircraft. She listened for the transmission between the tower and the aircraft, then checked her watch. *8:22. This must be it.* When she heard air traffic control contact the Falcon 50, she looked toward Mac's position then back to the inbound plane. It would all be over in a few minutes. So far, her meticulous planning and attention to detail had been flawless and was about to pay off.

The jet responded and Gretchen verified the target. *Mac, you're up. Don't be asleep. There's only one chance at it.* She picked up the two-way radio and held it close to her head. She squeezed the transmit button twice to break squelch—the signal to Mac that this plane was his target. He immediately broke squelch once to acknowledge her signal.

She switched off the radios and lifted the binoculars to search for Mac. Once she had him in view, she saw him rise on one knee, and shoulder the SA-16. She turned her attention to the jet, then back to Mac and then back to the aircraft. As she panned back, she saw the contrail as the missile arced upward at more than Mach 2. Focused on the jet, she anticipated the impact. Her anxiety peaked as the contrail entered her field of view. In an instant, it would hit. She expected the explosion. But the SA-16 missed its target. No sooner did she realize the missile had missed its mark than another entered her field of view.

The formerly tranquil environment morphed into chaos with the blasts from the two SA-16s as they unleashed their deadly cargo. Startled animals, frightened by the explosive noise, scattered in all directions and birds filled the night sky.

Mac had demonstrated his professional skill once again. Not relying on a single shot from the Soviet-made antiaircraft missile, he fired two. His next task was to evacuate without detection, then collect the rest of what was promised him.

The second missile connected with the aircraft's center engine at 8:23 p.m., igniting the fuel. The ensuing fireball temporally lit up the jungle and cast giant shadows, which finally dissipated. The once sleek Falcon 50, its tail separated from the fuselage, fell from the cloud of smoke and fire and crashed to the ground, erupting in fire as the remainder of the fuel was consumed.

Gretchen looked back to Mac's position and saw him sling the launch tubes of the spent SA-16s across his back. With an abrupt turn of his head, he made a quick search of the area before he darted out. He sprinted in one direction then another in a meandering course designed to throw off anyone who might be following. The limited visibility of the dark sky afforded him some concealment as he moved. Gretchen strained to follow his movements but lost sight of him when he disappeared into thick vegetation. She examined his route to see if anyone was following him and was satisfied he was alone. After several minutes of scanning the area, she caught a glimpse of him moving rapidly across the terrain. He stopped and went to one knee. She knew he was searching, using his senses, to determine whether he was still alone. Methodical and disciplined in his egress, Gretchen knew it wouldn't be long before Mac arrived.

She smoked a cheroot as she sat on the side of the Land Rover seat with the door open. Her green shirt was unbuttoned enough to partially expose her bulging breasts. Mac appeared out of the darkness, walking up the rise to her location. His camouflaged shirt was drenched in sweat. He removed the two tubes from around his neck as he stopped in front of her to drop them at her feet, a signal of mission complete. Next he slipped off his rucksack and set it on the ground. He reached for his canteen and quaffed almost half of its contents before lowering it.

"Glad you could make it, Mac," she said, then took a drag on the cheroot.

"I'm getting too old for this shit!" He took another drink.

"You did well. Two quick shots."

"I never trust those pieces of crap."

Mac removed his wet shirt and examined it for a dry place, wadded the shirt in his hand with the driest place out, and wiped his face and arms and down his chest. His muscles glistened in the moonlight. He took another long swig from his canteen and set it on the Land Rover's fender. After another swipe of his face, arms and chest, he stepped between her legs, reached for her cheroot, and took a drag from it.

"Have you ever made love in the moonlight?" She began to give him all the signals he hoped for.

"I'm looking forward to the first time." A slight smile began to emerge.

Gretchen slid her hand on top of his and took the cheroot between the first two fingers of her right hand. She lifted it slowly to her lips and, holding her gaze steady on him, took a drag.

"Did you bring my money? We need to settle up and get the hell out of here," he said, wiping his face again.

"What's your rush? We've got plenty of time. Besides you've got one more thing to do."

"What?"

"Bury the tubes. Then we'll settle up."

Mac retrieved the short, D-handle shovel from the back of the Land Rover and started digging. He dug a trench the width of the shovel blade and about a meter and a half in length. Occasionally he paused to wipe the sweat from his body and drink more water. Gretchen lit another cheroot and stepped close to the hole when it was about eighteen inches deep.

"Gretchen, I don't usually ask questions but my curiosity has got me on this." He jabbed the shovel into the bottom of the trench. "Who did I shoot down?"

"The president of Rwanda," She blew cigar smoke upward and adjusted her glasses. After she dropped her two radios and Mac's into the hole, she pulled an envelope from under her shirt and handed it to him. "The rest of your money, Mac."

"Shit, Gretchen!" He stood stock-still and held the envelope in his right hand. "What'd he do to piss you off?" He pitched the envelope of money into his open rucksack.

"He decided he didn't want to play ball."

"Huh?" he responded as he dropped the spent launch tubes into the trench.

"The peace between the Tutsi and Hutu is very precarious at best. Selling arms to both sides is worth a lot of money. In fact, the hostilities all across Africa are good for business." She paused to take another drag on the cigar.

"But the president?"

"Last August the UN-brokered Arusha Peace Agreement was signed in Arusha, Tanzania. President Habyarimana agreed to share power with Hutu opposition leaders and Tutsi RPF guerrillas. The agreement integrated the armed forces and called for twenty-five hundred UN soldiers to be deployed in Kigali to oversee the peace process."

"Yeah, I remember. So?" Mac responded. "They'd still buy weapons."

"My boss had tried to persuade Habyarimana not to go forward with the peace agreement. It seems that the President developed a conscience. That was going to cost him a lot of business if the UN Peacekeeping force came in. When the president refused his persuasion, and bribe, that pissed him off."

"I'm no fan of Habyarimana, but that's a pretty dramatic step," Mac replied.

"My boss is a ruthless bastard you never want to cross. When he learned of this trip he had me planning, checking, and rechecking the assassination. I didn't have any other choice. He didn't want any mistakes and wanted to influence the outcome. This was the planning trip for the interim government."

"I remember hearing about it. It was a big deal in the news," Mac said.

"The interim government for Rwanda was to be in place until multiparty elections could be held. That was supposed to bring peace to the region. That meant no arms sales or, at best, very limited sales.

"The power and privileges of the members of the government were threatened by this power-sharing agreement, and the Hutu extremists were enraged by the arrangement. My boss understands the situation and how fragile the peace is, if that's what you would call it. The president's key staff, most of who were in agreement with the president, was on the plane with him. That was all the better."

"Nice company you keep, Gretchen."

Gretchen withdrew a small tube that appeared to be lip gloss from her pocket and twisted off the cap, exposing the small ball on the top used to apply the liquid. Just as she was about to touch the tube to her lips, she paused. Instead, she reached toward him and slowly rolled the ball down his chest to his waist.

Mac read her intentions and smirked as his excitement began to build. He allowed the liquid to remain on his chest as a sign of acceptance, figuring that wiping it off could be a subtle signal of rejection. "Gretchen, as long as I have known you, you have never mentioned anything about your background." He paused to wipe his face again. "How did you get in this business?"

She recapped the small tube and returned it to her pocket. "There isn't much to tell, really. I lived in Hanau until I was about thirteen when my parents were killed in a car wreck, I was put in a foster home, and about a year later I ran away. I couldn't make the adjustment, too young I guess." She paused, then flicked the ashes off the cheroot. "I met a lady in a Frankfurt park not long after I ran away, and she hired me to help her around the house. We got along great. Sometimes we'd talk for hours. She convinced me to go back to school and on to Cambridge. That's it really."

"Well, how did you get into this business?"

"Enough questions. Break out that bottle of bourbon you keep in your rucksack."

He picked up his rucksack and pulled out the bourbon and a canteen cup, which he poured about a third full. After he took a sip, he passed it to Gretchen. She took a sip, and then held the cup in front of her.

"Have you got another one of those?" Mac pointed at her cheroot.

"Sure." Gretchen stepped to the Land Rover and refreshed her cologne before removing one of the small cigars from the pack.

"Bring your binoculars back with you," Mac said as he covered the hole.

"Here you go." She pitched the cigar underhanded to him.

He moved toward her, gazing into her eyes, and touched the glowing end of her cigar to his. Once it was lit, he cupped his hand around the end of the cigar to shield the red glow from observation. He raised the binoculars to observe the crash site. "It's getting busy down there," Mac said as he handed the binoculars to Gretchen.

She inspected the site and studied the people who searched for survivors and worked to extinguish the fires. Satisfied they were still interested in the crash site, she checked the rest of the terrain to see if their position had been compromised.

"Damn this stuff has a kick to it," Mac said as he lowered the cup after taking another swallow.

He examined the bottle to confirm the brand he was drinking. Surprised at the sluggishness and slight dizziness he was experiencing, he sat on the ground by his rucksack.

"You probably just got overheated," she said, looking at him. "It is pretty steamy."

"Maybe." He took another drink of bourbon.

"Just relax for a minute. You'll be fine." She kept him thinking he was being affected by the heat more than anything else.

He was smart and might figure out what she had done. She wanted to keep him off base as long as possible. If he figured it out too soon, he would kill her. She had to continue her seduction as long as possible. She watched him dig into his rucksack and pull out three aspirin tablets, which he popped into his mouth and washed down with bourbon.

Headache, good, she thought, maintaining her demeanor. *Abdominal pain and nausea should be next. It'll be no time now until he starts convulsing.* She used every opportunity to flirt and make sexual innuendos. Knowing her cologne would envelop him in the humid night air, she moved close to him and slowly stroked his arm. Then sliding her hand down across his, she took the cup and pretended to take a drink, but really only wet her lips. She then kissed him gently so that he tasted the bourbon. As he reached for her, she returned the cup to him. "Don't rush things," she said. "I like to enjoy the buildup. You won't regret it." She took a drag on the cheroot.

Her breasts heaved with each breath she took and inflamed his excitement. Mac drank from the cup without dropping his eyes from her. He enjoyed her toying.

As the cup passed back and forth between them, she kept up the pretense of drinking and continued to flirt. With each of his responses, she closely monitored his motor skills and eyes. As the progressive signs of poisoning became increasingly apparent, she began to relax.

Mac drank from the cup several times, and Gretchen refilled it twice. Finally, he put it down and looked her in the eyes. A blank expression washed over his face. "You bitch!" he said, his teeth clinched and brow furrowed. "You poisoned me!"

She stood and picked up the shovel. He struggled to stand and staggered toward her only to fall to the ground, clutching his stomach. Gretchen turned and dropped the shovel into the Land Rover as Mac tried in spite of his pain to crawl toward her. Glancing at him, she picked up his rucksack and made a systematic inspection of its contents. When she saw nothing inside to tie her to Mac or that location, she pocketed the envelope of money. Mac began to convulse slightly at first, then progressed to violent muscle spasms.

"I told you I was going to rattle your bones like you've never been rattled," she said to him with the rucksack in hand. "I guess you never will make love in the moonlight."

He was in a coma by the time she had the Land Rover ready to depart. After making a final check to ensure no trace of her was left, Gretchen pulled out of the camouflaged position without lights. She was more than a mile away before switching them on. The rucksack and its contents were scattered along the way.

Mac had entered the ecosystem and become a part of it. Before his remains could be found there would be nothing left—the bones stripped clean and scattered across a wide area. Most would never be found. If they were, there was nothing to tie him to the crash. Everyone would assume he died or was killed by an animal and his body eaten by scavengers.

The broadcaster interrupted the radio in the Land Rover with the breaking news of the jet crash, which was flashed around the world:

President Juvénal Habyarimana of Rwanda and President Cyprien Ntaryamira of Burundi, along with their key staff representatives, were killed in a plane crash. The two presidents and their staff were killed when their jet went down as it was on final approach to the Kigali Airport. President Ntaryamira of Burundi was a last-minute addition to the manifest....

Gretchen switched off the radio. *President Ntaryamira was on board, too. Hmm. Clay has his confirmation and Ntaryamira could be an added benefit. That should get him off my back for a while,* she thought.

Within hours of the crash, the organized slaughter of the opposition leaders, the Tutsis, and the moderate Hutus began. Civil war was what she and her boss expected to happen, and it was good for business. Almost one million Rwandans would be killed before the carnage would end.

Part Two

3

May 2, 1995
Brussels, Belgium

The young concierge watched the striking woman as she stepped down from the dining room level. She carried her slender body with poise, moving with confidence onto the marble floor of the reception area of the five-star Hotel Le Plaza on Boulevard Adolphe Max in Brussels.

"Would you like a taxi, madam?" he asked with a smile, eyeing the diamond pendant suspended on a gold chain nestled in her cleavage.

"No, thank you." She smiled in return but never broke her stride as she proceeded toward the brass-trimmed revolving glass door.

She carried a leather briefcase in her right hand as she walked along Boulevard Adolphe Max toward the Grand Platz. A few puffy clouds drifted high in the blue afternoon sky and a slight breeze swirled about making it a perfect day for a walk. People strolled along the wide pavement; some stopped to window-shop or enter one of the glass-front businesses. She hadn't gone more than a block when a Mercedes limousine with darkened windows slipped up beside her. The window on the back right opened and bluish cigar smoke wafted out.

"Get in," a man's deep voice said. His tone was harsh.

She paused to look at the man inside. Two gold chain bracelets around her right wrist sparkled in the sunlight as she brushed her auburn hair back and reached to open the door. As soon as she was inside, the car pulled away. Dydre Rowyn sat across from Clayborne Zsigmond.

She shifted her position, adjusted her dress, then looked out the limo's window as she waited for him to speak.

Although Clayborne Zsigmond was the name on his business card, he was commonly referred to as the Fat Man. His close associates called him Clay. He was a large man with a thick, full neck and thinning dark hair, gray at the temples. His title read International Trade Consultant. In reality he was a black market arms broker; he also maintained an impressive private military company, sold intelligence information, and created markets for weapons, ammunition, and explosives—a power broker.

The surprising end of the Cold War had left both superpowers not only without plans to demobilize huge armies and navies but also ill-prepared for the power vacuums that suddenly appeared in the new nonbipolar world. Prosperous defense contractors were suddenly faced with the loss of their biggest customers. Their survival depended on developing new opportunities, and scaling their operations to meet the changing demands. Developing countries seeking to rid themselves of the vestiges of colonialism and emerge from the superpowers' sphere of influence were now free to pursue regional interests, unconstrained by colonial-era borders or the interests of their patron states. Many regional people also saw this as an opportunity for independence from states dominated by dictatorship, or a ruling minority. Exploiting these cultural and political fault lines would build a fertile ecosystem for the arms trade.

Zsigmond used the situation to create opportunities for both supply and demand—often supplying both sides like he did between the Hutu and Tutsi civil war in Rwanda.

He puffed his cigar a couple more times, then said, "Dzhokhar Dudayev sends his regards. He's very pleased with the trainers you sent for his forces."

President Dudayev, she thought. *Don't like him, but he paid well. The only chance he had against the Russian army was to fight a guerrilla war and demoralize the Russian soldiers. My guys were the best ones to teach his military to wage that type of fight.*

Zsigmond had arranged for Dydre to meet with the president of Chechnya, Dzhokhar Dudayev, the previous November—just prior to the Russian invasion. When she met with him in Grozny, President Dudayev, a former Russian air force general, contracted with her for military trainers. These corporate soldiers from the West were the best trained experts in guerrilla warfare. The term "military trainer" skirted the definition of mercenary—the more politically correct term for these contract experts.

"Clay, please, that cigar!" She lowered the window and fanned the strong smoke. "Roll down a window or put it out!"

He glared at her, then placed the Montecristo Gran Corona in the ashtray and brushed an ash from the leg of his custom-made suit. Offering her a manila envelope, he said, "Your next task, my dear. Bosnia. A Saudi Arabian named Osama bin Laden has a nice little setup going in Bosnia, Chechnya, Pakistan, and several other countries. He's the kingpin of a terrorist organization called al-Qaida and has a humanitarian agency fronting his operation. He's using the money he gets to arm the Muslims. He'll be good for business."

She just looked at the envelope and said, "Clay, I've told you before I don't like doing business with those fanatic

Muslims, and besides, they don't like doing business with women."

"Dydre, take the envelope. I'm in no mood to repeat myself!"

"I don't want to do this anymore—"

"You what?" His face turned red with rage. Exploding in anger, he slapped her; his large hand with thick fingers covered half of her face. "You want to quit me? You don't just quit me! You'll do what I say, when I say. I don't give a damn whether you like them or not. If it wasn't for me, you'd still be on the streets. It was my money that put you through school and took care of you when you got pregnant. Besides, I told you to stay away from that army captain."

Dydre struggled to maintain her composure. As she glanced to the front of the car, she caught the watchful eye of the driver. She stared angrily at Clay, then at her briefcase. *Now's not the time*, she thought. She slowly took the envelope. Her thoughts shifted to Johanna Zsigmond. *Why did you have to die, Johanna? I need you now.* The childless woman had seen in Dydre what she thought her daughter might have been like. The woman hired the homeless and dirty teenage Dydre as a live-in domestic and assistant. Their relationship grew and Dydre ultimately filled a void in the older woman's life. At that time, Johanna was struggling with cancer and wanted to spend the rest of her life as a mentor to the young girl.

Johanna taught her the romance languages and sent her back to school. At every turn she stressed the arts and languages. Dydre developed her talents in theatre and martial arts, focusing on jujitsu in high school. Upon graduation, she was immediately accepted into Cambridge, where she continued with theatre and jujitsu and became accomplished in both. During her junior year the woman died and Dydre, grieving, took the rest of the year off. *Johanna was so proud of me*, Dydre thought. *She was more than a mother. She was my best friend.*

Dydre scrutinized the Fat Man's expression as he released the envelope, then said, "That army captain had a name—Michael Barron."

"Hmm," Clay said, his face wrinkled.

"Did you kill him?"

"Don't be ridiculous, Dydre!"

Halfway through her senior year, Dydre had become pregnant. She and Michael were to marry just before graduation, but he was killed in Bosnia a week before the wedding. Following graduation, she moved back into Clay's house, where he supported her during her pregnancy and taught her his business. When her baby was born, he employed the best au pair for the infant boy until he was old enough for a private school. It wasn't long until Dydre was well immersed in the business, increasing Zsigmond's profits. Professionally, she was skilled and talented but her personal relationship with Clay steadily deteriorated.

Clay had become contemptuous and bitter after Johanna died, and sensed Dydre was about to leave him. He became so cold and ruthless that he no longer had friends, and she found it difficult to be around him. Although she managed to stay at arm's length, she was in no position to leave him. His hold over her was too strong and, for now, they had a compromise. He penetrated her only weakness—her son.

Zsigmond picked up the cigar, inserted it in the center of his florid face, puffed a few times, then returned it to the ashtray. "I'll tell you when you can quit, Dydre. Besides, you've got David to think about," he said, referring to her son.

His message was clear. She knew exactly what he meant. She just stared at him.

"Your dossier could end up, anonymously, with Interpol," he added. "So don't get any ideas about being gallant."

"When am I supposed to contact Kingpin?" She asked without opening the envelope.

"Kingpin—an appropriate name—is expecting you to call the al-Qaida facilitator in Bosnia, Yasir Rashid Jamaal, and set it up." Clay withdrew a photograph from inside his coat and handed it to her. It was the photograph of a young boy of about six years of age wearing a school blazer from Switzerland. The boy was standing in a park and smiling, a photograph taken for Dydre. "David sends his love."

She traced the photograph of her son as if to feel his skin, then slipped it into her purse. "Can I see him this weekend?"

Her thoughts drifted back to when David was still a baby and she would hold him. *His soft skin, and the way he smelled.* She had nurtured him and watched him grow. *He was so funny and awkward when he was learning to walk. I'd get tickled, and he'd laugh with me. Then I'd scoop him up and wiggle my nose in his little, round stomach, and he'd laugh more.* The two played for hours, his smiles and laughter vivid in her mind. She never wanted Clay to hire an au pair, but he wouldn't have it any other way. Even after the au pair arrived, at every opportunity, she'd spent time with the boy, bathing, dressing, and feeding him. Then Clay had her traveling and doing more for his business. The nights and weekends away from her son were the hardest for her; she tried to make up for the lost time when she returned, but she seemed to be spending less and less time with him. Then one day Clay sent him to a private school in Switzerland, which crushed her. David was growing fast and she felt both of them were being cheated. This made her resent Clay even more.

She missed the woman who had changed her life. If Johanna were still alive, Dydre knew that she would love and care for David as a grandson. Clay never showed affection, and didn't love the boy. She knew Clay used David as a pawn to keep her from leaving, something that wouldn't be easy and could be deadly. He was capable of killing her or, worse, her son. She tried once before to leave and break his control over her, but he sent two of his thugs to bring her back. Fuming, Clay slapped her around but stopped just short of beating her. He warned her at that time to never try to leave again, and she knew he would go to any length to keep her there. Dydre vowed that day to escape Clay's hold. Even though she knew she was watched at all times to ensure she wouldn't take David and leave, she planned to do just that—somehow.

Clay smirked when she tucked the picture into her purse. "I'm sorry my dear, he's going on a field trip this weekend. I'll arrange a visit when you finish this task." he said with a sneer in his voice.

"Drop me off at the Grand Platz."

"Do you have any questions?"

"I assume you gave me a complete package and all the details are inside?"

"Yes." Clay picked up the cigar and placed it in his mouth.

Dydre frowned. "I have a little problem."

"What is it?"

"My information supplier at the Pentagon wants out."

"Offer him more money."

"He's scared. Ever since the arrest of Ames in February last year, they're all under intense scrutiny. He's worried they will find him."

"You know what to do." He puffed on the cigar. "How long will it take you to develop another source?"

"It shouldn't take too long. I'll just need to spend a little time in DC. Tysons Galleria is always a good place to start."

"While you are in the States, check out this company and see what you can work out with them." He handed her a copy of the international defense magazine *Armada International* and a large manila envelope. "They're promoting a new tool they've developed. You can read about it. I've received several inquiries already. In the envelope is detailed information on the company and background. I think you'll find them eager to take our money."

Dydre glanced at the dog-eared page as his large finger tapped the small article halfway down the page circled in red. "Do you want to buy their product?"

"No, Dydre," he said, puffing the cigar. "If their product is what they say, buy the damn company or at least controlling interest."

"If he won't sell?"

"Do what you have to do to get control of it. Their product will be good for our business. They're a defense contractor, which gives us another avenue into the US government. There's a big emphasis on IT security. The new term is *cyber security*."

"We're branching out to computer security?"

"No, we're expanding our information capability, Dydre. Keep me informed. I'll probably need some information soon about NATO plans in Bosnia." His tone, more of an order than request, meant fast.

"I'll call you if I have any questions." When the car pulled to a stop, Dydre got out and walked into the Grand Platz.

4

Austin, Texas

Two large men in their midthirties, with broad shoulders, narrow waists, and close cropped hair, entered the double glass doors of IT Security Solutions, Inc. The company's name in six-inch letters spanned the wall behind the receptionist's desk, and an overstuffed chair with lamp and table set to the side of the desk. Against the wall, beneath a colorful painting of a pheasant, a large bowl of chocolates sat on a narrow, glass-topped table. Several community and industry awards hung on the opposite wall.

A slight bulge beneath the left arm of the men's dark suit jackets revealed they were not paying a social call. One of the men, a couple of years older and slightly taller than the other, cupped a folder in his left hand. Their expressions were serious.

The twenty-two-year-old blond receptionist looked up from her computer and greeted the two men with an instant smile. "Good morning!"

"George Reynolds, please," the older of the two said.

"May I give him your names?" She appeared unaware of the 9mm beneath his left arm.

"Kennedy and Clayton."

"I'll let Mr. Reynolds know you wish to speak with him." Stepping from behind her desk, she swiped her security badge on the reader next to the door, then opened it. She didn't see the two men step behind her and follow her into the corner office.

George Reynolds, an overweight man in his midforties, worked at his computer terminal with his back to the door. The fashionable office was well furnished and several paintings, awards, framed newspaper articles along with his university diplomas hung on the walls. A couch and two side chairs framed a glass-topped coffee table. His curved, modern desk faced the door, while the computer sat on the credenza behind his desk. Two floor-to-ceiling adjoining glass walls formed a corner behind the credenza and offered an impressive view from his ninth-floor office.

Reynolds was the CEO of IT Security Solutions, Inc. Since his early retirement from the air force seven years earlier, he had worked to build up the company he founded. The majority of their contracts were with the Department of Defense. Reynolds, holder of a PhD in computer science and a master of science in electrical engineering, had developed a software tool that could search out and identify all the vulnerabilities in a computer system—the product in *Armada International.*

Driven by the need to survive in the marketplace against the larger, more established companies, Reynolds had focused on becoming more efficient in the performance of his work. He started out manually performing computer certifications and accreditations for the military; part of this process was securing computer systems and fixing all the known vulnerabilities—both unclassified and classified. He spent his evenings and weekends writing computer code and experimenting with different routines. He then developed the algorithms that led to the creation of a software program that could identify all the vulnerabilities in the system automatically. He used the program, testing it on each system, in the performance of his contracts. It wasn't long before he had sufficient capital to hire someone to help him with his business so he could concentrate on further development of his program. He realized he had invented leading edge technology that could be used by the military as a weapon to bring down an adversary's computer system, gain information from them, or simply rearrange data on any of their systems or industrial processes.

The business plan he devised for his new product enabled him to obtain investor capital needed to take his product to market. For the past six months, without success, Reynolds had targeted his efforts on selling his invention to the American military.

The receptionist entered Reynolds's office and said, "George, Mr. Kennedy and Mr. Clayton are here to see you."

"What company are they with?" he said without turning around.

"They didn't say."

"Thank you," he said with a hint of frustration in his voice. He let out a sigh before he stood to turn and face her. The sight of the two men directly behind the young woman gave him a start. With brown eyes open wide, he stared through the gold-framed aviator-style glasses that emphasized the bags under his eyes. The company name, embroidered in red, embellished the white polo shirt he was wearing.

The receptionist turned, only to bump into the man with the folder. Red-faced with embarrassment, she said, "I'm so sorry, excuse me." She left the room.

"Yes, I'm George Reynolds. What can I do for you?" he said in a stern voice.

"I'm Kennedy, this is Clayton," the older man said. The younger man closed the door.

"What is it you want?" Reynolds made no gestures to the men to sit.

"I'm from the Defense Intelligence Agency," Kennedy said. "And Special Agent Clayton is from the FBI."

Special Agent Clayton showed his credentials to Reynolds.

"Here is a number you can call to verify who I am," Kennedy said as he showed Reynolds a slip of paper. "I'm sure you will recognize the area code and prefix as that of the Pentagon."

A stunned expression crossed Reynolds's face when he saw the 9mm pistol beneath Kennedy's arm and the bulge beneath Clayton's arm. The two men sat down and Reynolds followed suit. "What do you want with me?"

"We came to talk to you about your product—Ranger, I think you call it."

Reynolds immediately relaxed and launched into his well-rehearsed sales pitch. He assumed the brash young men were there to talk to him about buying his product.

Kennedy interrupted. "Our meeting isn't to buy your product. Nothing related to our meeting will leave this room."

Reynolds tensed. He leaned back and crossed his arms over his chest.

"This meeting didn't happen," he continued, then sat momentarily in silence. "We have reliable information that a foreign entity is interested in Ranger." He flopped an open copy of *Armada International* magazine on his desk. "Ranger has garnered some interest from some people whom we would prefer not to have such a capability."

"Well, is the Defense Department going to buy it?" Reynolds shot back in defiance.

"Our engineers have their doubts about Ranger and your claims." he replied, his stern demeanor unchanged. "However, they did check with some of your current customers and your performance is good."

"What's your point?" Reynolds glowered at him.

The phone on Reynolds's desk rang. Kennedy looked at the phone, then to Reynolds—his eyes said it all. Reynolds got the message and didn't answer it.

"We've researched your company," Kennedy said. "We know you're out of money and spent your investors' capital foolishly, and without accountability. We know your investors are pressuring you and are probably about to call their notes due, which will force you into bankruptcy. You are behind on paying expenses, and on three occasions over the past six months, you were late on paying salaries. We also know you diverted some of the investor capital for your own use and you are living beyond your means. We consider your company at risk, and if Ranger is as stated, we view you as a security risk."

Then the stone-faced Clayton took over. "We have a proposition for you."

"What is it?"

"We want to put someone in your office to handle the transaction if the company is contacted as we suspect. You'll train the person to become an expert on Ranger. Of course, our person will be undercover and work as a business development person—in every respect. Everyone in your company has to believe our person is a business developer for your company. No one can suspect a thing."

"Okay, guys," Reynolds said. "I don't believe any of this bullshit. I'll call your bluff. Where's that phone number?"

Reynolds took the slip of paper from Kennedy, punched in the numbers on the phone, and locked his gaze on the two men while he waited for someone to answer.

"Operations, DIA, Colonel Jamison speaking," the voice on the phone said.

"My name is Reynolds and I—"

"Yes, George. I thought you might call." The voice was sharp but professional. "I take it that Kennedy and Special Agent Clayton are there talking with you, and that's why you're calling me, correct?"

"Yes...they are."

"They're a couple good men. They're on the level and straight shooters."

"How do I know you're really who you say you are and this is the DIA?"

"What kind of proof do you need, George?"

"Well…I'm not sure…"

"When you figure out what proof you need, feel free to call me, anytime. For the meantime, I suggest you hear out those two men. Is there something else you need, George?"

"No, not for now."

"Good day, George." The phone went dead.

Reynolds returned the receiver to the cradle, then sat back in his chair. "The man said I should listen to you. So, continue."

For the next several minutes Clayton and Kennedy outlined the planned sequence of events and emphasized that no one from his company was to be involved. They reviewed in detail what they expected Reynolds to do and what they would do. "Any questions, George?"

"Look, guys, this cloak-and-dagger shit could get one of my employees hurt. I think I'll pass. Good day, gentlemen."

"George," Clayton said. "We're actually going to rent your company for this operation. Besides paying you, we'll have DARPA test your product. If all goes well and Ranger is as claimed, you'll receive a nice little contract from the Pentagon."

"If I don't agree?"

"Well, let's see…. You failed to register and license this technology with the State Department, you failed to notify the government that you have an officer in your company who joined the Communist Party several years ago, if you don't take our offer you'll be bankrupt and forced to close your doors in a week. We'll pull your security clearances, have your existing contracts cancelled for nonperformance, and you'll be placed on the suspended contractors list. Ranger, along with all of the programming code and records, will be confiscated for national security reasons. Oh, and by the way…you're a retired officer. Better check your retirement papers—remember they say 'subject to recall to active duty at the discretion of the Secretary of Defense.' The Antarctic is nice this time of the year. Does that answer your questions?"

The humbled Reynolds had no choice but to agree.

5

May 12, 1995
Washington, DC

Steve Albritten sat across from Melinda in a secluded, dimly lit section of the Old Ebbitt Grill. It was a trendy place known for excellent food and impeccable service, where the wait staff catered to every detail, including discretion. The ambience was of Victorian décor with high ceilings; and paintings, reminiscent of the city, adorned the walls. The award-winning restaurant, only two blocks from the White House, was a popular meeting place for politicians, locals and tourists. Steve and Melinda sat in the Atrium dining room, their table draped with starched linen and heavy silver dinnerware.

"Bourbon on the rocks," she said to the waiter. As she leaned toward Albritten, enticing him with her partly exposed breasts, she said, "Steve, have a drink. Relax." She placed her hand on top of his and stroked it lightly.

"Bourbon for me, as well."

"Why are you so uptight tonight?" she asked as soon as the waiter left. She then grasped his hand with both of hers and leaned in closer to make sure he was enveloped by her exotic perfume.

"You have no idea how tight security is now at the Pentagon."

She ran her fingers across his cheek, allowing her hand to linger on his face.

"I shouldn't be here," he said.

"It'll be fine. You're allowed to have a personal life," she said, her voice soft and sensual.

"Would you like to order now?" the waiter asked as he set the drinks on the table.

"Not just yet," she replied.

"I, I…Melinda, I don't know." Taking the glass, he downed half of the drink.

"That'll make you feel better. Now just relax and don't worry about anything." Melinda rubbed his leg with her foot and added, "Let's have a nice evening. I'll take care of you." She motioned to the waiter to bring another round of drinks. At every opportunity, she played to his masculine instincts— displaying intriguing amounts of cleavage, touching and stroking.

Not allowing his bourbon to run dry, she ordered a third drink before he knew it. She refrained from business talk, which would come later, and gradually transformed the nervous man into an eager male. She continued to work him through the course of dinner and bottle of wine. When the waiter brought dessert—crème brûlée and a glass of dessert wine—she knew it was time to strike.

Melinda sat poised, then leaned forward to offer him another alluring glimpse of things to come as Albritten finished the last of his wine. She brushed her wavy black hair behind her ears and withdrew a cheroot from her bag.

Albritten lit the small cigar with one of the matches from the restaurant matchbook he had picked up when he entered. In an almost continuous motion, he leaned forward on the table and crossed his arms, dropping the matchbook into his shirt pocket. A subtle move she had missed when she returned the packet of cheroots to her bag. The alcohol and Melinda's flirtations had cleared all worries from his mind for the time being. His guard was down, and other things were on his mind.

"I'm sorry you want out, Steve," she said. "We were getting along so well. I can give you…well, let's call it a retainer for the future."

"No, I can't. It's too risky. I should've never done this in the first place." He glanced around to see if anyone was paying attention to them.

"Why? You needed the money and I provided it. No one will ever know who you are, unless *you* tell them."

"It's just too risky. I told you, they're scrutinizing everyone in the command center as well as information recorded in the command center's logs. Nothing is being overlooked. I just want out." He took a drink of his water.

"All right, if that's the way you want it." Melinda took out a small bottle that looked like lip gloss and removed the cap. She started to apply the liquid but stopped just before she touched her lips. "Let's go back to my hotel." She leaned close and whispered, allowing him to take in her perfume again. Then, with a flirtatious laugh, she rolled the end of the tube down his face.

Smiling, he turned and signaled for the waiter; Melinda replaced the cap and returned the tube to her purse. He wiped the liquid from his face with his hand and looked at it, grinning, then wiped his hands with the linen napkin and dropped it on the table.

The two walked out of the restaurant toward the parking garage just down the street. "Follow me to my hotel," she said.

"Which one, in case we get separated?"

"The Sheraton, by the Navy Annex. But don't worry, I'll keep you in my rearview mirror."

Steve Albritten, Division Chief, National Military Command Center, J-3 Operations Directorate at the Pentagon, never made it to her hotel but he did make the morning paper.

7:05 a.m.
May 13, 1995

"Yes, sir. I'll pick up Hector and we'll check it out," FBI Special Agent Alice Johnson said into the phone. The tall, thin woman stood, drank the last of her coffee, then dialed a number. Alice, on a special assignment, worked on the Aldrich Ames case and was instrumental in the arrest of the Central Intelligence employee on espionage charges. She was more butch than feminine and had a foul mouth that would embarrass any sailor. The forty-three-year-old agent was brutally abrupt and direct, which caused her more problems than anything else.

On the third ring, Hector Sanchez answered. Working with Alice on special assignment, the Miami-born Cuban was a senior analyst and Human Intelligence (HUMINT) expert from the Defense Intelligence Agency (DIA). He had the keen mind of someone much more senior with twice the experience.

"Hector, Alice," she said.

"*Alleese!* Good morning, *dahling*," he replied in a high-pitched voice full of surprise.

"Cut the shit, Hector. Meet me at the office ASAP."

"Now? I was just going out for a run."

"Fuck the run!" she said, her tone harsh. "Listen, you little shit, get your tight ass in gear and meet me at the office. We've got some work to do."

"On Saturday?"

"Yes, sweet pea. Now get going."

Alice picked up Hector at their office in Tysons Corner and tore out of the parking lot before Hector closed his door. She wasted no time in heading down VA-123 toward DC.

"Alleese," Hector said. "You know, you should do something with your hair. And I think if you added a little color to your face, you'd look pretty good." Hector fingered her hair as he offered his grooming tips in reference to her short, brown hair and lack of makeup.

"Knock it off, Hector!"

"Alleese. I'm just saying I think you should try some makeup."

"No thank you," she said, her voice sharp. "And my name is Alice. Can't you say Alice? For as long as we have worked together, you still won't say Alice."

"I did, Alleese."

"Hector, you're a case. How did you ever get a master's degree if you can't speak correctly?"

"I went to college, Ms. Johnson. Where are we going?"

"To the emergency room at George Washington University Hospital."

"Ooooh! Alleese, I don't do emergency rooms. They have that smell."

"Tough shit! Suck it up, bucko. Steve Albritten was killed in a car wreck last night. The boss thinks it's under weird circumstances and we need to check it out."

Alice identified herself as FBI and introduced Hector when they met the attending physician just before the end of his shift. The doctor told them that it appeared to be a typical car accident where alcohol was involved.

"He was drunk, high blood alcohol, .09% I think. Suffered head and neck injuries, and internal bleeding. He probably died on impact. From his injuries; I'd say he wasn't wearing his seat belt."

"Anything else?"

"That's about it. Pretty straightforward—drunk driving."

The information seemed cut and dried, but Alice remembered what her boss said just before she called Hector:

It just seems odd that he was on our watch list and met with a fatal accident—just too coincidental. But the evidence just didn't support anything else.

"Doctor, could I see what was in Albritten's pockets?" she said. It wasn't a question.

The doctor paused. He started to ask why, but knew the FBI woman wouldn't give any answers, only ask more questions. "The nurse will give you a bag with what little he had in his pockets." He nodded to the nurse behind him.

Hector took the bag from the nurse, stepped to the counter, and dumped the contents out. He made a list as he examined each item. Alice checked the wallet.

"It's just the usual stuff," the doctor said. "Billfold, comb, penknife, matchbook, change, and a tube of ChapStick."

"Thank you, Doctor," Alice said, then left.

From the hospital they drove to the Arlington police station, a place she avoided if she could. Alice knew she would probably run into Captain Jordan—she would rather eat worms than meet up with him—but she needed to read the accident report and talk to the officer who worked the accident.

As soon as they entered the police station she heard Jordan's voice. She followed the sound to his office where she found him on the phone with his back to the door. The captain's desk was a mess. The in-basket overflowed with papers. A small mound of folders spilled their contents, and two dirty coffee mugs added to the clutter. Memorabilia from his years of service were displayed on the wall and on a nearby bookshelf. Two chairs were in front of his desk and a couch hugged the wall.

The husky Jordan turned around as he hung up the phone and saw the two standing in front of him. "Well, well, well, Special Agent Johnson…to what do we owe the honor of the FBI's presence in our station today?" Jordan's sarcasm was thick.

"Cut the crap, Jordan. We're here on business."

"Who's your protégé?" he said with a nod of his head.

"Hector Sanchez, DIA—"

"You poor son-of-a-bitch," he said, then smiled at her.

"Jordan, I need to look at last night's accident report on Steve Albritten and talk to the investigating officer."

"So, you finally pissed off one of the big guys and they assigned you to look over the shoulders of municipal police. That's beautiful!" He laughed.

"Jordan, are you going to help me or continue to stand there and be a pain in my ass?"

"Why is the FBI interested in a DWI accident?"

"Don't get your balls in a knot. There's nothing to it. Since he was a DOD employee, I have to check out what happened," she said.

He studied her in silence for a moment. "Come with me. You be sure and let me know if there's more to this than just fact-finding. This is my turf, you know."

The police report read like the doctor's report—a case of drunk driving. The investigating officer estimated the speed at sixty-five miles per hour. The officer believed Albritten lost control of the car, struck the guardrail, then overcorrected, which caused the car to roll over. The police listed it as DWI.

6

At her office, Alice again studied the contents of Albritten's pockets, including the matchbook from the Old Ebbitt Grill. She sat behind her tan metal desk and leaned back with her arms crossed.

Hector, cross-legged with his feet propped on her desk, studied her for a minute. "What's next, Alleese?"

"I'm not sure. Nothing supports anything other than a car wreck, but I agree with the boss that it's too coincidental."

"Follow your hunch," he said. "If Albritten was the one who leaked information and you didn't want him revealing who he leaked it to, what would you do?"

"But why would a government kill him if they received information from him? If he gave them info once, he'd probably do it again."

"That's what we need to find out, but first we need to make sure this wasn't an accident."

Alice requested a copy of Albritten's photograph from the Pentagon. Their next visit was to the Old Ebbitt Grill. *It could be the lead we need*, she thought. *Or just a dead end. Dinner at that restaurant doesn't necessarily mean anything, but we need to check it out.*

The police wrote it off as a DWI. Nothing justified anything else. If, on the other hand, Albritten had had dinner with someone, that could be significant. If that was the case, she needed to keep her investigation quiet. After all, she hadn't briefed the boss yet. He encouraged initiative but he also expected to be kept informed. She didn't want him receiving any phone calls until she could brief him personally.

Alice and Hector entered the Old Ebbitt Grill. She flashed her ID to the young waitress and said, "I'd like to speak to the manager."

The unnerved waitress scurried off to look for the manager, who appeared within a few minutes. Alice once again flashed her ID. "Did this man eat in here last night?" she asked, showing the photo to the woman.

"I don't recognize him," the manager said, taking the photo from Alice. "But let me check with the staff."

She returned a few minutes later with a tall, slender waiter.

"You are asking about this man?" the waiter said with an Italian accent. He handed the photo back to Alice.

"What can you tell me about him?"

The waiter paused to consider. "Yes, I served him," he finally said. "He had drinks before dinner and wine with the meal. Dessert and wine afterwards. He seemed nervous and tense when he arrived, but as the meal progressed he relaxed. What did he do?"

"Was he with someone?"

"Yes. Normally, I wouldn't have paid any attention to them, but she was all over him."

"Can you describe her?"

"Yeah, she was white, slender, shoulder-length black hair, probably in her midthirties. They sat at a table in the Atrium dining room. It has an outdoor atmosphere and more privacy. She smoked a cheroot after dinner," he said. Hector jotted down the details as the waiter spoke.

Alice and Hector questioned him for several more minutes to see if there was anything else he could add to what he already told them. He couldn't. But as they turned to leave, Hector stopped and asked, "Did you overhear anything they said?"

"I got kind of busy...back and forth to the kitchen." He paused, with a grin spreading across his face. "Then it started getting interesting. I think she did invite him to her hotel."

"Did she say which hotel?"

"I think she said the Sheraton. I'm not sure...I think she said the one by the Navy Annex."

Alice wheeled into the portico of the Sheraton National Hotel located just up the hill from the Navy Annex and screeched to a stop in front of the entrance. She and Hector walked into the grand entrance with its high ceiling and marble-tiled floors. The well-lit, spacious, and inviting interior immediately conveyed a relaxing atmosphere. They marched to the front desk, her heels clacking on the shiny floor, where Alice produced her ID and demanded to speak to the manager. The woman behind the desk escorted the two across the expanse to the wide staircase with its glass sides and brass handrails. At the top of the stairs the desk clerk led them through a glass door into a small reception area outside the manager's office. She asked them to wait there, entered the office, and within a few minutes reappeared.

"Ma'am, this is Carlos, my manager," she said, then excused herself.

Alice made a quick study of the stocky Hispanic man with dark hair. He was smartly dressed in a blue blazer embroidered with the Sheraton logo on the pocket.

Alice produced her ID and said, "We're looking for a woman that we think stayed here the last couple of nights. Can you help us?"

"I'll do my best. What did she do?"

"She's white, slender, has shoulder-length black hair, and is in her midthirties," Hector said.

"That's hard to tell. You've just described many of the women that stay here. Can you be more specific, or is there anything special about her?"

"I'm afraid that's all we have right now."

"Let's check with the bell captain. He has closer contact with the guests than I do." The man led them back downstairs.

But after talking with the bell captain for several minutes, they were no further along than when they first arrived.

"I'm sorry, I just don't remember the woman," he said. "I'll check with the night shift and give you a call. I'm sorry I can't be of much help, but sometimes people come and go without our seeing them...although there was one lady last night I remember. It could be the woman you are looking for. Your description vaguely fits her. I never saw her check in but I saw her leaving a couple of nights in a row. I haven't seen her check out."

"Thank you," Alice said. She turned to Carlos. "I'd like you to check the registrations to see what women checked in, alone, over the last three days."

"I'd like to help you but—"

Hector squinted his eyes closed and tightened up his face, bracing for Alice's wrath on the man.

"But, my ass!" she said, her voice carrying across the room. "I'm conducting a goddamned investigation and I don't have time for your namby-pamby shit! If you don't help me, and right now, I'll cause you more aggravation than a bad case of hemorrhoids. Have you got that?"

The man paused. His expressionless face turned red, and he muttered under his breath, "*Puta!*" He took in a deep breath, looked her straight in the face, and replied, "Yes, Ms. Johnson!"

"Good. Then check the list and tell me what women have checked out since last night. I also want to know if any women who checked in within the last three days are still registered. Have you got that?"

"It'll take a little while but I'll get it as fast as I can."

"We'll wait over here." She pointed to the couch and two wingback chairs by the revolving door.

Within ten minutes the manager returned with a computer printout. "Seven women who checked in over the last three days are still registered in the hotel," he said. "Seventeen have checked out between last night and this morning."

Alice handed the printout to Hector. "Go back to the office and research these women. Find out all you can. Don't leave anything out."

"*Dahling*, you know I'm good and thorough. What you gonna do?"

"I'll stay here and check out the seven women still registered."

"You could probably get your hair done while you are waiting on me to get the information."

"Get a move on, Hector!" she said.

7

Alice wandered through the lounge area, bar, and restaurant without success. None of the women there resembled the description. After finding the restrooms vacant, she headed to the elevators to check out the seven rooms, all dispersed throughout the hotel's sixteen stories. Four women were in their rooms but none of them matched the description. Frustrated and tired, Alice returned downstairs to watch for the three absent women to return. She sat on the couch by the front door reading the *Wall Street Journal* and observed the people as they entered and left the hotel.

Hector called her about the time she finished the paper.

"Alleese, *notting* has turned up so far on any of the women. I'm waiting for verification on the three that gave overseas addresses but don't expect to get anything back until tomorrow."

"Okay, good," she said. "Go on home and call me in the morning. I'll wait here for a while longer. Maybe the women will turn up."

"Do you need anything?"

"No, I'm fine."

"Alleese, you be careful."

"Good-bye, Hector." Restless and realizing she hadn't eaten all day, Alice went to the restaurant, checking the bar and lounge on her way.

When she finished dinner, she returned to the last three rooms again. Two women had returned but didn't match the description. She stood by the large window on the fifteenth floor, down the hall from the final room, and looked at the evening Washington skyline. For a few minutes she allowed herself to mentally enter the nightlife in the city. "Another Saturday night home alone," she said to herself. "Damn, it's been over six months since I've heard from Andy, and before him, Chuck. Why am I having so much trouble keeping a man? It seems like it's getting harder to find one. I guess it'll be me and the two dogs at home, again. They just don't quite do it even though they are always glad to see me. God, what a life."

As Melinda entered the Sheraton's lobby, she scanned the spacious room and noted the normal routine before she stepped into the elevator.

When she exited on the fifteenth floor, she looked down the hall and saw a tall, thin woman in black pants and jacket, looking out of the window. After a few steps toward her room, Melinda saw the woman turn around. Melinda smiled. The woman started toward her. Melinda sensed danger but maintained her stride and pretended not to notice the woman. *I bet she's FBI*, Melinda thought. *They all seem to dress the same, like they were stamped out by machine and there was only one outfit for women and one for men—black.* Her poise intact, she calculated what to do. She didn't want to act too soon in case the woman in black was a guest and no threat to her. But the woman could be following her. *No way they can link me to Albritten's death*, she thought. *But what's she up to?* Melinda, who had been trained by the best in Europe, remained alert. Although she was tired, she wasn't about to relax as long as she sensed danger. Most people get caught when they let their guard down for just a minute or get overconfident. She was not about to do either.

As the woman neared, Melinda saw the bulge on her right hip. *I knew it. She's FBI. Now what's she doing?* Melinda, undaunted, continued to her room and when she turned the corner, she caught a glimpse of the FBI woman following behind. Keycard in hand, Melinda inserted it and entered the suite. The door latched and she flipped the night lock over for the added security. A few seconds later came a knock at the door.

Melinda ran her eyes around the room to make sure everything was in order. When she opened the door, she found herself face to face with the tall woman, holding up her FBI identification.

"I'm Special Agent Johnson and I'd like to ask you a few questions."

"All right. Come in."

Melinda checked the hall to see if anyone else was there. She then turned and sprang toward the agent. She grasped the lapels of the woman's jacket, dropped to one knee, and flipped her. Johnson, caught off guard, tumbled over. Instinctively, she grabbed Melinda and flipped her over. Johnson was now in the dominant position and as she lunged forward, Melinda blocked her advance. She threw the agent off by pushing to the right and bringing up her left knee. Johnson crashed into the ottoman, turning it on end, sliding it back. Melinda came across with her foot and struck Johnson in the face—her body went limp. She was out cold.

Melinda stood and exhaled. She removed the woman's 9mm SIG SAUER P228 pistol and pitched it on the bed. She then reached behind the woman, retrieved the agent's handcuffs, and slid them into her own pocket. She grasped the woman's arms and dragged the limp form into the bathroom. "This must be your lucky day," she said to the unconscious woman as she handcuffed her to the water supply pipe of the toilet. "I don't have time to fuck with you now, and this is the wrong place to leave a corpse. You should never have followed me."

Melinda wiped the pistol as well as everything else she touched to remove any fingerprints. She then removed her black wig and stripped off her clothes, laying her dress on the bed. She stepped barefooted to the bathroom and wasted no time peeling away the latex on her face. After she washed away the residue, she combed her auburn hair, donned her dress and jewelry, and applied a light amount of makeup. Not quite content with her hair, she brushed and blew it again with the hair dryer. Satisfied with her appearance, she packed the remaining articles, leaving no evidence behind. Once again she checked to make sure the handcuffed woman was still out cold. She grasped her bags and left the room, hanging the Do Not Disturb sign on the door. Dydre Rowyn walked out of the hotel.

"Alleese! Alleese, *dahling*, are you all right?" Hector asked as the paramedic finished cleansing Alice's cut lip.

"It's Alice, and hell no, I'm not all right! I just spent the night cuffed to the goddamn toilet after getting the shit kicked out of me."

"She's fine," Hector said as he straightened up. "Alleese, your eye…I think you're going to need to wear some makeup. You're going to have a real pip."

At that moment Captain Jordan sauntered into the room. "I'm glad to see you had a peaceful night there, Johnson," Jordan said, unable to resist the opportunity to razz her. "What the hell happened? Did you finally find someone you couldn't whip? Did you try to run some prostitute out of here or was it the *trick* that fucked you over?"

"Fuck off, Jordan. I'm in no mood for you."

"I told you this was my turf. Now what's going on?"

"Just an identification problem," she said, through clenched teeth.

"Johnson, you're on my turf and I want to know what's going on."

"I'll tell you when I have something."

"If you don't I may blacken the other eye myself."

"You'd better bring an army."

Frankfurt, Germany

"Don't worry, Clay," Senator James Griffith said. He settled his burly body more comfortably in the limo's leather seat and inspected his cigar before putting it in his mouth. "The US sees Chechnya as a Russian problem."

"Thank you, Senator," the Fat Man said, as he topped off his passenger's glass of single-malt Scotch.

"And here's the latest CIA assessment on Africa." Griffith pulled a thick envelope out of his inside coat pocket.

The Fat Man frowned. Griffith hadn't bothered to disguise the contraband documents—he was handing over an envelope with the logo and address of the Senate Select Committee on Intelligence in the upper left corner. Careless. But if the fifty-two-year-old Democratic senator was a careful man, he wouldn't be riding around the streets of Frankfurt in Zsigmond's Mercedes.

The Fat Man pulled an envelope from inside his own coat and handed it to the senator.

"Another contribution to your campaign fund," he said.

The senator took the envelope and tucked it unopened in his coat pocket. He patted his neatly trimmed hair, no doubt checking that his receding hairline was still camouflaged. Zsigmond suspected Griffith was anticipating the other rewards he would receive tonight in return for his latest installment of intelligence—dinner at one of Frankfurt's most exclusive restaurants followed by the expensive prostitute who would be waiting when the senator returned to his suite at the Le Méridien Parkhotel.

Griffith would never know about the suite's other amenities—the hidden cameras and microphones to record the evening's adventures—unless, of course, he ever developed a conscience and balked at fulfilling one of Zsigmond's requests.

"I want to know if the US plans on putting the CIA back on the ground in Afghanistan," Zsigmond said. "Keep me up to date. Osama bin Laden is buying a lot of arms and has several training camps set up there for his terrorist, fanatical brothers. I want to know what is going on there before the president knows."

"Have I ever failed you, Clay?"

"No. I just don't want there to be a first time."

If the senator perceived the note of menace in those words, he forgot about it as the Fat Man refilled his glass. Griffith leaned back and watched the streetlights of Düsseldorfer Strasse slip past outside the limousine's smoked-glass windows.

8

Monday, May 15, 1995
The Pentagon
Office of Assistant Secretary of Defense for Command,
Control, Communications, and Intelligence (C3I)

Roger Newport entered the conference room within the sensitive compartmented information facility (SCIF), a secure vault where the most highly classified information was discussed, processed, and stored. It had been specially constructed to prevent eavesdropping by any means, and all communications devices—computers and telephones—were specially certified to be used in this environment. No mobile phones or any other wireless devices capable of sending or receiving messages were allowed. The conference room, furnished with the most modern presentation equipment and an oval-shaped walnut conference table and chairs, resembled most any corporate boardroom.

Hector Sanchez stood, examining the paintings of military themes and crests of the different branches of the military that adorned the walls.

Already seated and talking with Special Agent Alice Johnson at the conference table was FBI Senior Analyst Mary Ellen O'Malley, a plump Texas woman with the reputation of being able to ferret out information. It was said that she could find the needle in a haystack, then link it to the thread in a haystack ten miles away.

"Good morning, everyone," Assistant Secretary Newport said as he entered, pausing to greet each one of them. Newport, a retired US Army lieutenant general, always took the time to know his subordinates. "That's quite a shiner, Alice. How are you doing? Feeling okay?"

"I will as soon as I get my hands on that bitch."

Distinguished looking and cordial, Newport—the kind of person that you immediately felt comfortable with and trusted—didn't display the ego as did many of the senior executives in the government. The handsome man instilled in everyone who worked with him a desire to excel above and beyond their self-imposed limitations. Detail oriented with an almost computer-like mind, he remembered minor details from conversations that happened a year before. Very little escaped his observation and nothing escaped his recall.

Newport officially formed his top secret team after the Department of Defense concluded their formal, four-month investigation into the humiliating debacle in Mogadishu, Somalia, in October 1993. The investigation found no internal leaks or security lapses that would have resulted in the failed operation. Even so, Newport was never convinced of the investigation's accuracy and suspected someone was leaking classified information. Unofficially, he formed this team when he was briefed approximately one month prior to the final release of the probable results of the Defense Department's investigation. Renewed emphasis on internal security leaks began as a result of the arrest of CIA employee Aldrich Ames. This arrest gave Newport the ammunition he needed for creating his team.

This select team was so secret that, other than these four, only the secretary of defense, the directors of each of the agencies of the individuals in the room, and the president knew of its existence.

Newport sat at the head of the conference table, opened his folder and said, "Alice, I saw your notes this morning. Is there anything else you can add to your report?"

"No, sir. I've gone over the entire sequence a dozen times and I still can't come up with anything else. We know she was seen with Albritten, then disappeared after we tangled. We're running the name she used to register at the hotel and I'm sure it's bogus since she paid for the room in advance with cash. The only other thing I can tell you is she's got some impressive martial arts skills."

"Mary Ellen, run the description worldwide," Newport said. See if it turns up anything. We need to find this woman ASAP."

"I've already sent it out. I'll find her if she exists."

"Hector, has anything else...anything surfaced on our leak?"

"*Notting* yet, sir. I'm still coming up with a blank."

"Hector, it's *nothing* not *notting*," Alice said in a low voice as she leaned close to him.

"Stay focused on this woman, everyone. She is our key...and all we have. I also think it is too coincidental that Albritten had a fatal accident when he was on our watch list. Alice, does Captain Jordan have anything else on the accident?"

"He's convinced that it's drunk driving."

Their meeting continued for more than an hour as they explored every avenue. This was the first solid lead the select team had had since they started their investigation into possible security breaches. Their patience and discipline were finally starting to reveal new information, however so slowly. They wanted whoever was leaking the classified information alive so they could learn the extent of the penetration and what was divulged. A dead suspect reveals nothing.

"Alice, you and Hector search Albritten's house," Newport said. "Look through everything and see what you can piece together...he must have left something behind that will give us more to go on. I don't want the local police or anyone else to know what you're doing. Don't tell them anything. We must keep this investigation quiet as we don't know who else may be involved.

"Mary Ellen, can you dig into Albritten's finances and see if he had unusual expenditures or income? If he had any, follow the trail."

"Yes, sir. I'll get the subpoena right away."

"Don't let the bureaucracy get in the way with our investigation. If anyone runs into a roadblock, let me know immediately," Newport said. "Also, get his phone records. Check if NSA has anything on his mobile phone. This doesn't make sense. Normally, when an insider commits espionage he isn't killed off. He goes dormant to be used again later."

"Yes, sir, that's what has me confused," Hector said. "If he was about to be caught and they knew it, whoever was running him would just have backed away and let him take the fall. Killing him doesn't fit."

"I know. But it's all we have so far. Does anyone have anything else?" Newport asked. He made sure each understood their respective instructions on what needed to be done. They all agreed that finding this mysterious woman Alice had tangled with could be the break they needed to get their investigation moving. Newport knew his team would find the woman and he could put his plan into effect. What he didn't know was when they would find her and where she would lead them.

"Mary Ellen, let me know as soon as you get anything on the woman," Newport said. "This is the best lead we've had in months. Stay focused everyone."

9

Austin, Texas

Dydre checked into the four-star Hyatt Regency under a false name as usual. Timing her arrival for when the clerks were busy made it less likely for them to remember her. Prior to departing Washington, DC, she had arranged to meet George Reynolds, CEO of IT Security Solutions, for dinner at Fonda San Miguel. When he suggested a one o'clock meeting at his office, she told him that business in DC would prevent her from arriving before five, and that she had only a short time in Austin.

"I've got to return to Europe," she said. "But I do want to meet with you as soon as possible."

"Well, why don't we meet for dinner?"

"That would be great, George. I am looking forward to meeting you and discussing your product, Ranger." She went on to ask numerous questions about Ranger, just as he would expect from a potential client. He gave a pitch short and businesslike in response to all her questions and said he would tell her more over dinner.

Fonda San Miguel, located in south central Austin, received consistent ratings as the top Mexican restaurant in the area. The décor resembled an Old Mexican hacienda—plants filled the courtyard, and the restaurant's decorations featured Mexican antiques, hand-thrown pottery, and Talavera tiles. Mexican paintings hung on the walls throughout. Waiters lit the candles on the tables as the guests were seated.

Dydre, dressed as Sam, with a wig of wavy brown hair and extra padding in the right places, would play her part perfectly. To be sultry on this first meeting was not part of her plan. That would come later. Timing was everything in her business and she knew how to deal with men. No man was immune to her charm after she got to know him, which didn't take long. From information provided by the Fat Man, she knew Reynolds needed money and sales—that was to her advantage. She pegged the CEO as a techie that was naive about the business world but very smart in his field. She pictured him with a big ego as well.

Reynolds, although instructed by FBI Special Agent Clayton to notify him or DIA Officer Kennedy immediately if someone inquired about Ranger, neglected to do so. He planned to meet Sam alone as she requested. Wearing a blue blazer, blue shirt and khaki pants, Reynolds arrived at the restaurant at 7:30 p.m.

As he approached her table in the secluded corner she had chosen, she stood and extended her hand. "Mr. Reynolds? I'm Sam. It's a pleasure to meet you."

"George, please," he said as he took her hand. "Thank you, the pleasure is mine. Did you have any problems getting here?"

"No problems. George, again, I'm sorry for the quick meeting, but I'm interested in your product and wanted to have this meeting before I head back to Europe."

Businesslike and slow in her approach so as not to alarm Reynolds, she directed the conversation. Dydre kept it light as they ate queso flameado and sipped margaritas. Gradually, she began to inquire about Reynolds and his background.

"My last assignment in the air force was at the Air Intelligence Agency in San Antonio and before that I spent six years at NSA," he said.

"All of your career has been in computers?"

"Computer security, actually. I was a computer security expert in the air force and got to work on some pretty big programs. Then about seven years ago, I took early retirement. I took what I learned in the air force and started my own business."

"Well you certainly have the background. What's next for you?"

"I'll ramp up my company, sell it, and retire on the beach someplace."

"Sounds like a nice plan." Dydre took it all in as she got to know the man—his likes, dislikes, and plans for his future. All of which could be useful in due course.

Reynolds tried to be evasive as to his future plans, but he was no match to her and yielded quite a bit of information. *His comments beg more questions,* she thought. *He's trying to be someone he isn't.* When the main course of Enchiladas de Mole Poblano arrived, Dydre said, "I've read about your product Ranger in *Armada Magazine.* Tell me about it. I'd like to know more. I'm very interested."

Excited at what seemed to be a prospect, Reynolds fell into his sales pitch. "Every computer has security vulnerabilities in the software that runs the hardware. When the different pieces of the system are put together, additional vulnerabilities can be created by the addition of these components...like the printer, routers, hubs, even copiers and scanners. New vulnerabilities are being discovered daily."

"Really? I had no idea," she said, her tone convincing.

"Most people don't. That's the problem. It's a full-time job to patch these vulnerabilities, and most organizations don't put the effort into keeping their computer systems up to date with the latest patches. Even the diligent system administrators within the government and military have problems keeping up with the new vulnerabilities."

"Another drink, ma'am?" The waiter stood next to Dydre as he interrupted Reynolds's spiel.

"Please," Dydre replied with a smile.

"Sir?"

"I'll have another, thank you," Reynolds said. Turning back to Dydre, he picked up where he left off in his presentation. "As I was saying, system administrators are human and they can get complacent, don't have the time or just aren't diligent enough to apply the patches to their system. No computer system is one hundred percent secure."

"That's where Ranger comes in?" she asked.

"Correct. Ranger is a revolutionary device, about the size of a handheld personal organizer that can reveal all the vulnerabilities. We keep the product updated with the latest information. As new vulnerabilities are discovered, we update Ranger with the new information regularly—either through the Internet or we can send out a disk."

"So, that should make computer systems more secure," she said. "I see. And if the computers are not up to date—"

"You got it! Within a few minutes I can gain access to a computer system by exploiting its vulnerabilities. Then, if I want, I can rearrange or delete files on the computer, change data, add information to a document, or plant a malicious code in the computer. I can do all this without the system administrator or database administrator knowing."

"I'm impressed. How is that possible?"

"A computer, as you type the keys, releases electronic emissions that can be captured with sophisticated equipment. These emissions contain data from the computer. They exist, for example, at the 55 to 245 megahertz range from the monitor. The RS-232 cables emit this electromagnetic radiation as well as the CPU."

"Really? So my neighbor can see what I'm doing on my computer?"

"Well, not really. Usually, only governments can afford such special equipment. The military and government computers of the United States are shielded to limit these emissions from being captured. The code name for the technology related to limiting the unwanted emissions from computer systems is TEMPEST, which stands for Transient Electromagnetic Pulse Emanation Standard. NSA oversees and is responsible for certifying government computers that are protected to prevent the capture of these electronic emissions. I worked in the directorate of the program office for the TEMPEST project for three years in the air force."

"Well, if the computers are shielded, what does it matter if the vulnerabilities are fixed or not? I could see it in the corporate world, but I don't understand for government computers."

"Good question. I discovered how to send an electronic emission back to the computer and gain control of it. I worked several more years developing this technique and computer code to access any computer by directing coded responses via emissions to control it as though I was sitting at the keyboard of the system. I could gain access by exploiting any of its vulnerabilities...then I own the system. The military must stay ahead of any adversary and that's what I did. If I was working on it, so were other governments." Reynolds stopped talking when the waiter returned and set their fresh drinks on the table. "Thank you," he said.

Dydre smiled at the waiter. "Thank you," she said. "George, this really works? It sounds more like science fiction."

"I assure you it works. I can give you a little demonstration."

"I have a plane to catch later tonight, so I don't have much time," she said.

"No problem. I can demonstrate it here for you."

"Really? All right, go ahead."

Reynolds retrieved what looked like an oversized handheld personal organizer from his tattered leather case. He pressed the power button and the display window came to life as a green light flickered. "It will take just a minute to boot up. Come with me. I think I can get close enough to their computer to gain access. This is my demonstration model. The one we are marketing has more power and can do its thing from a much greater distance."

The two stepped into the hall where the restrooms were located. The staff, busily attending to the full house of customers, had no time to pay attention to the two standing near the restrooms. The door to the manager's office stood slightly ajar. Reynolds pushed the door open a little farther revealing the restaurant's computer with the monitor perched atop the manager's desk.

"This won't take long," he said, pushing a couple of buttons. Seeing the green light flicker, he stood with his back to the door and Ranger in his hands behind him. "First, it is analyzing their computer. As soon as I know their vulnerabilities, I'll know how to get into their computer. Their system is small and can be checked rather quickly."

When Ranger completed its analysis, Reynolds turned to the side and shielded Ranger between him and Dydre. He studied the display briefly, pushed a few buttons, then scrolled down the displayed list. "These are the system vulnerabilities," he said as he discreetly showed her the display window. "Typical. Their computer has a lot of problems. I can get in easily." He clicked one of the identified vulnerabilities in the list and then pressed another series of buttons. "Stand on the other side of me," he said. As soon as she moved to his other side to conceal what he was doing, he pointed Ranger at the computer and pressed another button. The monitor flickered, coming to life. Typing on Ranger's keypad, Reynolds opened the directory.

"Company Payroll." He opened the file and turned Ranger toward Dydre. She glanced at the monitor to verify that what she was seeing in Ranger's window matched the information on the monitor. Reynolds opened two different employee files to show their contents. "Just think what I could do with this information," he said. "I can download any information I choose or I can leave a program behind to activate later. I have full control of their system and can do anything I like. Watch this." Pressing several buttons, he accessed a floor plan indicating the table numbers.

"Watch those two tables over there." He looked up, nodded across the room, then entered several more key strokes. "I just cancelled their drink orders and sent them a free pitcher of margaritas."

Several minutes later a commotion erupted at the bar. The bartender, waiter, and manager were trying to sort out a problem. Then the waiter, followed by the manager, approached the two tables that Reynolds had pointed out to Dydre; their mannerisms displayed their apologies to the patrons. Grinning at what he had done, Reynolds asked, "Any questions?" He switched Ranger off and led Dydre back to their table.

"I wouldn't have believed it if I hadn't seen it," she said as she smoothed the linen napkin on her lap. "I'm impressed with Ranger's capability. What's the export license requirement? I know the US State Department has some strict export requirements for technology."

"No problem. It's not licensed."

"With Ranger's capability, isn't your government concerned? I would think the US military would scarf up the technology and lock it away."

"There are some, well…not-so-bright people in decision-making places. They don't believe Ranger exists. But you saw it work. I'm a businessman and I'll go overseas if the US government doesn't buy it. When they decide Ranger does exist, it will cost them more." Reynolds finished his margarita and signaled the waiter for another.

Reynolds's frustration with the US government was a signal Dydre didn't miss. Also, finding out Ranger was not licensed by the US State Department told her that Reynolds was not as sharp as one would expect, or he might be trying to play two ends against the middle with the government. In any event, it made her job easier and Reynolds wouldn't be that difficult. She already knew he was practically broke.

"George," she said. "I like what I see. I'd like to take one back so my IT engineer can evaluate it. If he gives me the go-ahead, I'm prepared to make an investment in your company.

I also have some clients that are interested in Ranger and will want to take delivery, if all goes well."

"How much are you talking about?"

"If your product checks out—$3 million. You can call me a white knight or simply an investor. We'll work out the details later, but it must remain confidential." She looked up at him with her brown eyes.

"Obviously. This one is my demonstration model. I'll have to go by the office and pick up one that is ready for shipment."

She sensed his struggle to remain calm. Expecting Reynolds to haggle or at least counter her offer, she was surprised when he didn't. Again, the Fat Man's information was correct. Although Reynolds tried to portray his company as solid and meeting its obligations, she knew otherwise. His desperation made him easy to maneuver.

Dydre looked at her watch and said, "That'll be fine." She withdrew an envelope from her purse and slid it toward him. "I would like our business to be off the books. If you can arrange that, we can do business…lots of business."

He took the envelope and peered at the cash inside. Pausing, he looked up at her.

"That should be more than enough to cover any security deposit," she said. "Plus a little more to cover any expenses."

"I think I can arrange to do business with you," he said.

"Good. No one is to know about our meeting or our business relationship. I'll deal only with you…in cash. No records. Is that understood?"

"It's a deal."

"Good. Let's go by your office. I have to catch a plane. I'll call you later in the week to set up our meeting for some time next week. I should have the results back from the evaluation by then."

10

Dydre returned to the Hyatt Regency just before 11:00 p.m. Once inside her room, she removed the wig and makeup, and took a cool shower. After slipping on a robe, she sat at the desk and picked up David's picture. She smiled and laid it beside the stationary, then wrote him a letter. For a few short minutes she escaped the present and was with David. There were many things she wanted to tell him but, for the time being, couldn't. She needed to be cautious in what she wrote or said to him as the slightest slip could give her away and she would never see him again. A news story on CNN about the Balkans broke her spell. After listening to the story, she reread the letter and added, *I will see you soon. With love, Mommy.*

After sealing the envelope, she called the Fat Man on her mobile phone to brief him on her meeting with George Reynolds.

"I have a working copy of Ranger. He gave me a demonstration and it did what he advertised. I was quite surprised."

"Was he receptive to your offer as an investor?"

"I offered him five million and he accepted."

"Good. Get Ranger checked out. We don't need any surprises."

"Yes, I know. I know someone who can check it out. I told Reynolds I'd be back next week."

"You didn't leave me much time to arrange for the money."

"Clay, you can do it. Besides, you said you wanted to move quickly on this. Do you have anything else? I'm flying back to Washington in the morning."

"I want you to pick up a package for me that the senator left. You know where to pick it up."

"I do. Clay, this weekend can I——"

"It's arranged. David is looking forward to seeing you this weekend in Lucerne. Now, get that package back here as soon as you can. It's the latest imagery and intelligence for the Croatian army's offensive *Operation Flash*. As you know, it's very time-sensitive information and I'm getting pressure from them. What about your meeting with Kingpin's man?"

"I meet with one of his representatives on Thursday in Sarajevo."

"Good work, my dear. Have a good flight."

George Reynolds hadn't broken any laws yet, but DIA Officer Kennedy didn't trust him. He needed more than just a feeling to get a wiretap or justify the additional expense of having him followed; however, when Reynolds left work early and neglected to tell him or Paul Stevens, the undercover FBI agent assigned to his company, Stevens followed Reynolds to his meeting with Dydre. At first, Stevens believed Reynolds was discreetly meeting a girlfriend, but after observing them, he decided otherwise. The agent made his report and forwarded it, along with photographs, to Kennedy at DIA headquarters.

Wednesday, May 17, 1995
The Pentagon

The dry filtered air of the SCIF greeted Mary Ellen O'Malley as Assistant Secretary Newport held the door open for her. "I'm sorry I'm late, sir. The traffic was terrible."

"You're right on time. Don't worry about it." He smiled and greeted Alice and Hector who were already seated at the conference table.

"Mary Ellen, it's your meeting. What do you have?" Newport said.

"Albritten was divorced a couple of years ago," she said as she stood and passed folders to Newport, Alice, and Hector. "From his finances, he seems to have recovered quite well after the divorce. For about the last eighteen months or so, he does have some regular deposits of odd amounts, but always in cash and under ten thousand dollars, so a currency transaction report was not required to be filed with the US Treasury. He's paid all of his bills and built up a nice little savings account. I believe he was receiving money and tried to cover it up by making deposits under ten thousand. Hector agrees with my assessment."

Newport looked at Hector. "*Yezs*, sir. I believe he was on the take from someone."

"Go on, Mary Ellen," Newport said as he scribbled a note on his notepad.

"Next in your folders are these photographs I received after circulating Alice's description of her attacker," she said. "Alice has confirmed this is the same woman."

They each turned over the financial synopsis page and saw an eight-by-ten photo of a small group of people. Several in the group were identified with their names near their heads, and one woman with black, shoulder-length hair had a red circle around her head.

"Alice, are you sure this is the same woman?" Newport said as he examined the photo.

"That's the same little bitch."

The photo was a CIA photo taken two years before in Somalia. In the center of the photo was warlord Mohamed Farrah Aidid. It appeared to be more of a social gathering than a business meeting of Aidid's thugs and lieutenants. To the right, and rear of the crowd stood the woman.

"I have some other reports that a woman matching her description was in Rwanda and Chechnya." Mary Ellen continued. "We don't think she works for Aidid and we don't know why she was in this photo."

"This is a start. My guess is that Albritten was our leak, was on the take, and probably paid by this woman. We have a photo of her. Now who is she and who does she work for?" Newport said.

"Sir, I have sent a copy of this photo out, but as of yet no one has come back with any more information," Hector said. "She just appears, then disappears. I did receive a short report from the DIA about a woman in Austin, Texas, who sort of matches the description of our mysterious woman. What's the DIA got going on in Austin?"

"I'll find out and get back to you." Newport looked at Alice. "After I find out what is going on in Austin, you and Hector follow up with the DIA and see if the woman in their report is the same woman we're trying to find. If it is, we need to know what they have on her. Let's keep digging. No one just appears then disappears. I have an army officer I am putting to work on this with you. He'll be here tomorrow. As soon as you find out who she is, where we can find her, he'll get close to her and find out who she works for. We'll get the whole lot."

11

Tysons Corner, Virginia

Later that same day, Alice was at her office, going over the
items she and Hector brought back from Albritten's
house. They hadn't found any smoking gun that tied Albritten
directly to the internal leaks they were investigating, only a
few circumstantial and questionable items. She stood to take a
step in Hector's direction but the phone rang. She sat and
answered it on the second ring. "Special Agent Johnson."

"Johnson, this is Captain Jordan." His voice was polite
and cordial.

"Hello, Jordan. What's up?" She was guarded, not
knowing what to expect from this uncharacteristic call.

"We need to talk."

"We do? About what?"

"The case you're working on."

"I'm not working on any case."

"Come on, Johnson. I think you'll want to talk about
Albritten."

"Albritten? You said it was drunk driving."

"Well, it would have been."

"Would have been but for what?"

"That's what I want to talk to you about."

"Drunk driving. That's what you guys said."

"How about murder? Or do you want me to go to the
DA first?"

"Okay, Jordan. I'll play. When do you want to meet?"

"In about an hour, say, at the Mall in Tysons Corner."

"Too many people. I'll meet you at Arlington Cemetery."

Alice hung up the phone and checked the clock. "Hector," she said over the cubical wall. "We're going to meet with Captain Jordan. He says he has information about Albritten's death. I'm going to call the boss, then we're going."

"Jordan?"

"Yes. Jordan. I'll tell you about it in the car."

Alice told Newport about her phone conversation with Captain Jordan.

"See what he has before you tell him anything," Newport said. "He may just be trying to fish something out of you. If he has something, we need to know what it is. If you have to tell him, make damn sure he knows to keep quiet about it."

"Yes, sir. I'll brief you when I get back."

"Be careful."

Alice and Hector met Captain Jordan at the cemetery as agreed. They strolled along the sidewalk to a secluded place on a small knoll well into the sea of headstones and markers, where no one could overhear them. A slight breeze drifted through the tranquil setting. People, respecting the dead, quietly walked along, visiting the well-known graves—President John F. Kennedy, Robert F. Kennedy, Audie L. Murphy, and the Tomb of the Unknown Soldier—as well as fallen soldiers, sailors, marines, and airmen. No one seemed interested in Jordan, Johnson, or Sanchez.

"Okay, Jordan, what have you got?" Alice asked, her eyes fixed on him.

"When you first came over to inquire about Albritten's accident, I didn't pay it much attention. But when we got you out of the hotel room at the Sheraton, I knew you were investigating something in connection to his death." He paused and studied Alice and Hector.

"I explained all that to you," Alice said. "The hotel was a misunderstanding and I just needed to check out Albritten's death because of his position. So what's all this about?"

"Well I had a hunch. I went to the medical examiner and persuaded him to do some more tests." He handed Alice a folder. "See for yourself. He was poisoned."

"Poisoned?" Alice opened the file to read the examiner's report. She flipped through several pages and returned to the summation. She then handed the report to Hector.

"Yes," Jordan said. "When they initially examined him, everything pointed to drunk driving and there was nothing to indicate otherwise. So they didn't look any further. Basically, he died from paralysis from powerful neurotoxins, strong procoagulants that interfered with his blood clotting and myotoxins that caused muscle damage."

"Shit, Jordan, the killer wasn't fooling around. What kind of poison was it?"

"Snake venom."

"Snake venom?"

"Yes, snake venom. It came from an inland taipan snake from Australia—which, I am told, produces the most potent venom in the world."

"And there were no fang or puncture marks on the body, correct?"

"Correct. They did find traces of emu oil on his face. Emu oil allows a transdermal effect because its pH characteristics are similar to human skin. It readily penetrates the epidermis and enhances the absorption of other chemicals without interruption. The medical examiner said that the CIA experimented with mixing snake venom and emu oil for assassinations. It's very difficult to detect unless you are specifically looking for it."

"Are you saying the CIA killed him?"

"No, I'm saying he was killed by a technique that the CIA once experimented with."

Alice looked at Hector, but before she could speak, Hector said, "I'll get with Mary Ellen and we'll check this out at the CIA."

Alice turned to Jordan and asked, "Is this my copy?"

"If you'll level with me and bring me in on this."

"Okay, but this is highly classified. There'll be some things I can't tell you, but you'll be in on the case. And when the arrest or arrests go down, you'll be there. You'll need to handpick your men—only those you absolutely need and can trust. Lastly, you won't do anything without us."

"It's a deal."

"Send me their names and social security numbers. I'll have to do a screen on them first."

"Agreed. What can you tell me now?"

"Albritten was on a watch list of possible leaks of classified information. We think there could be others. Before you say it, Jordan, we know that they usually don't kill their source. That's what has us puzzled. We need to nab the entire lot. We only have one lead on this so far, the woman that gave me the black eye."

Jordan smirked. "Your eye is looking much better. What can you tell me about her?"

"You know most of it. She went to dinner and as far as we know was the last person to see him alive."

"Now she's a murder suspect," Jordan said.

"Remember, if you see her, don't bring her in without checking with us first," Hector added. "Send us those names and we'll get started on them."

"Got it."

12

Thursday, May 18, 1995
Ilidža, Bosnia-Herzegovina

Seated in a café that struggled to stay open with its limited clientele, Dydre, dressed as Sam wearing additional padding to make her look stocky, sipped a cup of tea and listened for anyone approaching as she scanned for her expected contacts.

The siege of Sarajevo and its nearby international airport had inflicted large-scale destruction in the suburb of Ilidža. The damaged city was practically deserted, enveloped by an eerie calm, empty of the usual city noises of traffic and children playing. Death seemed to hang in the air like a foul smell. Bombed-out buildings everywhere. The pungent odor of burning rubble and rotting garbage permeated the cool, moist morning air.

The café's awning was blown away, pockmarks covered the front of the building, and a blackened hole gaped in one side wall. The interior also showed the signs of fighting as evidenced by the broken glass and mirrors. An old ceiling fan, missing a blade, hung limply from the ceiling and two lightbulbs dangled from bare wires. The floor had been swept clean of debris from the fallen ceiling and the hole in the wall. The café was one of the few places open. A man seated across the room from Dydre was the only other person in the room besides the proprietor. Late morning rain began to fall, leaking water from the roof, which pooled on the floor about ten feet from where Dydre waited.

Wearing black cargo pants and a khaki shirt, Dydre carried a 9mm Walther P5 pistol in her right pants pocket. She knew the meeting she was about to have could turn fatal at any turn. The fanatics she had to deal with didn't like doing business with women at all, but in this instance Dydre had something they wanted and she came highly recommended. She had to be careful, showing no weakness, to maintain that leverage or she would be dead.

An expressionless, scraggly bearded, young Arabic man of not more than twenty-five, carrying a Kalashnikov assault rifle, stepped into the room. His clothes were tattered and dirty. He scrutinized the room and its contents. Turning toward Dydre, who sat alone with her back to the corner, he marched up to her and grabbed her shirt by the shoulder. "Come with me!" he said.

Dydre stood without resisting his tug on her shirt. As she stepped from behind the table and quickly pivoted toward her left, closing in on him, she positioned herself with the rifle outside both of them where it was no threat to her. Immediately, she grabbed him, thrusting her knee up as she pulled him downward, catching him in the solar plexus. She flipped him to the floor and followed him down, where she blocked his arm holding the rifle. To free it from his grip was not difficult as he was in great pain, gasping for air. "We play by my rules."

Before placing the Kalashnikov on the table, she checked to verify the weapon was loaded and the safety off, just in case she needed the firepower. A glance around the room told her no one else had entered the café during their skirmish. The other customer, watching what was happening, scurried out of the café, while the proprietor dashed into a back room. Knowing that reinforcements would arrive any minute, Dydre pulled up the dazed and defeated man and got him in the chair. "Just sit there!" she said. "Don't make a move or I'll blow your balls off. You got that, cockroach?"

The man nodded, still gasping for air. Dydre sat and faced the door with the AK47 by her right hand, pointing toward the entrance. Just as she suspected, two more Arab men, in their midthirties and also carrying Kalashnikovs, soon appeared in the doorway. They had heavy black beards, and their clothes were dirty and worn as well. One of the men, slightly taller than the other, cautiously approached Dydre, as the other man stepped to the left. The expression on their faces revealed their perplexity at seeing the younger man seated at the table in pain, struggling for air, while Dydre sat calmly as if nothing unusual was happening. "Stand up! Hands in the air!" he ordered.

"I came here to deal with Yasir Rashid Jamaal. I didn't come to this hellhole to let one of you cockroaches get cheap thrills by feeling me up and call it 'checking for weapons.' We talk here and now or this meeting is over." Dydre slipped the P5 from her pocket, pointed it toward Tall Arab from beneath the table, and was ready to shoot. She studied him and then the other one as they stood, pondering their next move. "Do we talk and do business, or meet Allah together?"

Tall Arab focused his eyes on Dydre's as he stood in front of her. No one moved in the deadly quiet room where tension was tighter than a piano wire. The two men contemplated the mysterious woman. Short Arab looked at Tall Arab and nodded toward the younger man who grimaced in pain. Tall Arab slung the rifle over his shoulder, grabbed the seated man, and took him to the door. Short Arab slid the chair out and sat. "I am Jamaal. We will talk," he said.

Dydre didn't trust the men, but felt herself relax when he said he wanted to talk. She was still prepared to shoot her way out if necessary. Gunfire, followed by several loud explosions and more gunfire, rang out a couple of blocks away from their meeting. She considered the man and how oblivious he was to the gunfire and explosions. He wasted no time in coming to his point, telling Dydre he needed ammunition, arms, RPGs, plastic explosives, blasting caps, time fuses, and detonators. "We were also informed that you could provide us with a computer device called Ranger that is made in the United States. Is this correct?"

She nodded and said, "Do you have a list with the quantities you want?"

The man pulled a piece of paper from his pocket and handed it to her. She looked it over, finally saying, "I'll call you with the price and we'll work out the transportation details. I require cash before the shipment leaves. Understood?"

"Understood. We will expect your call. May Allah be with you."

"You'll need him more than I will," she said then thought, *cockroach!*

Jamaal stood and stared at Dydre before joining the other two who waited by the door. The three Arabs walked around the corner, disappearing from sight. Dydre breathed a sigh of relief, returned the pistol to her cargo pocket, and drank another cup of tea. She wanted to be sure they were gone before she made her way out the door.

13

Friday, May 19, 1995
Palace Luzern Hotel
Lucerne, Switzerland

Seated on the balcony of the five-star hotel, Dydre sipped her morning coffee as she overlooked the lake below, the early morning sun reflecting off the blue water. She had checked in the evening before and phoned Zsigmond to give him the results of her meeting in Ilidža while she drew a bath. Her call complete, she slipped into the warm water to wash the events of the last couple of weeks away. Although her bath was long and relaxing, she was only able to get the surface cleansed. It would take more than a bath to wash the sights, smells, and sounds of Ilidža, Bosnia-Herzegovina from her body. She had several things to do before her weekend with David began.

Hearing the phone ring, she stepped inside to pick it up and heard Zsigmond's gravelly voice. At first she thought he was reneging on her weekend with her son. Her fear subsided when he provided the price and arrangements for the shipment to the Arabs in Bosnia-Herzegovina. "You have done well, my dear," he said. "Enjoy your weekend with David. First thing Monday, go back to Austin and make arrangements with George Reynolds to have Ranger shipped."

"Clay, I don't have the report back yet from the IT engineer." She ran her fingers through her hair as she paced the floor.

"You'll have it soon, won't you?"

His words meant that she was to push the engineer and make it happen quickly. Clay always moved fast, and he pushed everyone else to do the same, a trait that frustrated and often angered her. She knew she was on the front line and would take the fall if something went wrong, but this was a scenario she was determined to prevent. Better to be cautious in her approach than to operate on the edge as Zsigmond did.

"Yes, but there'll be some pissed-off people if it doesn't work when they get it."

"Have Reynolds cover the order for Bosnia-Herzegovina and complete your arrangements with him after it checks out. Go ahead and give him what you need to control him. He will get the balance when it checks out."

"If it doesn't check out?"

"You know what to do."

Dydre's phone conversation with Zsigmond put her in a foul mood, one that threatened to spoil the two precious days she planned to spend with David. Trying to block everything from her mind except her son, she forced herself to forget the phone call with Zsigmond. But she knew that he would never let her be completely alone with David. The call was no accident. He didn't have to say it, but it was his way of exerting control—if she didn't cooperate, David wouldn't arrive.

Dydre awaited David's arrival as she sat beneath a large umbrella in the Le Maritime garden restaurant on the hotel's terrace. The Saturday morning sun felt warm and the air smelled fresh. She sipped a large mug of coffee with cream, thinking only of seeing her son. The time in between their visits had increased to the point that their separations were becoming unbearable.

Whenever they did get together, she always felt that the time flew by. She found it impossible to do all the things together they talked about. With each visit she noticed slight changes in him, not just in his growth but also in his temperament, attitude, and personality. He needed a family. He needed to be in a situation where he could be nurtured, not in a situation where he was treated like a pawn. With this in mind, her determination to break away from Zsigmond grew.

Dydre checked her watch for the third time in five minutes, and took another sip of her coffee. She looked around to see if David had possibly arrived and was trying to locate her. Only unfamiliar faces were visible. *Where are you, David?* She checked her watch again. *It's my time, Clay, you promised!* She began to have doubts that David was coming after all. It could be one of Clay's power trips. She began to feel let down and even more despondent.

"Mommy!"

Dydre, with tears of joy immediately welling in her eyes, looked around to see her six-year-old son. She ignored the two brawny thugs, or chaperones as Zsigmond referred to them. One stood back several feet from the other clutching David's backpack in his hand. Dydre knew why these men were there. They would use whatever means necessary to prevent her from taking the boy and disappearing with him— even killing her, and David too, if necessary. They rarely spoke to her when she was with the boy, but stayed in the background and watched her every move. They didn't intimidate her, but she remained ever cautious around them, as she didn't want David harmed nor did she want to be denied visits with him.

For almost a year Dydre had kept her eye on the two chaperones so as to learn every detail about the men—a habit she developed through her training. They treated her son well and he seemed to get along with them. Locked into their routines, the two men probably didn't realize how much useful information they revealed to her. She'd honed a sixth sense, anticipating and predicting their moves, subtly testing their weaknesses. She would need that information one day.

Backpack thug examined the area for any threats and, after deciding there were none, leaned to the other one and spoke softly in his ear. The second thug made a quick scan and nodded. Backpack thug then headed toward the hotel, presumably to deposit the backpack with the concierge just as he had done on each previous visit.

David ran to Dydre as she squatted with open arms in greeting. He grasped her neck and she stood with her arms firmly around him, hugging and kissing him. Smelling his hair, his skin—the soft, fresh smell of the young boy—Dydre forgot about everything else but being with him. She kissed his cheek and whispered, "I've missed you."

"I missed you, too. Are we still going to the carnival?"

David had learned that a carnival was going to be in town, and told her about it in his last three letters. He even included crayon drawings of the rides and animal attractions. Touched by his letters, she was thrilled not only to take him to the carnival but just to be with him.

Putting him down, she kissed him again. "Let me look at you. You are getting to be a big boy." He was growing up and she wasn't there for him. "Yes, we are still going to the carnival." She grasped his hand, and the two walked to the entrance of the hotel en route to the festival.

The music blared as people in costumes milled about. Several bands played their trumpets, kettles and drums. In a different direction, another band blared out with alphorns and cowbells. Yodeling echoed across the carnival. Young men and women held competitions of flag throwing. Sideshows and vendors hawked their wares, competing for customers. There were games of chance of all sorts, food and beverage peddlers, and various rides. "Mommy, can I have a balloon?" David asked as he pushed through the turnstile.

"Pick a color," she said with a smile.

He touched his finger to his chin as he contemplated the cluster of helium-filled balloons in the clown's clinched fist. "The red one!" he finally said, full of excitement. His exhilaration built as the clown pulled out the chosen balloon and guided its string into his small hand. With a firm grip on the string, David led his mother forward. They strolled and occasionally stopped to enjoy the merry-go-round, the spinning tea cups, or any other ride that caught his eye. The pony ride was a must for him.

Dydre bought them a soft pretzel and orange Fanta to drink. They sat in the shade enjoying their snack and each other's company. This was the life she yearned for—a family with David—mother and son. She never wanted the weekend to end. As she looked around and her eyes fell on the two guards in their dark sport coats and turtleneck sweaters, her mood broke. They were a constant reminder that her time with David was limited and her real-world life was on temporary hold. "Finish your drink so we can go," she said as she dropped her eyes to him.

The two continued their adventure, going from ride to vendor. They ate bratwurst on a brötchen with pommes frites and topped it off with ice cream. As the day passed, David never seemed to slow down. He rode most of the rides, some of them twice. He collected trinkets and souvenirs from the carnival, but somewhere during the day he lost his red balloon. Finally, when the sun sank low in the sky, Dydre said, "It's time for us to go back to the hotel. I'm tired." She looked down at him as they walked together hand in hand.

"I'm not tired. Do we have to?"

She smiled. "Yes, we do. Tomorrow I'll show you where the dragon lives."

He knew exactly what she meant as he had heard the tale many times before. In medieval times, according to the legend, dragons with special powers lived in the rugged cracks and crevices of Mount Pilatus. And the next day they would be going to the top of that mountain.

The two left the carnival. As a final treat for David before the end of the day, Dydre decided to hail a horse-drawn carriage to take them back to the hotel. The carriage lurched forward as soon as they sat. By the time the carriage traveled the first block, the rhythmic clacking of the horse's hooves had lulled David to sleep.

14

Sunday

Dydre and David boarded the paddlewheel steamer *Unterwalden* from the pier by the train station where the Reuss River meets the lake in Lucerne. The two chaperones trailed behind. Although the train would have been faster, the seventy-minute boat ride down Lake Lucerne to Alpnachstad was a special treat for David. As soon as he finished his hot chocolate, he turned his attention to the huge steam engine, which propelled the steamer as it glided over the aquamarine water.

Dydre took him to a point over the engine room for a better view. He knelt on the grate and looked at the engine with its gauges, pipes, and moving parts. The brass cover on top of the engine was embossed with raised letters: Built in 1902. The large steel rods that pumped up and down on the engine, turning the shaft to the paddlewheels, fascinated him as did all the pieces that worked together to make the steamer go. He could have spent the entire ride watching the machine work, but Dydre coached him along to see other parts of the steamer. As she took his hand, she saw the ever-present guards following behind.

They disembarked at the pier in Alpnachstad and crossed the street to catch the cogwheel train to the top of Mount Pilatus. Their seat in the last car's rear compartment offered a breathtaking panoramic view, as the steepest cogwheel train in the world ground its way upward.

David folded his arms and leaned on the rear window to watch the scenery. He watched the landscape pass as the lake below seemed to get smaller. A few cows grazed at the lower altitudes and an occasional mountain goat appeared higher up.

"Tell me the story of the dragon again," David said, turning to his mother.

"David, you know the legend of the dragon."

"I know, but tell me again. Tell me that part about the brave boy."

"All right," she said. "Once upon a time, a long, long time ago, there was a pair of dragons with special powers that lived in the rugged cracks and crevices around here." Dydre waved her hand across the view of the landscape, her face full of expression.

"On one sunny day, one of the dragons landed next to a farmer named Stempflin. Seeing the dragon, old Stempflin was so frightened that he fainted. Tears came to the eyes of the good-natured dragon when he realized he scared the old man. When Stempflin woke up, he saw a small stone in the dragon's footprint. He picked up the stone, not realizing its power, and wiped it off. Then he stuck it in his pocket to prove to others that he had seen the dragon.

"One fall day a brave young boy fell into a deep cave in the mountain, probably right over there"—Dydre pointed across the landscape, her expression serious—"landing between two dragons. They didn't harm him but took him into their nest and cared for him. When spring arrived, one of the dragons flew away. The other dragon told the boy it was time for them to leave, too. The dragon handed the boy a stone, told him to clutch it in his fist, and it would give him courage. Then the dragon extended his tail and told the boy to hold on to it with his other hand. The dragon flew out of the cave, taking the brave boy to safety.

"No one knows what happened to the dragons." She smiled and clasped her hands.

"I like that story," David said with a grin. "People say they still live in the mountain."

"I'm sure they do," she said, then hugged him.

Reaching the station, the two had lunch in the restaurant inside Hotel Pilatus-Kulm at the summit. They had a stunning view of Lucerne and the lake below. After lunch Dydre took David out on the terrace. "David, there are seventy-three mountain peaks of the Alps. Can you count them?"

Holding up his small finger, he started to count as he pointed to each one. Dydre corrected him only twice. When he finished, he leaned on the rail to admire the views of the lakes and central Switzerland below.

Taking his hand, Dydre said, "Are you ready? Let's move along." They strolled along the path through the rock gallery, then took the trail that crossed the mountaintop north to south. Once they finished that circuit, Dydre led him on the short trip to get a panoramic view of the mountain range. "Look, David." She stooped next to him and pointed to the mountains. "There's Eiger, there's Mönch, and over here Jungfrau. Look at the six lakes below. Can you see them all?"

"One, two, three…six," he said out loud.

"It's time to head down the mountain, David," she said, grasping his hand. "Let's take the cableway back down the mountain to Kriens and take the bus back to Lucerne."

"Do we have to? I'm not tired."

"Yes, David. It's going to be late when we get back."

Dydre sat next to David in the gondola with her arm around him; he sat quietly and leaned his head on her lap. She looked at her reflection in the gondola's window. *In just a short while they'll take David and I'll go back to my real-world life*, she thought. *I don't want it to end…I can hardly stand to think about it.*

Later, the two sat together on the bus, both knowing their time together was near its end. The excitement of the weekend was now a memory. When she glanced at her reflection in the glass, Dydre saw the two goons seated behind her and David. It was all she could do to fight back the tears.

Upon their return to the hotel, the shorter of the two men held out his hand. "It's time to go, David."

The other goon stepped to the concierge desk and retrieved David's backpack that they deposited that morning. It was the same routine as each previous visit—quick, efficient, and with minimum drama.

"No! I don't want to go," David said. He began to cry.

Short thug shot Dydre a look that commanded her obedience.

"Give me a big hug. It's time go, honey."

The boy continued to resist and plead, but she knew what she had to do, no matter how much it pained her.

"Give me a kiss," she said from behind tear-filled eyes. As they embraced, she whispered in his ear, "We'll be together soon, I promise. I love you."

The man took the crying boy from her and they disappeared around the corner.

15

Sunday Evening

Dydre laid David's photo on the desk. Just as she picked up a pen to write him a note, the phone rang. She stared at it through two more rings. There was only one person who would be calling her there, and she didn't want to talk to him. Her mood soured, she finally answered on the fourth ring. The last person she wanted to talk to was Clay Zsigmond. She despised him for using her son like a poker chip.

"Hello, my dear," Zsigmond said. "I trust you had a good weekend with David?"

"Yes."

"Good. You're going back to Washington in the morning, correct?"

"Yes, I'm working on someone for a replacement as our supplier."

"Good. Your suitcase is at Union Station."

Zsigmond was referring to a suitcase containing $5 million Dydre needed to pay Reynolds to control his company. Enlisting the help of Senator Griffith, Zsigmond had him arrange to put the suitcase, containing the $5 million, in a diplomatic pouch and ship it from Frankfurt to Washington. When the suitcase arrived, it was put in a locker at Union Station.

"I'll take care of it."

"I want Reynolds in the bag as soon as possible," he said. "Our Balkan customers want Ranger right away."

"Clay, I still don't have the report back on Ranger."

"Give him what is needed to keep him happy until you get your report. We had this discussion before. How much do you think he is going to want to keep him happy until your report comes back?"

"I don't know! He was pretty tough and wouldn't budge much before, so I'm guessing he'll be the same."

"What'll it take?"

"To get him on my side and to ship four Rangers…maybe half of what I offered him," she said.

"That seems a little steep, Dydre. Don't give him anymore than you have to. But bag him quickly."

"I know, Clay. I will. I know what to do."

"Tell me as soon as you have him under control. I may have several other Rangers sold and everyone is anxious to get their hands on one."

"Good-bye, Clay."

"Good night, my dear."

Austin, Texas

George Reynolds leaned back in his chair behind the walnut desk in his study and fixed his gaze on the picture opposite him on the wall. The picture was of his vacation home in the northwestern province of Guanacaste in Costa Rica near the Gulf of Papagayo. "It won't be long now," he said to himself. As he took another drink of Bud Light, he admired the lush green foliage and palm trees that surrounded the stylish, tropically designed house with its arches and open architecture. The deep blue water of the gulf provided a splendid backdrop to the white house.

After several minutes he stood and stepped over a bulging black trash bag to get to a large potted plant on the floor. He lifted and placed the pot to one side, then knelt at the opening of the floor safe. With his chubby fingers, he spun the dial through the sequence of numbers to unlock the door, and pulled out a stuffed envelope. Oblivious to his wife's presence, he returned to his desk and withdrew $5,000, which he placed on the desk. He put the envelope on the right side of the desk to be returned to the safe later.

"Dinner will be ready in a few minutes," Janice said, watching him. Because he didn't acknowledge her and she saw the preoccupied expression on his face, she said again, "Dinner will be ready in a few minutes."

"What?" He looked up at her.

"What're you doing? What's the money for?" she said in a tone that sounded more concerned than curious. "You were in here most of the day going through the files and throwing things out. Is something wrong?"

"No, everything is fine. Just cleaning out some things."

"What's the money for?"

"Janice, how would you like to move to Costa Rica?"

"What? What're you talking about? Move to Costa Rica?"

"I might sell the company. There's someone who's interested," he said.

"Really? Are you sure? I mean, do you really want to sell your company? You've worked so hard to build it."

"We've always talked about retiring to Costa Rica. We'll have the money now. I think it's time we get away from this rat race."

"When? This is so sudden."

"The buyer is coming this week. I have a couple of things to do and then we're finished."

"I…I don't know what to say. We need to talk about when we are going, and this house. I just can't think right now."

"I want you to go down to Costa Rica right away and get our house there squared away. I'll be down in a few days."

"George, this is so sudden. I can't just walk away like that."

"Why not? We'll have the money and there'll be nothing holding us here."

"It's just a shock...so sudden."

George opened the center desk drawer and pulled out two passports and an airline ticket folder, which he placed by the money. "You're all set. Your passport is up to date and you have a ticket to fly down on Tuesday."

"Tuesday! I can't just hop on a plane on Tuesday and walk away from here. I need more time. I have friends I'd like to see first. My family. There are things we need to settle...I just can't go that fast. Why do we need to rush out of here?"

"There'll be nothing holding us here. Let's just go."

"What about this house?"

"I'll call a Realtor. They'll handle everything."

"George, what's wrong? Are you in trouble or something?"

"Everything is fine, Janice. Let's have dinner." He stood and gave a gentle push on her shoulder to nudge her toward the kitchen.

George continued his charade the rest of the evening and avoided answering any of his wife's questions. He was focused on his final move—turning their vacation house into a permanent residence. He had already shipped several boxes of files, computer disks of code, as well as the schema and schematics of Ranger to Costa Rica. He had set his plan in motion and he was not leaving any clue as to where he was going.

The call to a Realtor would not happen.

16

Monday, May 22, 1995
Tysons Corner, Virginia

"Alice, better have a look at this." Mary Ellen said as she swung her chair around. "It's a report back from the San Antonio field office."

"What does it say?" Alice asked as she took the message out of her hand.

"They confirmed it. It's her, the same woman. Good going!"

Alice grabbed the files on her desk and shoved them into the safe. "I'll call you."

"Where are you going?"

"To bag a bitch! Austin."

"Be careful. Let me know where you're staying and keep me posted." Mary Ellen knew not to advise the headstrong Alice against going to Austin. Better to let her go than to suffer her wrath.

"Will do." She felt for her pistol at her side as she took a quick look around her area.

"Hector!" Alice called out over the blue cubicle divider. "Are you over there, sweet pea?"

"Yezs, Alleese."

"Get your shit. We're going to Austin."

"Austin…Texas? It's so hot there. Why Austin?"

"The sunshine will do you good. Now move your ass! We're going to go bag the bitch that gave me this pip."

"But, Alleese, that's not procedure. Have you briefed the boss yet and gotten his approval?"

"I'm not going to let some pimple-faced, young jerk-of-an-agent just barely into puberty from the San Antonio field office nail her. Not on your sweet ass. I've got a score to settle with her."

"I *don* know...the boss, he's not going to like it."

"Hector, using his own words—we'll do it and ask for forgiveness afterwards."

"Alleese, I *don* like it. You're going to get in trouble."

"We've got a plane to catch, now get a move on!"

"What about the new guy?"

"Newport's giving him his instructions now."

Major John Steadman, US Army Special Forces, wearing his dress-green uniform and holding his beret in his hands, sat in the leather chair in front of Assistant Secretary of Defense Roger Newport. Major Steadman was the handpicked officer Newport had brought in to work on his classified team. The thirty-five-year-old broad-shouldered bachelor was a Rhodes Scholar—a handsome man of six feet and about 190 pounds with features of a definite Mediterranean heritage. He was smooth and knew women—knew just how to treat them.

"Major Steadman," Newport said. "Your mission is sensitive compartmented information. No one outside me and the team members you have met are to know about your assignment and what you are doing. You report directly to me. Understood?"

"Yes, sir."

"You have read the report Hector gave you, correct?"

"Yes, sir."

"I'm not convinced that Steve Albritten was the only leak nor do I know whom he was passing information to. I need you to find out the identity of Albritten's contact and which government was involved. Then maybe we can find out if we have any other holes."

"Did Albritten leave any clues?"

"We haven't found any yet if he did. I just think it is too coincidental that he was under suspicion and in a fatal accident. The only lead we have is the woman in the photograph Mary Ellen gave you, and it's a weak one at best. The DIA and FBI are working an operation in Austin, Texas. A woman matching the description of the woman in the photo was seen there. You're booked on a flight to Austin in the morning. See if you can locate the woman. Stay away from the DIA and FBI boys down there. I don't want them to know about you or what you're doing."

"Got it, sir. How far am I to go with her?"

"That's the tricky part. You're not allowed to do any police work or aid the police inside the US. Stay clear of law enforcement and don't get caught. Keep Alice informed and she will make the arrest at the appropriate time. Wherever our suspect goes, you go. Again, try to get involved with her, but be careful. We don't know anything about her."

"If she goes outside the US?"

"*Wherever* she goes. Stick with her. Most likely she will lead you somewhere overseas. We just don't know. Keep in touch with the team here and they'll provide you all the help you need. Mary Ellen is a whiz, so rely on her. What she doesn't have, she'll get. They're all very good, but not magicians, so give them whatever you come up with and they'll take it from there. You have pretty much an open ticket on this. I want her alive...at all costs."

"Understood. I'm undercover the entire time?"

"Correct, from this moment on. I don't know who else may be involved and I'm not taking any chances. I don't want some inquisitive senator or congressman, let alone a snoopy reporter, getting wind of this. There's no telling where this may take us. One slip can put us out of business and our only lead will get away. Hector will give you a special number to use to call in. It will connect directly to me.

"Hector has given me my cover. Simple enough, just a business executive from a computer company on holiday."

"Good luck, Major. Take care and be safe." Newport stood and extended his hand. "Finance is waiting for you so stop by there as soon as you can to pick up what you need from them."

Major Steadman shook his hand, thanked him, and took a large envelope from Newport. The envelope contained his orders, additional detailed instructions, and the latest intelligence on the woman as well as basic information on the DIA and FBI's operation in Austin. Also in the envelope was a passport, a stack of business cards, and several other identification documents as part of his cover. The name on the passport and business cards was Anthony Mangiano.

Monday, May 22, 1995
Washington, DC

Dydre picked up the suitcase from Union Station in Washington, DC, and took it to the Ritz-Carlton in Pentagon City where she was staying. There, she removed the money from the suitcase and put it into four cardboard boxes. Three of the boxes were about the size of a briefcase containing $1 million in $100 bills. The fourth box, twice the size of the others, contained $2 million in $100 bills. When she was satisfied with the packing, she took them to a Federal Express office and shipped the three smaller boxes to the Hyatt Regency hotel in Austin where she would be staying. The largest box was shipped to her private home in Bressanone, Italy.

Tuesday, May 23, 1995
Austin, Texas

Dydre collected the packages as soon as she arrived at the hotel in Austin and took them to her room. After she stripped each box of its outer wrapping, she rewrapped it with brown paper. One of the packages was the deposit for Reynolds to pick up at the Hilton Austin. He would receive the other two as soon as she received the report from her IT engineer, which she anticipated would be the following day. A dinner meeting was arranged for that evening with Reynolds at Fonda San Miguel restaurant.

Out of habit, Dydre had made detailed observations of the restaurant her first time there. She identified escape routes, blind spots, places where someone could hide, and those that offered the best cover if needed. Being cautious had kept her alive. Always sensitive to security, she wasn't about to overlook even the slightest detail, nor violate her rule to never meet someone to exchange money or solidify a deal in unfamiliar surroundings.

One more task was yet to be completed before the dinner meeting—scout out the area surrounding Reynolds's office and the restaurant. Walking into a trap was not in the plan.

17

Seated with George Reynolds in his office at IT Security Solutions were Alice Johnson, Hector Sanchez, and Paul Stevens.

Prior to the meeting, Paul had told Alice and Hector about his operation to prevent Reynolds's invention, Ranger, from getting into the hands of adversaries of the United States. Alice didn't give details to the extent Paul did, nor did she mention Anthony Mangiano. Although she was brief, she did tell him that Reynolds had dinner with the same woman who had been seen with Steve Albritten shortly before his fatal car crash, and that they wanted to question the woman about her relationship with Albritten and what she knows about the wreck. Alice didn't say how she got her black eye, nor did Paul ask—he knew her reputation.

"George," Hector said, "we know that in the wrong hands, Ranger would dramatically change the power base and, with its destructive power, is the equivalent of a nuclear bomb." Each watched Reynolds for his reactions. "In a matter of minutes, the military's computer system could be shut down, corrupted, or changed to make it ineffective. A rogue state or terrorist organization, for example, could go unchecked and wreak havoc without fear of retaliation by the United States." Reynolds shifted in his chair and maintained an expressionless gaze. "We cannot, and will not allow this to happen," Hector said.

"I know its capabilities," Reynolds said. I invented it, remember? What're you driving at?"

"Nothing," Hector said. "We do understand the gravity of the situation."

Paul took over, and for fifteen minutes repeatedly questioned Reynolds, without much success. "What do you know about this woman?" Paul tapped his finger on the photograph.

"Like I told you before, she told me her name was Sam, and contacted me to provide IT services to the companies she represents."

"What companies and where?"

"I...I didn't get that far."

"That's kind of weak, George," Alice said. "As the head of this company, you'd have more information on her than that, even for a first meeting. Besides, as a defense contractor, you know you're to report any contact with foreigners."

"I thought she was legitimate," Reynolds said. "And was looking for the services my company offers. She didn't give me any indication otherwise. If I'd thought differently, I'd have told you."

Alice stood, her patience gone. "George, now cut the bullshit and give me some straight answers!" She slammed her fist down on the table.

Paul and George flinched at her sudden outburst. Hector winced as he knew what was coming.

"I've told you..." George said and shifted in his seat again, his eyes darted to each of them then back to Alice. He wiped the sweat from his forehead.

"You haven't told me shit. I want answers! Now who is this little bitch?"

"An international business development consultant is all I know. She said her clients wanted a reliable American company for their IT security and we are the best." He looked at their faces as if trying to judge the success of his lie.

"Who are her clients?" Alice said, her eyes narrowed and teeth clenched.

"I don't know. I guess I forgot to ask."

"What's her last name?"

"I don't remember...I guess I lost her business card."

"George, that's the weakest line of bullshit yet. The last time I looked in the mirror, *stupid* wasn't tattooed on my forehead. You don't really expect me to believe that, do you?"

"I'd like to call my lawyer. I think this has gone far enough."

"You might want to call your travel agent instead. You're getting very close to taking an extended trip to the Antarctic. You do remember getting briefed about the Antarctic, don't you, Mr. Reynolds? Or should I say Captain Reynolds?"

"I can see how you got that black eye," Reynolds replied, glaring at her.

"Go ahead. Call your fucking lawyer! Tell him to bring his parka and long underwear."

"Look, all I know is the woman called, we talked, then she suggested dinner. She was interested in our services for her clients."

"What about Ranger? Didn't she ask about Ranger or inquire about buying it?" Paul asked.

"Just in passing. Naturally she was curious, but Ranger didn't seem to be her main focus."

"How're you supposed to get in touch with her?" Alice asked, her face in front of his.

"I'm embarrassed that I lost her business card. But she said she'd call me," he said.

"That's flimsy, George. I'm not buying any of your shit! When is she supposed to call or meet you again?"

"We're supposed to have dinner again tonight."

"That's good, George. Maybe I'm getting through that bowling ball you call a head. Let's see if you can do it again. Where are you meeting for dinner?"

"Fonda San Miguel."

Alice questioned Reynolds for another half hour, but couldn't get any more information from him. Finally, she stood up and said, "George, I want you to keep your dinner appointment with Sam. I want you to play it with her just as you have been, and you're not to mention any of this to her.

Also, you're not to go anywhere without notifying Paul first, and if the woman contacts you…let him know immediately." Alice leaned into his face. "Do you understand me, George?"

"I got it," he said as a sweat bead trickled down his white face.

"Good, now don't forget it or I'll rip your balls off!"

Alice and Hector left the meeting, while Paul remained with Reynolds for another round of questions in relation to his operation. When Paul indicated his plan to be at the dinner meeting and orchestrate what he wanted Reynolds to do, Reynolds frowned.

"Look, she told me to come alone or she wouldn't show," Reynolds said.

"All right then. I don't want to spook her," Paul said. "But I will be in the restaurant where I can see you. Do just as Alice instructed. We'll take the woman outside so as not to interrupt the restaurant's business or put any of the patrons at risk."

Reynolds nodded.

Alice and Hector sat in the car with the air conditioner on. Hector checked the notes he had taken and was ready to support Alice as she called Assistant Secretary Newport to brief him on the discussion with Reynolds. "They are to meet for dinner tonight at Fonda San Miguel. I'll work with the manager and make sure they sit at a certain table, which will have a listening device underneath. When she gets up to leave and steps out, I can go after her and bring her in," she said.

"Go ahead and be at the restaurant as you suggested," he said. "But don't arrest her. See what you can learn from what she says to Reynolds. Arresting her on assaulting a federal officer won't do us any good. We need to know who all the players are before we arrest anyone."

"What about questioning her?"

"After you find out what she tells Reynolds, then you can question her. She might lead us to who else is involved. Perhaps by bringing her in, she may want to make a deal. We don't have any other options or leads."

Alice ended the call and said, "Hector, get the address for Fonda San Miguel."

Within a few minutes, he was scribbling the address on his notepad. He ended the call, tore the paper from his pad, and said as he handed her the paper, "The address, Alleese."

"Let's go check out the restaurant," she said as she looked at the paper.

Dydre turned the corner, driving toward IT Security Solutions after checking out the restaurant. She traveled slowly down the tree-lined street and inspected the parking lot, the building, and the surrounding area for anything unusual. The mirrored glass façade of the building glimmered under the brilliant Texas sunlight and cast a blinding reflection. She noticed nothing out of the ordinary, but it was still early. The high-rise office building sat in a complex with several other buildings surrounding it. The grounds were immaculately landscaped with native plants, full of color and fragrance. A light wind danced through the branches of the trees as the late morning sun hung in the clear blue sky. In front was a sprawling parking lot about three-quarters full. *No work vans parked along the street or in the parking lots that might be used by the authorities as surveillance vehicles*, she thought as she entered the parking lot in front of IT Security Solutions. *No unmarked police cars. Good. Everything appears normal.*

Parked across the street under the shade of a live oak tree and in front of a sister office building of IT Security Solutions, Anthony Mangiano sat in his rental car. His vantage point allowed him to watch cars entering the parking lot as well as people entering and leaving the building. Cars parked on either side of him made it difficult for anyone across the street to see him. He had coordinated with Alice and Hector to arrive prior to their visit to the building, and he would continue his surveillance for an hour or more after they departed. If Alice could rattle Reynolds enough, they suspected he may try to slip out and lead them to the woman or another contact. It was a long shot and they had nothing to lose.

Anthony sat in the car for almost two hours observing the sparse traffic enter and leave the area. Austin in May can be quite hot and this day was no exception. The light breeze that swirled about did little to cool him. Wiping the sweat from his face and his short, dark-brown hair, he scanned the area again and saw a light-blue Chevrolet Malibu approaching. It turned into the parking lot across the street. Anthony studied the car and driver through the telephoto lens on his camera. *It's the same woman who circled by about forty-five minutes ago. She's pretty good–looking,* he thought as he snapped her picture. Watching her cruise through the parking lot, he saw the brake lights of the Malibu illuminate just as Alice and Hector emerged from the entrance of the building. *Well, Red, so Alice and Hector interest you. Why? What's your game?*

Anthony watched as the Malibu turned, then exited the parking lot, proceeding toward his left. *She doesn't match the description of our woman, but she might be able to lead me to her. That was a subtle little slip you made there, Red. I've got your picture and license plate number. I'll find out more about you later, but for now, I need to keep an eye out for the woman in the photograph in case she shows. I need to know who all the players are, and it now seems there are three.*

18

Dydre drove the rental car into a shopping center and parked in a row of cars; she needed a few minutes to think. Unmarked police cars, signaling that the authorities were waiting for her, wouldn't have been a surprise, but seeing the FBI woman there—the one she had cuffed to the toilet—was a different story. *How could she know I was coming here? Reynolds could've called the FBI, but he didn't seem like he would. He needed the money and was too eager to take it. He wanted more. So why is that woman here? I don't have much choice now. I need Ranger and I need Reynolds to go through with his end of the bargain.*

Dydre entered the mall and walked to a pay phone where she dialed Reynolds's number. On the second ring he answered, "George Reynolds."

"This is Sam. Are you alone?"

"Right now, yes."

"You've had some company."

"Yes, they're looking for you. But I didn't tell them anything."

"We still have a deal, George?"

"Yes, believe me, I didn't say a thing."

"What do they know?"

"Very little. They say they want to talk with you about someone that died in a car wreck in DC."

"Go on."

"That's it. They're also expecting someone from outside the US to buy some Rangers, which I guess that's you as well. That's it."

"George, if you're setting me up or trying to fuck me over, you won't live to see the sun set. Do you understand?"

"I do. Believe me, I haven't told them anything about you."

"Okay, George. I believe you but just remember what I said."

"I do. Not to worry."

"All right. Without being seen, slip out your backdoor and go to Ultimate Electronics, the one down the street from your office. Be there at 12:15. Look at the laptop computers as if you're going to buy one. You'll be met there and given instructions. Do you have my order ready?"

"It's ready."

"Good, George. If you do this right you're about to become a rich man. If you screw it up, a dead one."

Dydre didn't trust Reynolds but her plan was already in play, and she needed Reynolds to go through with his part so she could make it work. She didn't like dealing with weak, desperate people like him, but this was the hand she was dealt.

Dydre, confident they would be looking for Sam and not her, entered the Ultimate Electronics store about ten minutes before Reynolds was due to arrive. With that on her side, she felt like she had a very good chance of pulling off her meeting with him. She took the few minutes to scout out the store for signs of any authorities who might be waiting on her. She purposely gave Reynolds short notice for the meeting in the event he was informing the authorities; it would be difficult for them to try to set a trap for her. Meandering through the store, she analyzed every detail. *Nothing suspicious*, she thought. *People are calm and not interested in anything in particular, especially me. No one looking at laptops, two women buying office supplies; probably secretaries trying to get ahead of the noon crowd. No one with bulges under their arms...nothing resembling the FBI with their standard issue black wardrobe. Good observation point there, another here. Good cover. Last thirty feet to the exit open with little cover. Lots of places to stay out of sight.* With these assessments made, she noticed the noontime customers beginning to populate the store just as she anticipated.

And there goes Mr. Reynolds, Anthony thought as he observed George emerge from the side door. He snapped his picture and watched Reynolds check the area as he walked to his car. *My guess is you didn't tell anyone where you were going, did you, George? Let's just see where you're heading. Maybe Alice did spook you enough to go to the woman.*

Reynolds pulled out of the parking lot and headed into the main flow of traffic, Anthony followed at a safe distance. When Reynolds pulled into the Ultimate Electronics parking lot, Anthony thought, *Maybe he's not heading for a rendezvous with the woman. I doubt you spotted me tailing you. Never know though. This seems like an unlikely place to meet. I can't believe you're the errand boy, George. What are you up to?* He waited in his car for a few minutes as he watched Reynolds enter the store.

Once inside, Anthony observed Reynolds pretend to look at the laptop computers. So that he could better monitor Reynolds and anyone he may come into contact with, he walked several aisles over. The salesmen were helping a few customers in the vicinity of Reynolds, but no one was near him. From the corner of his eye Anthony saw a woman round the corner. *Well, hello, Red. Let's just see.* He watched her make her way to Reynolds. *I thought so. But who are you and where's the other woman? Maybe you're the go-between and you can lead me to her. Do you have any backup, Red? You're too good-looking to be his girlfriend.*

Dydre began to look at laptop computers as she meandered to where Reynolds stood. When she got there, she glanced around to ensure no one was interested in her. "George, Sam sent me. Be calm and keep looking at the computers," she said in a low voice. "Did anyone follow you?"

"No…I don't think so."

Dydre acted as if she was trying to decide on a laptop while she talked to Reynolds. She eyed the store again. "The order is ready to ship, correct?"

"Yes, they're at my house ready to go. I just need the instructions and some money."

"Good. Here are your instructions and a claim check for a package at the Hilton, Austin Airport. The report isn't back yet on Ranger, but you'll find the deposit quite suitable until the report gets back from the IT engineer. It's expected anytime. Then you'll be contacted to pick up the rest of your money."

"I don't ship until I have my money."

"Don't try to get tough with me. I want them shipped today. Got that?"

"If I have my money, I'll ship them all. How much is in the package?"

"A million."

"I'll tell you what, I'll go ahead and ship half of them. The rest go when I have the balance."

"George, you're pissing me off."

"I could call the FBI. Then you don't have shit."

"Neither will you, and you need the money."

"Get on your IT engineer then."

"Overnight them. Have the rest ready to go. I'll call you later. Don't let anyone see you pick up the package or ship the Rangers. And don't be late for your dinner appointment tonight with Sam."

"Don't worry. Just get me the money."

Although infuriated with Reynolds, Dydre maintained her composure as she walked out of Ultimate Electronics. Reynolds dealt her a card she didn't want, one that could cost her a day in the execution of her plan. Whether a day or a week, it didn't much matter if it foiled her plan or cost her life. She headed to the hotel to call the IT engineer to see what was holding him up.

Reynolds isn't going anywhere. Red is the link I need, he thought. Anthony waited until she was out of the store before he followed after her. Unable to hear the conversation between the woman and Reynolds, he knew instructions were passed. *She'll lead me to the other woman.*

Anthony, hanging back in traffic, followed the Malibu to the Hyatt Regency. He parked well away from her car so as not to arouse her attention, and slipped into the hotel unnoticed. Once inside, he made certain she was going up to a room. *Phony registration, I'm sure, but I gotta check,* he thought. He called Alice from the lobby phone to bring her up to date and asked her to get the information from the Hyatt. Alice urged him to let her bring Red in for questioning, but he resisted. "If we let her run for now, she'll lead me to the other woman," Anthony said.

"Well, you're right. As far as we can tell, the redheaded woman hasn't broken any laws and was only talking to Reynolds," Alice said.

"If we move too fast, we could lose the woman," he replied. "Reynolds, on the other hand, might be able to provide a few more details. I suggest you have another talk with him after you check out the hotel. Reynolds isn't going anywhere, but Red might be."

19

Dydre paced in her hotel room as she called the IT engineer doing the evaluation on Ranger. She was frustrated with Günter Schenck's uncharacteristically slow response, which cost her time. "Günter, the evaluation, are you finished? I need the info right away."

"Ja, ja, I am finished. I'm sorry to be so tardy. My wife, she was sick."

"Sorry to hear that. Now the evaluation, what about it?"

"Ja, very impressive tool. You will make a lot of money with this. It works just as you said."

"Good. Thank you, Günter. I'll see you soon."

"Auf Wiedersehen."

Dydre sighed after hearing his words. *Now I can get back on track and won't have to deal with a bunch of irate terrorists,* she thought. *Better call Clay to bring him up to date and tell him what Günter said. That'll get him off my back for the time being.* She knew Zsigmond well enough to know that he'd gloat for a while and relax his grip on her.

"Clay, Reynolds is on the payroll," she said into the mobile phone. "I just received the IT engineer's report and it checks out."

"Good. I told you, you worry too much, my dear. I'll call our client in Bosnia and let him know the Rangers are on the way."

"It'll be in two shipments, probably just a day apart."

"As usual, you have done well."

"Thank you, Clay. Can I see David this weekend?"

"I'll see what I can do. Are you going back to DC?"

"In the morning."

She didn't want to talk to Zsigmond but had to keep him updated. She was almost nauseated. *Clay's happy now that the Rangers will be on the way to the client and I've completed my task*, she thought. *Thank God he won't be focused on me for a while.* Dydre put the two remaining packets of money inside a suitcase she purchased earlier, then took the suitcase to the Airport Marriott to be picked up by Reynolds. Meeting him for dinner that evening was not in her plans. *Too bad, George, but I don't trust you. If I leveled with you, you'd slip and tell the FBI woman I'm not meeting you for dinner.*

Dydre didn't call Reynolds until later that night. "The balance is ready for you." she said into the mobile phone as soon as Reynolds answered. "You can pick it up at the Airport Marriott. I mailed the claim receipt to you." She ended the call as soon as she heard, "Okay—"

Anthony Mangiano emailed the photos he'd taken to Mary Ellen who sent them out on a worldwide message for identification and information. Alice ran them through the FBI's database. The next move was up to Red. Anthony took a room in the same hotel as Red and, turning on his charm, paid the night receptionist fifty dollars for her help.

"Sir I'm not supposed to say, but the redheaded woman checked in using the name of Debby Jones."

"Thank you…Judy," Anthony replied after reading her name tag. "You've been a big help to me." He winked at the woman.

"Please don't tell anyone I told you her name. I could lose my job," she said.

"Not to worry, Judy." He flashed a big smile that seemed to light up the lobby. *That's probably another bogus name, but I'll pass it on to Mary Ellen*, he thought.

"Ms. Jones is scheduled to check out in the morning," Judy added. "She asked for a wake-up call at six a.m."

"Judy, you've been very helpful," Anthony said, then mimicked a kiss. "Please give me a wake-up call at a quarter to six."

Next he slipped the concierge fifty dollars to find out where Red was going when she left the next morning. Then he headed to the bar for a drink and sat where he could watch the entrance just in case Red doubled back on him.

Wednesday, May 24, 1995
Washington, DC

Anthony followed Dydre to Washington, DC, where she checked into the Ritz-Carlton hotel in Tysons Corner. That evening he tailed her to Tysons Galleria and watched her stroll through three levels of the mall, occasionally stopping to window-shop. At first, he thought she was just passing the time, but after studying her for almost an hour as she milled around the mall, he thought otherwise. *You're looking for someone, aren't you? Well then, let me see if I can be of assistance to you, Red. I'll just make myself available.* He made his way slowly to where she was standing, looking at a jewelry display.

"They're nice, aren't they?" he said, looking at the display of diamond necklaces.

"They are. Your wife will like it."

"I'm not married."

"Your girlfriend, then?"

"No girlfriend either. I'm just killing time really."

Dydre looked at him, paying closer attention. "Oh, are you here on business?"

"I just finished up my business and I'm going to take some time off to see the city."

Not familiar with the city, she thought. "What kind of business are you in?"

"I work for an IT company. Most of our contracts are with the Defense Department. I am in DC a lot, but I've never taken time to see the city."

"Well, there's a lot to see."

"Do you live here?"

"No, I live in Europe. I'm here on business as well."

"Europe? Nice. Your accent is English though."

"I went to school in Cambridge and the accent stuck."

"What type of business are you in?" Anthony studied her.

"I'm an international trade consultant. I come over here quite a lot."

"I see. Say, I haven't eaten all day. Is there a good place to eat around here?"

"Well, there are several places that are pretty good. There's Maggiano's, an Italian place on the upper level. The food is good and the service is great."

"That sounds good. Why don't you join me?"

"Umm, well…" *Not exactly what I planned,* she thought. *I don't want to get stuck with this guy. IT contractor. I'll just see where this goes.* "Sure, that would be nice."

"My name is Anthony—Tony if you like."

"I think I like Anthony better. Mine is Diann."

He smiled. *Another alias or is this her real name?*

The two took the escalator to the upper level and were soon seated in a booth just off the main dining area of the restaurant. Anthony ordered a bottle of red wine and kept the meandering conversation going. Dydre remained guarded. She evaluated everything he said, constantly listening for any inconsistencies in his story.

"I'll have the special. It's always good," she said as she peered at him over the top of the menu. "You can't go wrong."

"Sounds good to me."

They continued to chat throughout the meal. Dydre still couldn't detect anything but sincerity in the man who sat across from her. *No obvious bulges that conceal a weapon which would indicate an FBI Agent or undercover officer,* she thought. *He's not pushy or rushed, just casual and self-confident.* She smiled and laughed as they talked.

Anthony divided the remainder of the wine between them. "You were right. That was good."

"I thought you would like it. Well, I—"

"Would you like to go get a drink, Diann?"

"I must be going. I've got an early morning meeting. Thank you for the dinner company." She smiled and stood.

"The pleasure was mine. Would you like to have dinner tomorrow night?"

"I would like to, but I have a commitment with a client tomorrow evening."

"What about Friday evening?"

"I'm sorry, I'm going out of town Friday. Perhaps when I'm back in town we could get together."

"Here's my card. I can be reached at that number. You may hear of someone that needs IT support."

"And my card," she said as she offered it to him. She took his card and glimpsed at it before dropping it into her purse. *He's a possibility,* she thought. *So far, so good. He might just work if his story checks out. He's a sharp guy, seems well educated. Could prove to be useful. If he works the DOD maybe he can introduce me to some key people inside the Pentagon. For the time being, I'll just see how this plays out.*

Dydre extended her hand and thanked him again for the dinner conversation. When he took her hand, she was delighted by his masculine touch.

She started to step away and he asked, "When do you think you will be back in town? Maybe we could meet again."

"I'm never sure of my schedule. It's very fluid depending on clients. Probably a few days."

"I see. Well, maybe next trip. Have a safe flight."

"Thank you. Good evening." She smiled and walked away. *He is a gentleman,* she thought. *But I'll have Clay check him out.*

20

Anthony sat at the desk in his hotel room and made a few notes on what he learned from Red—now calling herself Diann—which was virtually nothing, and even less about the woman in the photograph. The bits and pieces of information he learned were just that, bits and pieces. He still had not located the woman in the photograph identified as Sam, but believed Red would lead him to her. Learning of her departure was frustrating but patience was the key to discovering more about both women. *She said she would be back in town in a few days,* he thought. *If she will or not is another story. I need to find out where she's going.* When he was satisfied that he captured the few details, he called Newport.

"This is Newport," the voice said.

"This is Mangiano, sir. I have an update for you."

"Go ahead."

"I made contact with the redheaded woman tonight and only have a few sketchy details so far. She used the name Diann, said she lived in Europe and worked as an international trade consultant. She spoke with a slight English accent and said she went to school in Cambridge. All of that is probably fictitious, but it may be worth checking out. She did say she was leaving early in the morning and has a meeting with a client tomorrow evening."

"Did she say where she was going in the morning or whom she is meeting tomorrow evening?" Newport asked.

"No, I think she may have just been putting me off, but I'll find out. She's going out of town on Friday, and could be heading back to Europe, or anywhere for that matter. She's smart and hasn't really let her guard down."

"Good. It's a start. I'll pass this on to Mary Ellen. Maybe what you've learned will lead to something."

"I'll be watching for her in the morning and pick up her trail. Can you ask Mary Ellen to start working on the airlines and find out where she's going? I don't want to lose her."

"Mary Ellen and her crew will get to work on the information and be back to you soon."

Anthony hung up and leaned back in the chair. He reviewed each detail in his mind from the time he met Red in the mall until he left her. When he felt certain he hadn't forgotten anything, he switched off the light and went to bed.

Trieste, Italy

Günter Schenck, in the basement beneath his shop, checked his notes once more before departing for the scheduled meeting with his contact. Günter operated a small computer and electronics shop as a front for the CIA in Trieste. From all respects—including financials, checking account, and the like—it resembled a real business in case someone investigated him. He even sold and repaired equipment. The business masked his primary mission, which was to collect intelligence, plant electronic surveillance devices in electronics, and report back to Washington.

The purpose of his meeting was to update a report he had provided two weeks ago after learning about the Rangers from his network. His contact would send the update to CIA headquarters in Langley, Virginia. Günter's initial report led to the DIA and FBI's operation in Austin when he discovered that a terrorist organization planned to acquire several of the devices. This update would notify the CIA headquarters that the devices were expected to be delivered within the next two days. Unfortunately, that was too short of notice for a CIA response team to intercept the shipments before their delivery to the Arab terrorists in Bosnia-Herzegovina. Günter didn't want to deliver the message and Washington surely didn't want to receive it. The message quoted the subversive group's rhetoric that "they would defeat NATO forces with this product." Günter added in his report, "I believed that, and from what my sources told me, the terrorists planned to test out the product very quickly, then launch a major assault on NATO."

Günter's clientele ran the gamut of users—good and bad. The list of thieves, crooks, and subversive groups hostile to the US and NATO was the most impressive. With his true identity unknown to Dydre, he conducted the evaluation on the device for her.

With Ranger's functionality verified by Günter and expected delivery to the terrorists, the CIA and FBI scrambled to react. The size of Ranger made it extremely difficult to locate and the use of satellites or other overhead observation was useless. Günter needed to find out exactly where the terrorists were to take delivery of the devices and what their plans were. But obtaining this information presented a challenge as he was restricted in his ability outside of his shop to determine the location. He could rely only on his contacts and word of mouth.

5:07 a.m.
Thursday, May 25, 1995

An intrusive ringing woke Dydre from her sleep. Disoriented at first, she patted at the alarm not realizing it was the phone. Then finally, awake enough to know it was not the clock, she flicked on the light and read the numbers on clock before she picked up the receiver.

"Yes?"

"Dydre, Clay. We need to talk right away." The phone went dead—a signal for her to go to another phone and call him back immediately.

She splashed water in her face and ran her brush through her hair. *What's eating at him? Not how I wanted to start my day!* Throwing on her clothes, she grabbed her purse and headed out the door.

The lobby was vacant as she anticipated. Stepping to the lobby phone, secluded out of the main traffic flow, Dydre dropped her purse on the desk as she looked around the vacant room once again. She dialed Clay's special number.

"It's about damn time! What took you so long?" Clay said, answering on the first ring.

"What is it? Do you know what time it is?"

"Kingpin just called me. The devices Reynolds sent don't work!"

"What do you mean they don't work? I saw it work and Günter verified that it worked. They probably just don't know how to operate it. There was supposed to be an instruction sheet in the shipment. Maybe they can't read English."

"I told Kingpin you'd check it out. Call his man, the al-Qaida facilitator, what was his name...Jamaal, right away. He's expecting your call. Do you still have the phone number?"

"Shit! Yes, I have it. Anything else?"

"Just get this straightened out! I don't want them spreading the word that we're not to be trusted. I'm working on a shipment to Liberia and Sudan."

"I need you to check someone out. He might be useful to me."

"What's his name?"

Dydre withdrew Anthony's business card from her bag and read the information to him. "He seemed legitimate but I don't want to take any chances."

"I'll have the senator get right on it. Do whatever you need to do and get this mess cleaned up!"

"Clay, what about this weekend? I want to see David."

"You'll have to wait. This is more important. Now go straighten out this mess."

She dropped the phone on the cradle and looked at the clock on the wall. *This day has already gone to hell. Clay, you bastard, you're screwing up my plans. Reynolds, if you have something to do with this, you're dead meat. Dammit! I need a coffee.*

Picking up her mobile phone, Dydre dialed the number she had used before to contact Jamaal. Connecting on the third ring, a man's voice said, "Yasir Rashid Jamaal."

"This is Sam. I understand you have a little problem."

"I may have a little problem but you could have a big one. This shit, Ranger, doesn't work. None of them and we paid a good price for them."

"I'll be there as quick as I can to check them out."

"Come to the same café as before in Ilidža."

"No. Just bring them to the airport."

"I said the café."

The conversation was short and she didn't like the tone in his voice. She wanted a more populated place. The meeting was in their territory, by their rules, and they were not happy customers. *This is going to be dicey*, she thought as she hung up the phone.

Dydre returned to her room then called Günter. "I just got word the Rangers don't work. You told me they did."

"Ja, Ja, it worked. Just as you said it would. Who said it doesn't work? I checked it out myself."

"My client called my boss, then he called me."

"They probably can't read English. They're stupid. Can you bring it to my shop?"

"No, it's in Bosnia-Herzegovina."

"That's a very dangerous place. What do you want me to do?"

"Nothing for now. I just wanted to confirm that it worked when you saw it. I've got to check it out. I'll call you if I need your help."

"Be careful. Those radicals can be very dangerous and short on patience."

"I know. I've dealt with them before. You just be by your phone."

Dydre booked her flight to Sarajevo as soon as she completed her call with Günter, then showered and dressed. Lifting the receiver to call Reynolds, she looked at her watch. *Damn, it's too early to call,* she thought. *The one-hour time difference means he won't be in his office for two more hours.* She punched in the numbers to his mobile phone and it went straight to his voice mail. *Shit!* She walked to the window and gazed at the skyline. After a few minutes, she dialed room service and ordered a continental breakfast with juice and coffee. She turned on the television. She thought the news may help pass the time but nothing interested her. The minutes crept by while she waited to call Reynolds.

A little after 8:30 a.m. Dydre dialed Reynolds's number to see if he had failed to mention something on operating Ranger, even though she doubted it as Günter had been able to operate it without any problems. Her call went immediately to Reynolds's voice mail. She looked at her watch again. *George, where the hell are you? Well, maybe it's still too early for him. I'll try a little later. I've got to get to the airport.*

Anthony sat in his rental car where he could watch the front entrance of the hotel. At about 8:40 a.m. he saw Red leave the hotel and get into a cab. *I thought you had to leave early. This isn't early. Okay, now where are you going?* he thought. The cab pulled away and he followed at a safe distance behind. As soon as the cab pulled onto the Dulles Toll Road, he knew she was headed for the airport but beyond that he didn't know.

21

Tysons Corner, Virginia

Mary Ellen, at her desk, reviewed the information Assistant Secretary Newport gave her and made a few notes on Anthony's report from the night before. When her phone rang, she closed the file's cover and answered, "This is Mary Ellen."

"Mary Ellen, this is Anthony."

"Good morning! I see you are making a little headway."

"A little. Red's good and didn't let her guard down. She went to Dulles and I lost her in the crowd. That place was packed. I need to know where she's going and who she's meeting. Have you come up with anything on her?"

"Nothing yet. I'm working full-time on her and I'll let you know as soon as I find out anything."

"Thanks."

"Be careful." She hung up the phone, recorded the time and additional notes in the file.

"Alice, Hector," Mary Ellen said over her cubical. "I've got some information you both need to see."

"Is it about our little bitch and Mr. Reynolds?" Alice asked.

"You got it, kiddo."

"Hector, get your sweet ass over here," Alice said, sitting in the chair in front of Mary Ellen.

"Yes, Ms. Johnson." He quietly stepped from behind his desk and snuck up behind Alice.

"Hector, one of these days I'm going to punch out your lights. You scared the shit out of me." Alice had not seen him come around from behind and stand next to her.

Leaning over Mary Ellen's desk, Alice read Newport's notes and what Mary Ellen had added, then said, "I knew that chubby son-of-a-bitch Reynolds was pulling a fast one on us the other night. He knew the woman wasn't going to show for dinner. He just played us, made it look like she stood him up for dinner. That fat bastard shipped Rangers. Shit!"

"Hector, run these names and background information on the woman and see what pops up," Mary Ellen said, referring to the information in the report. "I'll be working on the airlines. I'm sure she used an alias there, too, and it's going to be a bitch to check out all the names."

"I'll check with the guys in San Antonio to see if they'll have another chat with Mr. Reynolds. He's playing us," Alice said.

About forty-five minutes later the three regrouped to exchange what they discovered.

"Reynolds wasn't at work when I talked to Kennedy," Alice said.

"I *don* have anything on the names yet and it's too soon to get anything back from the UK on Cambridge," Hector said. "It'll take a little time."

"Nothing else has turned up on the woman in the photograph, and so far, nothing even close to any of the names has turned up on the airline manifests," Mary Ellen said. "I've sent messages to the stations closest to the places, most likely, where she'll land. Hopefully, they can spot her when she arrives and find out where she's going. My guess is Europe."

"Mary Ellen, did you see this message?" Hector said, holding a piece of paper. "It's from our front, Günter Schenck. The Ranger devices are in Bosnia-Herzegovina. The terrorists received them, but are having some type of problem. They aren't working."

"They're in Bosnia but not working? I thought Günter checked them out and they were fine. That could be a stroke of luck for us. Send a note back to Günter and ask him if he did something to it." Mary Ellen said.

"Will do!"

"We don't have much time," Mary Ellen continued. "And they'll figure out a solution to their problem pretty quick. I'll brief the boss."

"Schenck also says that the woman Sam, who brought the device to him, is going to Ilidža, Bosnia-Herzegovina, to find out what's wrong and fix them," Hector said. "This is hot *sheet*!"

Alice, looked at Hector and started to speak, but then paused. "I've got to take care of Captain Jordan. He's eating my shorts over Albritten. Do you need me to go with you to brief the boss?"

"No, I'll handle it. You take care of Jordan."

Mary Ellen picked up the secure phone and dialed Assistant Secretary Newport. "Mr. Secretary, this is Mary Ellen."

"Yes, hold on a minute. I need to close my door. Go ahead, Mary Ellen."

"The terrorists have the Ranger devices but are having a problem with them. They're not working and our woman in the photograph, Sam, is on her way to Ilidža to fix them."

"That doesn't leave us much time. Maybe we can get them all," Newport said. "There's a Delta team on standby, which I can get to Sarajavo on short order. They're to recover or destroy all the devices and take out the terrorists. I want that woman. I'll notify the Delta commander to take her alive. I'll get you his address so you can transmit her photo to him."

"I've already sent a message to the station there to follow her and report the location back as soon as they can."

"Good! Where's Anthony?"

"He's still here in DC. He's just waiting for me to give him the woman's destination. I'll have him on a plane shortly."

'Give him the details and link him up with the Delta commander. I want Sam. We'll get the redheaded woman after we get Sam. Let's hope they can take the woman without killing her. She's no good to me dead.'

"Got it!"

"Tell Alice to get with the boys in San Antonio and to stick close to Reynolds. The terrorists may get in touch with Reynolds to fix the Rangers, if they haven't already. Or the woman could contact him and he could be going to meet her in Bosnia-Herzegovina to fix the devices. I'll notify the Delta commander about him as well.

"Good work, Mary Ellen."

"Yes, sir."

Frankfurt, Germany

Zsigmond sat in a wingback chair, perusing the latest copy of *Armada International* magazine, when the phone rang. Taking a sip of his Scotch, he looked at the number and placed the receiver to his ear. "This is Clay."

"Clay, this is Senator Griffith."

"Good afternoon, Senator, or, for you, good morning. What's on your mind?"

"Clay, I just learned that a Delta team is being sent to Bosnia-Herzegovina. They're headed for Ilidža. It's a suburb of Sarajevo close to the Sarajevo International Airport."

"Yes. I'm familiar with the place."

"Their mission is to take out a cell of terrorists there and then to either recover or destroy the Ranger devices—the ones you shipped."

"When are they supposed to be there?"

"Shortly! They're en route now."

"Okay, Senator, calm down. I want you to raise a stink with the president and see if you can get this stalled or cancelled."

"Clay, they'll be on the ground anytime now."

"I understand. Get to work on the president and keep me posted. What about the name I gave you to check out, Anthony Mangiano?"

"He's clean. He's a vice president of business development for an IT company that has several DOD contracts.

"Good, now get on the president." Without waiting for the senator's reply, he broke the connection and dialed Dydre's mobile phone to alert her. The call went to her voice mail. Clay left a message.

Tysons Corner, Virginia

"*Sheet!*" Hector said, as he read the message from DIA Officer Kennedy. "Alleese!" he said, his voice carrying across the room. "Alleese!" Not hearing her reply, he turned to Mary Ellen and asked, "Mary Ellen, have you seen Alleese?"

"She just stepped out. What's wrong?"

"I need to find Alleese right away. *Shezs gonna* be real mad." Hector began to pace, his purple Hush Puppies squeaking on the tile floor.

"Hector, what is it?"

"Reynolds is gone?"

"What do you mean, Reynolds is gone?"

At that moment Alice entered and said, "What's this about Reynolds?"

"*Hezs* gone."

"Gone where?"

"Alleese, I just got this from Kennedy." Hector handed the message to her. "He's confirmed that Reynolds disappeared and they don't know where he is. They've checked his house and with the neighbors. Poof!" Hector raised his palms upward. "Gone."

"That son-of-a-bitch!" Alice said, her voice harsh and her fists clinched. "I told those guys in the San Antonio office to watch him. I didn't trust him for a minute. It doesn't say anything about either woman. They're asleep down there. I can't believe this shit! Hector, let's go to Austin to see if we can get a lead on Reynolds. No one just goes poof and disappears!"

"Okay, Alleese. Are you *gonna* brief the boss?"

"No time, I'll call him. Mary Ellen, can you start checking to see if you can get a trail on Reynolds?"

"I'm on it," Mary Ellen replied.

"Alleese, *he's* not *gonna* like it." Hector said, squinting his eyes.

"He's really not going to like it if we can't find Reynolds. Let's go!"

22

Ilidža, Bosnia-Herzegovina

Dydre parked the car and walked toward the café—her Walther P5 pistol in her right cargo pants pocket and stiletto in the other—to meet Yasir Rashid Jamaal. This time she carried two extra magazines in her right rear pocket.

The sun was low in the late afternoon sky and the city was unchanged from her preceding trip there—it was a no man's land and it stunk. Occasionally, the sound of gunfire punctuated the silence. The last time, Jamaal and his men had wanted what she was selling, but were unprepared for Sam. This time it was different. Handing over $5 million for something that didn't work warranted no second chance, and forgiveness was a bullet. Dydre suspected she was being watched as she approached the café. Her senses strained to hear, see, smell, or touch the danger in time to react.

Just as she rounded the corner of the café, she felt a dull pain as something pressed firmly against her back. *Jamaal's welcoming committee*, she thought without turning around. *It's probably the same young scraggly bearded Arab that I worked over before and that's no doubt the muzzle of his Kalashnikov assault rifle poking me in the back.* Dydre froze. "Well, cockroach," she said. "What'll it be, you shoot me, or you take me inside to show Jamaal how to operate Ranger?"

"Shut up! Put *you* hands up."

"We went through this last time, remember? You aren't going to feel me up."

"Shut up! Put *you* hands up and lean against wall."

At that moment another man appeared, the same taller and older Arab as before. He shoved Dydre against the wall and stepped behind her. Placing both of his arms around her, he grasped her breasts to check for weapons, then stopped. He slid his hands to her padded waist, then stopped, not feeling her P5. Reaching up, Tall Arab grabbed her hair and pulled it back. The wig came off in his hand. His face registered a combination of surprise and bewilderment as he realized she was in disguise.

Dydre, who had sensed his surprise when he felt her padded bra, took advantage of the split second when the man hesitated. She sprang, kicking up and to the rear, catching him in the groin. With a hard push off the wall, she crashed into the groaning man, knocking him into the younger one. She drew the Walther and fired twice as the two men stumbled backwards. Her first shot hit Tall Arab between the eyes and killed him instantly. Her second shot hit Short Arab in the heart. Although he would be dead by the time he hit the ground, a look of shock covered his face as he struggled to take a half step forward before collapsing.

"Well, shit! This unraveled real quick," she said to herself. "I've got to get the hell out of here! There'll be no talking done today."

Dydre bent over to retrieve her wig as two bullets struck the wall behind her. Immediately she hit the ground and rolled into the shadow of the building. Springing to her feet, she darted behind the hulk of a burned-out car ten feet from her. She crouched down and scanned the area in an attempt to locate the shooter. Her heart raced. *No one in sight, no movement,* she thought. Her mouth was bitter with adrenaline and death seemed nearby. Another scan of the area revealed movement two blocks away—a person in black, then another. *Shit! Soldiers. That's why the shooter stopped. It's now or never.*

She advanced quickly and slipped along the shadows. Moving in the opposite direction of the soldiers, she darted in and out behind remains of cars, garbage bins, and piles of rubble. She paused only briefly to search for other snipers or for a blocking position established by the soldiers that would prevent her escape. Finally, she reached the car, slung the door open, and jammed the key into the ignition as she flopped behind the wheel. Dropping the transmission into drive, she floored the gas pedal and the tires squealed as it shot forward. She zigzagged as fast as she could through the vacant, debris-strewn streets to escape the perilous neighborhood.

Once clear of the area, Dydre slowed the car and breathed a sigh of relief. She retrieved the mobile phone from her pocket and switched it on. Within a few seconds the light flashed signaling a voice mail. She pressed the buttons and heard Clay's voice. "Dydre, get out of there! A US Army Delta team is on its way to take out the terrorists you're meeting with. Call me."

"Well no shit, Clay!" she said, looking at the mobile phone. "I figured that out. Thank you for the advance notice. Asshole!" *Now that this meeting is screwed up, I'll be on their list of people to take revenge on. The only way I can get back in their good graces, if at all, is to get their money back to them or get them working Rangers. I can't give the money back. Mr. Reynolds, it's time we had a little talk.*

Dydre looked at her watch and calculated the time difference between Ilidža and Austin. *Seven hours. Let's see if I can get George.* She punched the numbers into the phone. It went to voice mail. *Shit! George, I've tried to call you for two days.* Next, she dialed the main number for the company.

"IT Security Solutions. How may I direct your call?" the woman's voice said.

"George Reynolds, please."

"I'm sorry, Mr. Reynolds isn't in. Can someone else help you?"

"No, I need to speak to George. Will he be back today?"

"He's out sick and I don't know when he'll be back in the office. Would you like his voice mail?"

"What's his home number? I'll try him there. It's quite important."

"I'm sorry, but I can't give out his home number. Would you like to leave a message?"

"No, I'll check back tomorrow. Thank you." *Sick, my ass,* she thought.

Frustrated, she dropped the phone in the seat next to her. The drive out to the airport gave her time to think and plan her next step. George Reynolds topped the list. *Maybe he's sick and maybe he isn't. But I need to have a little talk with him.*

Hotel Le Plaza
Brussels, Belgium

Dydre set her bag on the floor as she entered her room at the Hotel Le Plaza. She kicked off her shoes and took a bottle of mineral water from the fridge. *Another weekend apart from David. It won't be much longer.* She sat at the desk with his picture in front of her, but before writing him, she had to try to get in touch with Reynolds again. She picked up her mobile phone and dialed the numbers to connect to information in the Unites States. When the operator for Austin information answered, Dydre asked, "Would you give me the listing for George Reynolds?"

"I'm sorry, that is an unlisted number," the operator replied.

Unlisted, shit! She dropped the phone to the desk. *Sick and an unlisted number. Too fishy. I've got to get to Austin to find out what's going on. Something isn't right. If Reynolds skipped, I'll have the terrorists and Clay after me. There's not much time to find him and get this Ranger crap cleaned up. If I am ever to break free of Clay, I can't stop now.* "Dammit, Clay!" she said. "I don't know whether to cry, be mad, throw a fit, or what. I've had all I can take from you. God, I've got to get away from you and your thieving, murdering world! I have nothing and no one except for a weekend every now and then." *I need someone to share my life with,* she thought. *I need to be held and have companionship from a man—one that isn't trying to kill me and one that would be good to me. Is there such a man?* She picked up the receiver and made a reservation on the next flight to Austin, which wasn't until Sunday morning. Once the flight was confirmed, she dialed Zsigmond's number.

"Hello, this is Clay," he said.

"Clay, Dydre. I have a little problem with Reynolds. I can't reach him. I'm afraid he may have skipped."

"What do you mean skipped? Where would he go?"

"You know, gone. Disappeared. His company says he's out sick and doesn't know when he'll return. His home phone is unlisted. I'm flying back to Austin Sunday to see what I can find out. Can you try to find out Reynolds's home address and call me back? Also, can you find out if he left the country? Leave me a message on my phone as soon as you get it."

"All right, but it'll be a while."

"Just get it, okay?"

"Kingpin told me that you killed his two men. He's quite unhappy about it."

"Things got out of hand real quick. I didn't have much choice."

"The only thing that's keeping them from going after you for now is that I told them the Delta team was on their way to him."

"I'd hope he'd be appreciative. You just saved his hide."

"Dydre, this is screwed up and has to be fixed immediately. I've got a lot of money riding on this. Are you getting sloppy?"

"Clay, get serious. I'm not sloppy and I'm working on it! You keep Kingpin off my back and I'll deliver Reynolds or replacements."

"Remember, Reynolds has $5 million of my money."

"I haven't forgotten."

"Be sure you don't! I'll call you as soon as I have his address."

The phone went dead before she could say another word.

A cloud of bluish smoke hovered above Clay's head as he ran his thick fingers through his hair. He gazed out the window for moment, then returned to his seat and placed his cigar in the ashtray. Turning to his computer, he opened his contacts and scrolled down the names until he found the one he was looking for. He dialed the number.

"Yes," the man's voice said.

"Rüdiger, I have a mission for you," Clay said. "Are you available?"

Rüdiger, an ex-Legionnaire, often worked for Clay when Dydre was unavailable or if Clay didn't think she could handle the job. Rüdiger anticipated the day when Clay would make this particular call to him. If anyone was up to the task, it was him, but Rüdiger was no fool. He knew she was dangerous.

"What's the mission?"

"I have an uneasy feeling about Dydre. I want you to follow her and see what she's up to."

"Sounds simple enough."

"She's on her way to Austin, Texas. How soon can you be ready to go?"

"In about two hours, if you'll send your car to pick me up. I assume you'll have all the details for me when the car gets here?"

"Yes, you'll have a complete package. Keep me up to date."

Clay went on to tell Rüdiger about the Ranger devices and the events leading up to his phone call. "I don't have a good feeling about this whole mess. I think Reynolds, and possibly Dydre, might be planning to make off with my money. Find out what they're up to. If they are going to pull a fast one, take care of them."

23

Sunday, May 28, 1995
Austin, Texas

Dydre drove slowly along Reynolds's street in search of the address Clay supplied. *I can see where you spent your money, George. Nice houses, Spanish-style, red tile roofs, and large lots. David would like it here.*

She located the house number and took a hard look at the area and yard as she drove past. *It's quiet, no one about and nothing in the yard. I don't like it. Are you really home sick, George? I doubt it.* Several houses down, she turned around and drove back to the house, where she parked in the driveway.

Dydre pushed the doorbell. No answer. She peeked in the sidelights. *No lights, no one in sight,* she thought. Again, she pushed the doorbell, but still no response. She twisted the doorknob and found it locked. Stepping to the front window, she looked in. *No one home.* She then went to the side of the house, unlatched the gate, and entered. *Thank God. No dog. The yard is vacant.*

At the first window, she peered in but detected no movement inside. She tried to open the window but it was locked, as was the adjoining window. She looked deeper into the bedroom and saw on the wall the keypad for the alarm system. *That figures,* she thought as she stepped onto the patio. *Dealing with the alarm will take too much time. Better check out the backdoor as well.* She stepped to the door and tried its knob. "The place is locked up tight," she said. "Shit! Where is he?"

She was well aware that she didn't have much time to find Reynolds, and get working Rangers, or Reynolds, to Bosnia-Herzegovina before Clay or the Arabs would start to get impatient. Either would be a problem. *I don't have time to screw around with Reynolds. He's going to get me killed.*

Dydre felt a play in the mechanism when she jiggled the door but it remained locked. As she anticipated, she felt the door move, which indicated it was away from the seals and needed adjustment. She looked at the bolt from the knob where it engages the strike plate. *This would be a piece of cake,* she thought. *But I can't risk the time to bypass the alarm system. I don't want the neighbors to get suspicious, seeing the car in the drive, and call the police. The neighbors may know something.*

In front of the house she paused and looked around the neighborhood. Not seeing anyone outside, she went to the house next door and rang the doorbell. No response. Again, she rang the bell but no one came to the door. As she turned she saw a woman's head in the window of the house across the street. *The neighborhood busybody,* she thought. Dydre crossed the street and as she stepped onto the drive, an elderly woman came out the front door and picked up a watering can with a long curved spout.

"Excuse me, the house across the street, the Reynolds—" Dydre said.

"The Reynolds? They live across the street but they're not home," the woman said, her voice full of caution.

"Can you—"

"What do you want with them?"

"I do business with George from time to time. I came through town and thought I'd stop and visit with him and his wife for a while."

The skeptical gray-haired woman studied Dydre briefly as she stood, pleasantly smiling at her. "Nice people. He's quiet but I don't know him very well. Janice, his wife, is real sweet. She brought me these plants." The woman pointed to several potted house plants on the porch and then poured water onto one of them.

"Yes, Janice is a dear, isn't she?" Dydre said. "What a beautiful fern! The geraniums look like they're on fire."

"They do. Janice has such a green thumb."

"I know. Can you tell me—"

"Do you have a green thumb?"

"I grow a few plants. Do you—"

"You aren't from around here, are you? You have an accent."

"I went to school in Cambridge and I guess the accent stuck. Can you—"

"There were some others here looking for the Reynolds, too. Is something wrong?"

Dydre's brow wrinkled. "I don't know. Who were they?"

"I didn't like them. A bossy woman and two other men. The woman said she was the FBI and the other two men with her said they were from the Defense Department."

"It was probably something to do with George's work. He did work for the Defense Department. It's probably nothing. They do 'checks' all the time."

"They went to the Reynoldses' house but nobody was home. Then they went to the neighbors asking questions. That bossy woman…well, she could've been a little nicer. I would've helped her, but since she was so brash, I didn't want to."

"What were they asking about?"

"Oh, I don't know…if I'd seen the Reynoldses and knew where they were. Things like that. I didn't tell her anything because she made me mad."

"Well good for you. I wouldn't worry about it." *So Reynolds has skipped out and the government is looking for him. I've got to find him first. I knew he was trying to pull a fast one.*

"Well…can you tell me when the Reynoldses will be back?"

"Don't know. It is strange though. Janice usually tells me when they're going to be out of town. She didn't say anything this time."

"Well, they're probably not going to be gone long."

"Probably. But Janice did give me these flowers."

"Maybe she forgot to tell you?"

"Perhaps."

"Do you think they went on a short holiday?"

"Well, like I said, Janice usually tells me when they're going away. I guess they could have. They have a house in Costa Rica, you know. They go there a lot."

"I've heard George mention it several times. By any chance do you have their address there so I can contact them?"

"Well, you look like a nice lady. Are you married?"

"No, my husband is dead. I have a son."

Just a minute." The older woman set her water bucket down and entered the house. She returned within a few minutes. "Here you go. I forgot where I put it," the woman said, handing Dydre a piece of paper. "I jotted their address down for you. I think their house is on the coast."

"I believe it is. Thank you very much."

"Good-bye."

Dydre hurried across the street, got into the car, and drove to the hotel. *Reynolds skipped out on everyone, but do they know where he went? If they don't know now, they will soon. Am I ahead of them?*

She made reservations on the Monday morning flight to Liberia, Costa Rica, the closest airport to the address the woman provided. Since she didn't want to go on a wild goose chase, she dialed the phone number the woman gave her. After six rings the answering machine picked up. Dydre cancelled the call.

Rüdiger, sitting in a rental car two blocks away, watched as Dydre pulled out of the driveway. As soon as she was out of sight, he pulled into the woman's driveway and got out of the car. "Excuse me, ma'am!"

The woman, with watering can in her right hand, rose up and said, "Yes, what is it?"

"I'm Special Agent Brown of the FBI," Rüdiger said as he closed the car door and held up a fake FBI identification card.

"I've been watching the Reynoldses' house. That woman that just left, would you please tell me what was she looking for?"

"Well, you sure are a lot nicer than that FBI woman that was here before."

"Oh, how is that?"

"She was bossy and cold. She made me mad."

"I'm sorry about that ma'am. I'll make a note of it. The woman that just left—"

"What're you watching the Reynoldses' house for?"

"It's just routine. The woman—"

"She was nice too. Pretty, wasn't she?"

"Yes, she was. Please tell me what she was looking for."

"The Reynoldses of course."

"Yes, of course. Did she say why she wanted them or where she was going when she left?"

"You FBI people sure are nosy."

"Sometimes we are. The woman—"

"She said she does some work with George and was coming through town. She just stopped by for a visit."

"I see. Anything else?"

"No, that's about it."

"Did the woman happen to say where she was going?"

"She said she was going to contact the Reynoldses in Costa Rica."

"Costa Rica? I didn't know they were in Costa Rica."

"If that other FBI woman wasn't so snippy and rude, I would have helped her but she made me mad. I'm not sure they went to Costa Rica, like I told the lady that just left. But they do go there a lot."

"Do you have their address there?"

"That other lady wanted it, too."

"May I have their address?"

"I suppose. Just a minute." The woman put the water bucket down and entered the house. Returning after a moment with a small piece of paper in her hand, she said, "Here you are."

"Thank you. I appreciate your time. Have a good day."

The woman picked up her water bucket, and watched the man leave before she continued to water her plants.

As Rüdiger drove away, he peered over the steering wheel and mumbled to himself, "So she's on her way to Costa Rica to find Reynolds. It looks like the Fat Man was right—Reynolds skipped out. He's rarely wrong. But which side of the fence is Dydre on?"

24

Washington, DC

Senator Griffith, wiped the sweat from his face and leaned forward in his chair as he patted down his dark-brown hair. He checked his contact list and dialed a number. While the phone rang, he downed the remainder of his Scotch, a hint of more sweat on his face already visible.

"This is Clay," he said.

"Clay, this is Senator Griffith. Your man Reynolds is a hush-hush topic. There's a high-level classified investigation going on. I can't even find out anything about it. I…"

"Well, man, go on!"

"I've got to back off of this. I can't risk having them start investigating me."

"I'll tell you when to back off! I need to know where Reynolds is and what's going on."

"Clay, they'll start investigating me if I start asking questions and pushing."

"Senator, I have taken care of you and made sure you got reelected. I want answers! I want to know where Reynolds is and what this investigation is. Do you understand me, Senator?"

"Clay, it's too risky."

"Senator, I have some pretty explicit video of you and a prostitute that would put an end to your illustrious career.

The *Washington Post* would love to have it. Do you understand me?"

Griffith sat back in horror. The thought of a scandal sent perspiration streaming down his red cheeks. He leaned forward to refill his glass from the bottle on his desk, but his hand trembled and he splashed more on the on desk than in the glass. "I'll see what I can do."

"Now that we have an understanding, I want you to make the rounds and keep your ears open. No need to push. Just visit and see where it takes you. I want to know what's going on."

Hesitating, Griffith finally forced the words, "All right. I'll see what I can find out."

The phone line went dead.

Clay, angered by the senator's call, slammed his fist on the desk. He stood and paced as he chewed his cigar. He needed answers. He feared the terrorists would come after him for not fulfilling the contract to deliver working Rangers as promised. The disappearance of both his $5 million and Reynolds distressed him. "If Dydre and Reynolds are together in stealing my money," he said to himself, "she'll be after the boy. She's a fool! She should know she can't get to the boy."

The phone rang, breaking Clay's train of thought. "This is Clay," he answered.

"This is Rüdiger."

"What do you have for me?"

"It looks like Reynolds has gone to Costa Rica. Dydre was here in Austin and is headed after Reynolds. It appears that she isn't in with him."

"Stay with her and be sure she isn't. I want to know every move she makes."

"Will do. I'll call you from Costa Rica when I know more."

Clay tapped the button to get a dial tone and entered a number. When the man's voice answered, Clay said, "Stay alert. In the next few days Dydre may try to take the boy. If she tries, don't kill her. Just keep her and the boy until I can get there."

"Yes, sir."

Clay hung up. He anticipated hearing from the terrorists at any time but hoped that it would be after he had answers; otherwise they, or their associates, may pay him a visit. Waiting was something he wasn't good at. He contemplated offering Dydre up to bin Laden so as to keep his men away from his doorstep. But in doing so, he was assured of losing his money. He decided to wait before making that call. He wanted his money back first.

Over the next several hours, Dydre called Reynolds several times, only to get the answering machine. Finally, a man answered. Dydre recognized the voice as Reynolds's and immediately terminated the call. *So you're in Costa Rica,* she thought. *You bastard, you're not going to get away from me and make off with the money. You've got some work to do. We'll have a little discussion tomorrow.* Knowing the FBI and Defense Department were on Reynolds's trail concerned her, but she believed she had the advantage. What did bother her was Clay. She hadn't called him as she had nothing more to tell him. Not wanting to suffer through his rage, she wanted to find Reynolds first. *Clay will start making demands and pushing for results,* she thought. *I'm too close to breaking free from him to be reckless. I'm not about to get killed or arrested.*

25

Monday, May 29, 1995
The Pentagon

Secretary Newport faced Mary Ellen across a table in the SCIF conference room. "I received a message from the State Department that Reynolds used his passport to enter Costa Rica," she said. "Anthony's on a plane to Costa Rica and I'll have an address on Reynolds soon."

"Good! The woman will probably be meeting with Reynolds there, but keep watching to see if his passport is used anywhere else."

"That's how we see it, too. Do you want me to notify the Costa Rican government?"

"No, not until we find our leak. If we notify them, word could get out and whoever is leaking the information will know what we're doing. That could cause us some real problems."

"Yes, sir, it would," Mary Ellen said.

"Tell Anthony to call me as soon as he locates the woman, and emphasize again that we need her alive if at all possible. I want to coordinate this. I'm counting on her leading us to whomever she works for. I want them all but we don't have much time. Alice and Hector—"

"Are on a conference call to San Antonio," Mary Ellen said.

"Tell her Senator Griffith was trying to pressure the president on the Delta team's operation in Bosnia. We didn't think too much about it until he started nosing around."

"What's he up to? Isn't he planning to run for president?"

"He is. Griffith was asking questions about Reynolds. I want Alice to start checking around and see if she can determine what Griffith's interest in Reynolds is. Also, get the senator's phone records. Tell Alice to get a court order to wiretap his phone. We've got to do this by the book. Tell her I said *by the book*."

"Yes, sir. So you think he's possibly tied to this or knows something?"

"I don't know. I'm not taking any chances. Let's see where he takes us. Tell Alice to be careful and be discrete, but stay on this. If it gets out she's checking on him or he thinks we're investigating him, we'll have to deal with Griffith and that will be a disaster."

"I know. He's always looking for headlines…a bid for the White House."

"If she finds anything, both of you get with me immediately and in person."

"Yes, sir."

"Have you uncovered any more information on the Rangers or where they might be?"

"Nothing except some chatter about them, and that the buyers think they got ripped off. They're a bit upset."

"Keep turning over rocks. No telling what you might find. With any luck, it'll be where the devices are. The Delta team is on standby and I want them to move as soon as you have something. We may have only one chance at getting those devices and everyone involved in this."

"I know—and may stop a White House hopeful." Mary Ellen saw a slight grin on Newport's face and smiled. She closed her file and exited the conference room with Newport.

Papagayo, Costa Rica

Dydre parked the car out of sight from Reynolds's house and was ready for a closer look. Covering her red hair with a large floppy hat and carrying a large stuffed bag, she walked to the water's edge in her bathing suit. She located the beachfront entrance of Reynolds's house and put up an umbrella, then put on her sunglasses and lay on a blanket. Blending in with the rest of the people on the beach, she occupied a good vantage point to observe the house. For the next half hour she watched. The house was quiet without any movement inside.

Standing and adjusting her hat, she took a casual stroll along the water's edge, all the while keeping an eye on the house. A large covered patio, flanked by tropical trees, was attached to the house and opened out to the beach. Two large wicker chairs offered seating on one side while a barbeque grill stood on the other corner. A picnic table in the center completed the patio's setup.

Dydre searched the people who lounged in the water and on the sand, but didn't see Reynolds. After walking about a hundred yards past the house, she turned and made her way back. Occasionally, she picked up a shell and then discarded it in an effort to mimic the others enjoying their day out in the sun. Halfway back to her place on the sand, she spotted Reynolds floating in the water. *There you are. Floating like a blob of protoplasm, you fat bastard.* She continued to her blanket, keeping an eye on him. *That must be your wife with you. Anyone else?* She studied him and his wife. *He's in his own little paradise, thinks he has no cares and no troubles. Well, now he does.*

For a few minutes, Dydre watched a young boy about David's age playing with his mother. *I can see David and me on a beach like this somewhere.* As the small boy and his mother made their way back to their place, Dydre snapped back to reality just in time to see Reynolds and the woman trudge ashore and walk toward their house. As soon as they disappeared inside, Dydre gathered her things and sauntered back to the car. She was ready for her next move.

Rüdiger appropriated a nearby beach house, the vacation property of an absent family. It provided good observation of the sand and surf as well as Reynolds's house—just what he needed to watch Dydre and close enough to act when the time was right. "I know you too well, Dydre," he said to himself as he laid his binoculars on the window ledge. "All quiet now, time to relax. Your move, Dydre. I expect it'll be dark before you make your play. Then I'll know what you're up to." Settling back, checking his suppressed Beretta 9mm pistol, he was ready to move when she returned. He didn't need to follow her as he knew where she was going and Reynolds was her target.

Part Three

26

The tropical sun was sinking below the horizon, dipping into the water like a giant orange ball of fire. Several people lingered on the beach and others on their patios watching the sunset. When the giant fireball finally sank, its light extinguished, the spectators left behind the tranquil rhythm of the waves and returned to their homes.

As night fell, Dydre, dressed as Sam, returned and parked in the shadows. She remained seated in the car briefly and examined the area, making sure no one else lingered about. She then headed toward the beach under the pretense of taking an evening stroll along the shore. When she ambled to the beach side of Reynolds's house, she remained ever cautious. Bumping into the FBI woman or the Defense Department men was not in her plan. Finally, she reached the corner of the house and crept to the rear window. She peeked in but saw no one in the room. The only light was from the computer monitor on the desk and what light spilled through the open door. She tiptoed to the door and slowly twisted the knob. The door opened and she slipped in.

As she neared the house, Rüdiger identified her. He picked up his Beretta the moment she went inside. Then he slipped out the door and headed for the rear of Reynolds's house where he could see her sitting in the darkened room. "I know how you operate," he said to himself. "You're waiting for him to come to you and you chose this room to meet him." He knelt beneath the open window so he could hear. "Is the Fat Man right, or do you live until another day?"

Dydre remained seated as Reynolds entered his office. When he flipped on the light and saw her, the color drained from his face. He looked around to see if anyone else was with her, then, with a trembling hand, closed the door.

"Hello, George," she said. "We have a little business to conduct."

"Just a minute." George turned around and stepped out the door. "Janice, I have a little work to do."

"Okay, I need to go over to the neighbors anyway. How long will you be?"

"Not sure exactly, hopefully not too long." George stepped back into the room and closed the door behind him as soon as he heard Janice leave.

"Very good," Dydre said. "Now sit down!"

Reynolds stared into her eyes, then stepped in front of her and said, "I've got a question for you first, Sam. What do you mean by coming here like this?"

"Three million dollars, George. I told you not to fuck me over."

"What are you talking about?"

"George, I'm not in any mood to play games. You know damn well what I'm talking about! You were to ship four Rangers to Bosnia, remember?"

"I did."

"Yes, George, but you omitted one little detail. They don't work. Now sit down!"

"And if I don't?"

"Don't be stupid. You've got ten seconds to sit down and cooperate or you're dead."

"Don't try and bluff—"

"You now have five seconds."

"They worked when I shipped them. You even had them checked out to verify they worked. I can't help it if—"

"You've got two seconds. Now sit down!"

"Get out of here or I'll—"

Dydre's kick connected with his crotch. As he doubled over, she thrust up with the heel of her hand and struck him on the chin. He fell backwards to the floor like a sack of potatoes.

Reynolds groaned and opened his glassy eyes. Grabbing him by the shoulder, Dydre helped him up and guided him to the chair behind the desk. "Are you ready to cooperate now or do you want to take another little nap?"

He nodded. "What do you want me to do?"

"That's better. The Rangers don't work. What did you do to them?"

"I inserted a program to shut them down after your engineer checked them out."

"Why, George?"

"I just couldn't give working Rangers to terrorists."

"That's very patriotic of you, George. Now we have a problem. How're we going to correct the situation?"

"I can give your money back. But it will be tomorrow."

"That's not an option. Let's try again. You ship working replacements or we're going to take a little trip to Bosnia so you can fix them."

Reynolds stared at her. This woman meant business, and his only choice was her terms. "That won't be necessary. I can write a code to fix them and transmit it to the devices."

"That's a good plan. You write the code and as soon as they're working, I get out of your life. Just remember you're dead if there are any mistakes. Next time I won't be so nice and warn you. Have you got that?"

He looked at her, then rubbed his jaw. "I've got it. Now I've got work to do. Come back in the morning and I'll have your fix."

"No, George. I'll be right here with you until I verify they're working. I'm not taking any more chances with you. Now get to work."

Rüdiger turned away from the window and returned to the nearby house he used earlier. Once inside he sat in a chair beside the window so he could continue to observe the house while he made a phone call. He dialed Zsigmond's number.

"Yes, this is Clay," the sleepy voice said.

"Dydre has met with Reynolds. He's writing a code that will fix the Rangers. He should have it finished in a little while. Then he's transmitting it to the devices. Dydre's going to verify they're working before she leaves."

"Very good. Perhaps I was wrong about her. I'd have hated to part with her."

"She isn't in with him. She's on her own."

A long period of silence ensued, then came Zsigmond's response. "What do you mean?"

"You gave her $5 million for Reynolds, correct?"

"That's right."

"She only gave him $3 million."

Once again there was a long pause before Rüdiger heard the response, the voice slightly trembling and full of anger. "Are you sure?"

"Yes."

"As soon as she verifies the devices are working, you know what to do. I don't want any more screwups. Getting them working will be my saving grace with the Arabs. Report back when everything is settled."

"Will do!"

Rüdiger sat back and stared into the darkness as he formulated his move. There could be no witnesses, no mistakes—quick and clean. Otherwise, he'd be dead instead of Dydre. Leaving the area without running into an accomplice of hers or being seen was his last objective. "Dydre is the challenge," he said in a low voice.

Dressed in shorts and a tropical shirt and wearing a small backpack, Anthony trolled the moonless, neighborhood street in search of the address Mary Ellen had provided. He could hear the gentle lap of the waves nearby. Suddenly, a dog's bark broke the tranquility of the night. He plodded on as though he was out for an evening walk. A porch light flashed on, and a man peered out the door and eyeballed the neighborhood. Anthony waved a friendly greeting to the man and kept walking. The man, apparently satisfied nothing was out of the ordinary, went back into the house and turned out the light. Anthony exhaled slowly, then continued.

The dim light escaping from the closed blinds caught his attention as he approached Reynolds's house. He listened intently and stepped closer. *Is she here? Or has she already gone? I doubt I'm ahead of her.* Hearing nothing from the front of the house, he continued to the rear. When he turned the corner, he saw the light spilling out of the open door and windows onto the patio. Near the back of the house, he paused and wiped his brow. He heard a man and a woman talking. *They're in the back. Is it Reynolds and the woman or his wife? Are they alone and are they the right ones? If not, I could lose the woman. There's no turning back once I execute.*

Hearing the woman's voice say the name "Jamaal" and "Ranger," Anthony thought, *Right people, right place...anyone else?* Just as he was about to move around the corner to where he could observe those inside, he saw a silhouette move in the darkness. But the bright light on the patio, spilling outward, prevented him from seeing into the darkness. He backed around the corner and waited for his eyes to readjust. Then he made his way around to the other side of the house. *I know you're there. Who are you? Are you her backup or someone else? Where are you?*

Crossing to the adjacent house, Anthony increased his distance while decreasing the angle of view from the back corner of the house as he approached. Just when he could see beyond the corner of the house, he spotted a man crouching below the window, apparently watching and listening to what was happening inside. He also saw the man's pistol with suppressor. *This guy means business. This could get nasty real quick.* Anthony slipped the Heckler and Koch, Mark 23, out of his backpack, then the suppressor, screwing it onto the threaded muzzle. The caliber .45 ACP Mark 23 was for Anthony's evaluation prior to the official fielding of the pistol to the US Special Operations Command the following year. Keeping his weapon at the ready, he moved further out on the beach, almost to the edge of the water, so he could look into the study directly and observe any activity in the rear of the house.

Once in position he knelt to retrieve a pair of binoculars from his backpack. *That's her, Sam, talking with Reynolds,* he thought as he observed Dydre inside the house. *But who is the kneeling man, and what's his connection? What gives here?* He watched the woman he knew as Sam pick up the phone and dial a number. *Overseas by the number of digits she's dialing.* Anthony turned toward the waves so as not to be heard by the kneeling man beneath the window. He spoke into the mike of a small transceiver that relayed his call via satellite to the special operations cell Newport had established in the SCIF. "She's making a telephone call from Reynolds's house. Can you capture it?"

"Stand by," the man's voice said in his earphone. "Tracing and recording started."

"I have the woman in sight, inside the house talking to Reynolds," Anthony said softly into the mike."

"Roger, over."

"A man with a sidearm is watching outside the house. I don't know if that's the woman's accomplice or someone else," he said into the mike.

"Roger, over."

"You'd better alert the Old Man," Anthony said, referring to Newport. "This could get nasty."

"Roger, out."

Anthony sat on the sand and faced the surf as though enjoying the evening on the beach. With a turn of his head, he could see the two people inside the house and the kneeling man beneath the window. No one else was on the beach. *I can't afford being discovered,* he thought. *The police would be a big distraction I don't need, and I don't want to get caught by a backup to either the woman or the kneeling man. Nice beach.* He grasped a handful of sand. *Too bad I'm here on business. I could spend about a week here. Umbrella, cooler of margaritas, and a babe....* He looked around once again. *Clear. Good! No one in sight. All is calm.* At that moment his full attention snapped back to what was happening inside the house. Dydre spoke into the phone and then waited as if expecting someone else to come on the line.

"They're about to send a patch to fix the Rangers," the man's voice said in Anthony's earphone.

"Roger, out," Anthony said. He watched Sam continue her phone conversation—speaking, pausing, speaking again, turning to address Reynolds and then back to the phone. *Shit! I can't charge in there until I know who Mr. Kneeling is. I'll have to worry about the patches later. First things first.*

27

Dydre nodded confirmation to Reynolds to proceed. After he checked the phone line to the computer, he tapped the Enter key, which sent the coded patch via the phone to the handheld device in Ilidža.

"Okay, now what?" Dydre asked.

"I just need to walk them through the process of installing the patch. Then they'll need to shut down the device and reboot it."

"So far, so good, George. Get going. Start talking." She handed the phone to Reynolds.

Within a few minutes he said, "That's one down."

She took the phone from him and placed it to her ear. "Does it work?"

"It is running," the man replied.

"Reynolds will tell you how to test it on your laptop. Then I want you to tell me if it's working." She handed the phone to Reynolds.

He began to give instructions on how to scan the computer, only to become frustrated at the need to repeat several steps because of the confusion of the person on the other end of the phone. Each time he looked up at Dydre, unnerved that she may not understand the man's incompetence. Sweat ran down Reynolds's head, more from the tension than from the humid, night air. Finally, he looked at Dydre and nodded, then handed the phone to her.

"Is it working?" she asked the man.

"Praise be to Allah! It works," he said.

"Very good." She returned the phone to Reynolds and said, "Now do that three more times, George, and I'm out of your life."

The sound of the back door opening startled Dydre and Reynolds. She backed up and turned toward the door. "Rüdiger!" she blurted out. "Why're you here?"

"It's good to see you too, Dydre. Reynolds, save a copy of that patch to a disk and give it to me. Then keep working. Dydre has a decision to make."

Reynolds struggled with his trembling fingers to tap the right keys and save the code. "What the fuck?" he mumbled. "First, Sam's unexpected appearance and now this man holding a pistol and calling her Dydre. This is unreal." He took a deep breath and continued at his task.

"So Clay's a little worried. As you can see I'm getting the devices fixed." Dydre looked into his eyes, touching the Walther inside her pocket.

"You and I both knew it would come to this one day. The great and deadly Dydre, master of disguise—*you* have a problem. Yes, the Fat Man is worried. He thinks you ripped him off...and rightly so."

"What do you mean?"

"We both know—$2 million. You told the Fat Man that Reynolds wanted $5 million but the deal you struck with Reynolds was for $3 million."

A slight squint of her eyes revealed her surprise. *How much does he know and when did he find out? How much does Clay really know? He'll be furious...David! What's Rüdiger's real game?*

Reynolds looked at Dydre then back to Rüdiger. The expression on his face said it all. He realized he was in way over his head and just might die. As cunning and daring as he thought he was, these people had proved he was an inexperienced and naive sap.

"Now it's up to you," Rüdiger continued. "I want a million dollars and I don't tell the Fat Man you ripped him off, or I kill you. If you kill me, the Fat Man will know he was right and send others after you. He'll be pretty pissed off and you can bet he'll kill your son, too. Or he could tell those Arab fanatics you ripped them off, and they'll take care of you and your son. They're still pissed off that you killed a couple of their guys. Or, I could shoot Reynolds then shoot you. I'll make it look like you broke into his house, and you killed each other. What do you think about that? You don't have many options."

"Here's the disk," Reynolds said as he held out his trembling hand. "I...I have the fix on the disk. I—"

"Shut up and keep working." Rüdiger took the disk and shoved it into his cargo pants pocket.

"Well, Dydre, what's it going to be? A million dollars for me and you live, or you die tonight. At least if you pay me, you and your son might be able to disappear. But you'll have to get him first. I might even be persuaded to help you. Is it worth a million dollars to disappear with your son like you planned?"

"What's to keep you from killing me after I give you the money?"

"I guess you'll have to trust me."

"Not good enough."

Swinging the pistol toward Reynolds, Rüdiger squeezed the trigger. Reynolds's body jerked and fell onto the keyboard. At that instant Dydre came down hard with a chop to his wrist, knocking the pistol out of his hand. Rüdiger came around with his left. Dydre blocked his blow and grasped his shirt. He came up with his arms before she could execute her move then kicked her front leg causing her to shift her weight and step back. She attacked but he was quicker. He flipped her over and she crashed into the wall. He dove for the pistol, grabbing it as he rolled, and came up to a crouching position. Dydre froze.

During the scuffle her wig came off and lay flattened on the floor. "You're getting me exited, Dydre. I've always liked you better as a redhead."

At that moment Janice opened the door from the main house and entered the room. "George, what are you doing? Who are you? What's going on? George—"

Rüdiger looked up at the woman and fired. Janice's body dropped to the floor like a rag doll. He pointed his pistol back at Dydre and said, "Well Dydre, what's it going to be?"

The Pentagon

Alice sipped her coffee as she entered the SCIF where the special operations cell was located and walked straight over to the watch officer. "What's going on with the good senator?"

"He's made numerous calls to a number in Frankfurt, everyone on the Intelligence Committee, the Speaker of the House, the majority leader, the secretary of defense, the director of the CIA, and almost anyone else of importance," he said. "He's been quite busy. Where's your sidekick?"

"Hector? He's keeping tabs on the senator. Do you know whose number in Frankfurt it is yet?"

"Hold on, let me pull it up." He tapped the keys to access the file. "You'll be interested to know that Anthony is on to the woman in the photograph. She and the redheaded woman are one and the same. Anthony just confirmed it."

"No shit? That's why we're having trouble finding her…disguise."

"Yep! She's at Reynolds's beach house. Anthony has eyes on her now but there's a third player there. A lone gunman as far as Anthony can tell. The guy just shot Reynolds and his wife. Anthony's afraid he is going to shoot the redheaded woman."

"What the hell is going on? If he shoots her, we've got a problem."

"The woman did make a call to Bosnia and we have a recording of it. Reynolds transmitted a fix to one of the Rangers before he was shot. Anthony thinks the gunman is trying to make a deal with the woman."

"Damn! Have you got a good number on the phone call she made?"

"No, the number went to a call center and was rerouted. The Old Man isn't happy about that. Anthony is going to stay close to the woman. She's got real possibilities. He thinks that she'll lead him to a key player and, if all goes well, to the devices."

"Shit!" Alice said under her breath. "Anything else?"

"Just bits and pieces right now. The senator is still snooping around. Here's the info on the person he's been calling in Frankfurt." He pointed to the monitor, then slid his chair to the side so Alice could read the computer screen.

"Clayborne Zsigmond," she said as she read the screen. "Black market arms broker. He's supplied arms to the conflicts around the world from Rwanda, Somalia, Chechnya, the Balkans, to the Palestinians…and is believed to be supplying terrorist groups globally. This slimeball is a real asshole!"

"I wouldn't invite him to dinner," the watch officer said. "He's probably got a private army protecting him. Mary Ellen will have a lot of work to do on him in the morning. The noose is getting tighter around the senator's neck. I'll probably have more later."

"Good. The Old Man is going to let the senator discover some information so we can make sure it's him. Then we'll see whom he gives it to. My money is on Mr. Zsigmond. We can't have any screwups on this. It's got to be tight. Keep me posted."

"That's a safe bet. Will do! Cheers," he said as Alice walked out.

The door to the SCIF conference room latched shut as Newport looked around at his assembled team. "I've initiated an agreement with the Bundesnachrichtendienst (BND), Germany's Federal Foreign Intelligence and Security Service, for their cooperation on this operation. I've only given the BND the details that led to Germany and Clayborne Zsigmond."

"Are we ready to go after the senator?" Alice asked.

"Yes, the SecDef is reviewing the hook now. We've made sure the information isn't available anywhere else. That'll be the evidence we'll need to arrest Griffith. Alice, that's you."

"Got it. I'm ready," Alice said.

"I hope this will end our security leak problem," Newport said as he looked at each of them. "Tomorrow morning, the SecDef and I are meeting with the senators on the Intelligence Committee and he'll include the controlled information that we believe will get Griffith's attention."

"The wiretaps are in place," Alice said. "Captain Jordan has been alerted, but he doesn't know yet who we're going to nab. He knows to keep it quiet."

"Good. Thanks, Alice. Mary Ellen, keep working on the terrorists in Ilidža. Also, send a message to Günter Schenck to see if he has anything."

"Yes, sir."

"When I was informed that Reynolds fixed one of the Rangers, I alerted the Delta team to move to Sarajevo and be ready to execute on order."

"The terrorist cell in Bosnia has been smart and stayed ahead of us so far," Mary Ellen said. "We've got a reconnaissance satellite and signal intelligence resources tasked to us for this."

"A human intelligence team is also focused on this," Hector said.

"My fear is they may move from Ilidža, Bosnia before we can locate them," Newport said. "So far, the terrorists have maintained discipline and patience, making themselves practically invisible. They may make the one mistake that would reveal their position. Everyone stay alert."

28

Reynolds's Beach House
Papagayo, Costa Rica

She's good, Anthony thought as he watched Dydre handle herself inside the house. *Mr. Kneeling may just end it all right here. Shit! If he kills her, I'm back at square one. This isn't how I wanted it to play out.* Anthony aimed his Mark 23 toward the house, and drew a perfect sight picture on the man. Flicking off the safety, he inserted his index finger through the oversized trigger guard and gently felt the match grade trigger. He applied a slight pressure with his finger, then suddenly released it. Anthony keyed the mike on the transceiver. *I've got to try this before I charge in like the cavalry,* he thought. "Dial Reynolds's number and let it ring. If someone answers, hang up. I need a diversion. When I tell you, call the police and report the shooting."

"Stand by," came the response.

Anthony watched the two inside the house as he waited for acknowledgment that the call was made. "Okay, Mr. Kneeling, all I need is for you to get slightly distracted and Red to make your move," he said to himself.

"Phone is ringing," came over Anthony's headset.

His attention focused on the two in the house, Anthony aimed his pistol and was ready to fire if Dydre needed the help. It was a gamble he had to take. He did consider that Dydre might be the loser.

Rüdiger crouched, waiting for Dydre's answer. "Well, Dydre, what's it going to be? You've got two options—live or die."

She focused on his eyes and saw them slightly widen when he glanced at the ringing phone. In that instant she lunged forward, bringing her left arm up and out, knocking Rüdiger's aim off. The pistol fired. Dydre came across with her right and turned slightly to her left, and placed her right leg behind his. Rüdiger fired again. He went down as she gripped his wrist, twisting and applying pressure. The pistol fell from his hand. Dydre kicked him in the kidney, in the midsection, and then on the chin as his head came forward as a result of her kick to the midsection. He lay dazed on the floor.

Dydre stood upright and took in a deep breath. She pulled the disk from Rüdiger's pocket, stuffed it into hers, and stepped to the door, picking up her wig on the way. She paused to look out to make certain no one was waiting to waylay her. Turning back to Rüdiger, she withdrew the small tube from her pocket and twisted off the cap. "You said just two options. There was a third—kick your ass and get out of here. You lose, Rüdiger. I'm not giving you a million dollars and I'm not going to die tonight. Even if I did pay you off, you'd try to kill me anyway." She rolled the liquid on the back of his neck and then down his side as she lifted his shirt. "I can't afford to have you after my ass for the rest of my life."

Rüdiger would never catch up to her or live to see the inside of the police station.

She stepped out of the door with caution and disappeared into the darkness. The incident with Rüdiger at Reynolds's house didn't go as she planned and, no doubt, compromised her ability to get David. Uncertain as to whether Rüdiger had acted alone, she checked to see if anyone followed as she made her way to the car. *Clay will be expecting a call from Rüdiger and I don't have much time. If he doesn't hear from Rüdiger soon, he'll know there's a problem and will have his goons waiting for me.*

A dog barked and she stopped, listened intently; her eyes darted in all directions only to see the deserted neighborhood in the darkness. The dog posed no threat to her but the sound of the approaching sirens did. She picked up her pace. *Damn dog! The Arabs are still a problem. They hold me accountable. Clay could use them to do his dirty work. I need some help, someone I can trust who can provide some backup. Ah! Ludwig Stäbler, Lucerne. But before I do anything, I need to get in touch with the Arabs first— and before Clay—or the Arabs will come after me for sure, if they haven't already decided to do that.*

Making the right decision—going for David first or taking care of the Arabs—worried her. A delay in meeting with the Arabs would make for a short meeting, deadly short. Fixing the Rangers first could also prove deadly as Clay would have more time to set his trap. She knew how the Arabs operated, and that their spies would be out. A wrong move with them would mean death to her and David, or they could be looking for revenge regardless of what she did. And if it came to her killing anyone, she didn't want David to see that.

Meeting with the Arabs would take time—a commodity that was in short supply. Clay was capable of killing David, as she well knew, but probably not until he had served his purpose. *He'll use David as bait*, she thought. *The more time Clay has the less my chances are.*

Anthony flattened himself against the cool sand and watched Dydre enter the doorway, stoop over kneeling man, and step out the door. When she was two houses down, he slung his backpack over his shoulder and spoke into the mike as he followed her.

"We're on the move. The gunman is down. She worked him over pretty good."

"Roger, over."

"She's probably going back to the hotel to update the other devices. Monitor the calls into and out of the hotel. I'll contact you later."

"We're set up and ready to go."

"Also, she probably won't stay in the area long."

"Mary Ellen is already working the airlines and will contact you as soon as she has something."

"Roger, out."

Anthony briefly lost Dydre when he went for his car but caught up to her shortly after getting on the road. She was heading to the hotel.

In the hotel room, Dydre called Jamaal. Convincing him of her trustworthiness and that she would repair the devices was the challenge.

"You have betrayed us!" Jamaal said. His words blared from her mobile phone.

"No, Jamaal! I'm your friend. I'll fix the other Rangers as promised. You must give me a little time."

"There is no more time. You killed two of my brothers when you were to meet with me. The Master is not pleased."

"Jamaal, they were going to kill me. They violated our agreement. I was going to you in honor of our agreement but they had other ideas. I had no choice."

"You lie! There is no more time."

"No! Listen to me. You were warned that US Army soldiers were heading for your position, correct?"

"Yes, Zsigmond called to warn me. He's our ally."

"No, Jamaal, he's not your ally. I called Zsigmond and told him to warn you about the soldiers. I fixed one of the Rangers and was going to repair the others, but Zsigmond sent a man to stop me from making the repair. I have the patch with me. That's what happened. He wants the devices and patch for himself. He has no intention of giving it to you."

"You told Zsigmond to warn us?"

"Yes."

"The Master will want proof of your loyalty."

"I said I'd fix them but I need just a little time to get to a safe place so I can send you the patch."

"There is no more time."

"Jamaal, I'm in Costa Rica and need a few days to get to a safe place to transmit the patch to you."

"There is no more time."

"Then I'll bring the patch to your location but you must give me time to get there."

"The Master will be pleased."

Dydre mechanically went through the motions of the remainder of the phone call and scribbled a new phone number for him as she was already planning her move.

Giving her instructions to go to Ilidža, Jamaal said, "Call me when you reach the edge of town."

This is going to be tricky and I don't trust them. When the phone connection went dead, she snapped back. *They bought it, for now, that Clay double-crossed them. Now to prove my loyalty.*

The next call Dydre made was to Ludwig Stäbler—not his real name, but it didn't matter as long as he did his job. He was a German soldier of fortune, not on the scale of Rüdiger but pretty damn close, and he had worked for her several times in the past. After three attempts and about as many hours, she finally reached him on the phone. "Ludwig, I have a job for you. Are you interested?"

"Ja, possibly. Tell me about it?"

"Not on the phone. But can I meet with you day after tomorrow night? The job will be a short one and I'll pay you well."

"Ja, sure. Come to my house around 2100 hours. We'll talk then."

"Thank you, Ludwig."

"Ich sehe dich dann."

"Auf Wiedersehen!"

29

Tuesday, May 31, 1995
Lucerne, Switzerland

The afternoon sun was dipping in the western sky over Lucerne when Dydre checked into a small, family-run hotel that she had identified months ago. She was careful not to leave any clues that she planned to use the hotel on such an occasion or even knew about it. Not her usual class, but the classically Swiss-style inn was immaculate and up to date with twenty rooms, a restaurant, and a bar. Most important, it didn't appear in tourism guidebooks and was off the beaten path, the sort of place only locals would know about.

Dydre took one of the rooms with a balcony that overlooked the city. She believed that no one would expect her to stay there. *A little sleep and shower. Then I can think with a clear head. I've got to do this right. Clay's probably put the word out on me by now and offered a lot of money to whoever nabs me. Most of those I know would turn me over to Clay in a flash for the money. Ludwig Stäbler owes me and he doesn't care much for Clay. He's about as good as it gets.* She sat at the desk trying to think things through before showering. *Not good. Clay could've talked to bin Laden, most likely put him onto me when he didn't hear from Rüdiger. Clay probably doesn't know about the patch. I just can't think clearly right now. Something to eat and a few hours of sleep first.*

Anthony followed Dydre to Lucerne, with Mary Ellen's help, undetected and waited outside the hotel until she went upstairs before he entered. He believed she sought out the safety of this hotel to rest before making her next move. Filling out the guest register he said to the clerk, "The lady that just checked in…she's my fiancée."

"Ms. Johnston?" the clerk replied.

He handed her a 50 Swiss franc banknote and said, "Yes. Please don't tell her I'm here. I want to surprise her at dinner."

"How romantic!" she replied. "Ms. Johnston asked to be called at 6:30."

"Thank you. Please call me at 6:00. I want to be waiting at a table when she comes down."

"I'll see to it." She grinned.

Anthony winked at the young woman, then casually went to his room. Once settled he called the special operations cell to update them, give his current location, and phone number of the hotel. "Monitor all the calls going both in and out from the hotel," he said. "If she calls anyone, I want to know who she calls and what was said."

"Roger. The Old Man sends his regards and reminds you to keep her alive. The terrorists have gone to ground and we haven't located them yet. There's been a lot of chatter about the devices, so we should pick them up again pretty soon. The Old Man believes the woman is the key to finding them and wants you to get close to her."

"Roger, but she could get spooked on seeing me."

"He knows but wants you to push it. The NATO commander is getting uneasy."

"Got it. Who was Mr. Kneeling at Reynolds's house? Let me know what you learn from him as soon as you can."

"That won't be much—"

"What do you mean?"

"The man is dead."

"Shit! How'd that happen? Was it from the woman working him over?"

"No, they don't think so. He had a seizure of some kind. An FBI liaison team is going to check it out and lend a hand. The Costa Ricans aren't as advanced as we are."

"Let me know the results of their investigation. I was hoping he could provide some information."

"Will do."

Anthony looked at the clock as he laid his pistol on the nightstand. *Jet lag. Get some sleep, then back to work.* He stretched out on the bed and closed his eyes.

The Pentagon

Alice, Hector, and Mary Ellen sat at the table with Secretary Newport for their status report and Anthony's progress.

"The man in Costa Rica died from paralysis from neurotoxins, procoagulants that interfered with his blood clotting and muscle damage from myotoxins. The same thing Albritten died from—snake venom." Hector said.

"Snake venom?" Newport said. "Make sure Anthony knows. Have they left the hotel yet?"

"No, sir," Mary Ellen replied. "We're monitoring all the calls in and out of the hotel but nothing significant yet."

"What about mobile phones?" he asked.

"We've got them covered, too. Do you want me to put someone on watching the hotel?"

"No, but have a couple men standing by to give Anthony a hand if he needs it."

"Yes, sir."

"What have you got on the senator so far?" Newport asked.

"Senator Griffith has taken the bait. He called Clayborne Zsigmond in Frankfurt," Hector said. "You have the file on Zsigmond."

"Yes, he's a black market arms broker."

"That's correct."

"We have the phone conversation on tape and it's conclusive," Alice said. "It's enough to get a warrant for his arrest. I have a brief ready to go to the attorney general."

"Okay, good work," Newport said. "Mary Ellen, send a message to BND to bring them up to date."

"Yes, sir."

"Get everything ready but don't arrest the senator yet," Newport continued. "I want to get the senator and Zsigmond at the same time. This must be tight and the Germans must take Zsigmond the same time we take the senator. But Anthony must locate the Rangers first. I'm hoping the woman will lead us to them. If Zsigmond and the senator aren't arrested at the same time, the one not in custody could alert the terrorists. Make sure BND is on track with us—we must have a news blackout on the arrests. If the arrests make the news, that could tip off the Arabs. It would be hell finding those devices then. Give Anthony all the support he needs and stay on the senator and Zsigmond. They may provide some clues to the location of the devices."

"Yes, sir," Mary Ellen replied. "The Brits gave me a bit of good news. Remember Anthony said the woman told him she went to Cambridge?"

"Yes. They turned up something?" Newport asked.

"Spy one-oh-one. Make your cover as close to you as you can and the best way to keep from being tripped up is to use parts of your real life. I had the Brits check her out and see if she did go to Cambridge. They found her and her name is Dydre Rowyn. She graduated from Cambridge...was also active in the theatre and in a jujitsu club. She left school during her junior year. Some of her school friends remembered her mother or guardian died that year—that part is a little fuzzy. She returned to school the following year and halfway through her senior year she became pregnant." Mary Ellen looked up at Secretary Newport, then continued. "One of her school friends recalled that she was dating a US Army officer, but he was killed in the Balkans before they were married. No one remembers what happened to her after she graduated, but everyone believes she had the baby."

"Well, we're getting somewhere with the woman. Now we have a name. See what you can find out about the baby and pick up the trail from there."

"I'm already on it. The Brits are working it now."

"Anything else?" Newport asked.

"Not much else has turned up on the woman. We're still working on her."

Their meeting lasted another fifteen minutes. Each had specific tasks to complete in order to coordinate the arrests of Senator Griffith and Zsigmond as well as to maintain secrecy. As a result of her involvement with the investigation and arrest of Aldrich Ames, Alice was charged with overseeing that all procedures were in place for the arrest of Griffith, and all rules followed. Hector was to focus on the senator and keep tabs on his every move until the arrest occurred. Mary Ellen was to continue her support of Anthony and research on Dydre Rowyn.

The lack of information on Dydre Rowyn frustrated Newport. Adding to his frustration was the fact that Anthony was limited by discovering everything on his own. Newport knew that the more information they could obtain about Dydre, the better they'd be at predicting her moves. He needed something he could use to his advantage to possibly induce Dydre to help them, and therein lay the challenge.

30

Lucerne, Switzerland

Seated at a linen-draped table with his back to the wood-paneled corner, Anthony observed the entrance to the dining room. The restaurant hosted many locals in addition to the hotel guests, and this particular evening was no exception. The restaurant was about two-thirds full, which allowed Anthony to blend in as he waited for Dydre to enter. The staff was busy waiting tables and the noise in the room rose proportionately with the arrival of more patrons. Anthony sipped wine and checked his watch, expecting her to arrive at any moment. Finally, the glass door swung open and Dydre, dressed in dark pants and shirt, entered. Anthony partly obscured his face by holding up the menu and pretended to study it. He watched her look about the room as one of the staff escorted her to a seat three tables over from him. She sat perpendicular to him with her face to the door.

Dydre looked over the room again, then took a sip of wine. *It'll take about half an hour to get to Ludwig Stäbler's house from here*, she thought. *I don't really trust him but I don't trust anyone else either. Hmm...fifty thousand for a night's work may keep him on my side.* There was no right or best solution as to whether she should go for David first or take care of the Arabs. It was basically a Hobson's choice as neither Clay nor the Arabs would stop until they had her. She figured going after David and possibly dealing with Clay would be the most difficult. *Fixing the devices may be the best course of action*, she thought. *If I took care of the Arabs first, they would probably be less likely to help Clay, unless he paid them a lot of money. Then I wouldn't have to worry about them.* Dydre set her glass on the table and tensed, realizing someone other than the staff had approached.

"I'm sorry if I startled you," Anthony said. "Diann, isn't it? We had dinner together in Washington."

"What? Yes, Diann," she replied, forcing a smile. *Why's he here and what's his game? Whose team is he on?* "And you're Anthony, business development for an IT company. This is really quite a small world, isn't it?" Her defenses up, she scrutinized him in detail and everything he said.

"That's correct. I thought it was you when I saw you come in. What a pleasant surprise. Are you here on business?"

This is no fucking coincidence. He's following me, she thought. "Yes, I'm here for a quick trip. What about you?" *Is he one of Clay's goons or is he with the feds? Time to go. This is not happenstance.*

"I'm still on vacation. I just decided to come to Europe and I've always wanted to see Lucerne."

"Well, I hope you enjoy it. I've got to be getting on," she stood and started to leave.

"Would you like to meet later for a drink?"

"No, thank you. I've got an early flight. I still have to pack."

"Okay, another time."

Dydre glanced over her shoulder as soon as she reached the lobby, and saw him leaving as well. She paused in the lobby as if searching for her room keys. He passed her by and disappeared up the staircase. Before going out of the front door, she looked for any threat. Once he was out of sight, she took one last look around before heading for the rental car and her meeting with Ludwig.

2100 hours
Ludwig Stäbler's House
Lucerne, Switzerland

Ludwig led Dydre into his spacious, well-appointed den, and said, "Please." He motioned for her sit in a leather wingback chair by the coffee table. "Brandy, ja?"

"Thank you." Dydre focused her attention on him and the room as he poured the drink.

"Here you are. Just a minute." He sat the two brandy snifters on the coffee table, and turned up the music on the surround sound with a remote control. "Just a precaution. One never knows who might try to listen in," he said as he sat in a matching wingback chair next to Dydre. "You have a job for me, ja?"

"Clay is holding my son. I want you to help me get him out."

"Ja, the Fat Man. He will be a tough one."

"I know. I'm offering you 50,000 Swiss francs for one night's work to help me."

"Who else do you have?"

"There's no one else I can trust."

"You pay me 75,000 Swiss francs and I will get two more to help us. You will pay them 50,000 Swiss francs each, ja?"

Dydre looked deep into his eyes as if searching into his soul. *I can take him if I need to. But if he has two men with him, that throws the odds in his favor,* she thought. *Could he be setting me up—take my money then bag me? He's playing it straightforward. I need help and he's the best shot I've got.* "Agreed," she said, nodding.

"When?"

"Two nights from tonight. I have another problem to solve first."

"Not much time, ja?"

"It must be quick."

She leaned forward and presented him with her plan. First she drew a sketch of the school, then pointed out David's location and routes in and out. Ludwig listened to the details and made a few suggestions that she adopted. Their discussion covered details of all logistics, including when and where he and Dydre would split up. Finally Dydre said, "You scout out the school. I have a little job to do. I'll meet you here day after tomorrow...say around 1000."

"Ja, at 1000. I will need from you 175,000 Swiss francs before I can start."

"Here's 50,000 Swiss francs." She withdrew an envelope from inside her shirt and flopped it onto the coffee table. "This'll get you started. I'll have the rest of your money when we meet day after tomorrow. Have the others here and ready to go. Agreed?"

He hesitated, an expression of contemplation on his face. "Ja, agreed," he said, leaving the envelope untouched on the table.

Ludwig sipped his brandy, then returned the snifter to the coffee table. The two stood in unison and he lowered the volume on the surround sound. He escorted Dydre to the door. "Auf Wiedersehen!"

"Auf Wiedersehen!" she replied and walked toward her car.

When she was almost there, she felt a sense of danger but had no time to identify its source for a crashing blow suddenly knocked her off her feet. The full weight of a large man was on top of her by the time she hit the ground. "Shit!" she said, fighting against him. *Where did he come from?* Trying to throw him off—kicking, grabbing, defending herself—was useless. She found herself unable to move. Then she felt the strength of another pair of large hands clamping on her wrists.

"Just relax," he said with a deep voice.

"Who are you? What do you want?"

Struggling, twisting against her attackers was futile. As strong hands twisted her arm outward and shoved her sleeve

180

up, she realized what was coming. Terrified, she fought with every ounce of her strength but couldn't stop him. Then a sharp, piercing pain in her right arm. *They've given me an injection of something.* "No! No!" Dydre said through clenched teeth as she continued to resist.

"Shut up! I don't want to hurt you. We're going to see the Fat Man," one of them said.

Lifting her to her feet, the two burly men ushered Dydre toward a large Mercedes parked on the street out of sight from the house. Dydre's arms and legs became heavy and uncooperative. Reaching the car, they slammed her against it, one of them pinning her next to the right rear door. Her strength was fading fast, her head was thick, and her eyes wouldn't focus. The car door opened, exposing the dark abyss and she knew that's where she was going. In the next instant she felt herself tumble onto the backseat. Hearing a familiar man's voice, Dydre looked up and through the drug-induced haze realized it was Ludwig.

"Ludwig, why...?" she said, the words slurred from her mouth and thick tongue.

"I didn't want to do this but the Fat Man is offering more, much more than you are. He has a standing reward out for anyone who helps you. Why, you asked. It's a simple matter of survival. If I helped you, Clay's army would be after me."

A brawny figure in black settled in the car beside her. Dydre slumped against him out cold.

31

Warehouse Building
Lucerne, Switzerland

Dydre sensed light as the drug began to wear off. She struggled to open her eyelids and found herself in a brightly lit, stark room. Her head felt heavy and sluggish, and the light penetrated her eyes like daggers. She attempted to move her arms and legs, but they wouldn't budge no matter how hard she tried. She willed herself to think, then realized the light was from an industrial ceiling fixture and she was seated in a chair with her arms and legs bound to it. *Where am I? What happened? Think, think…just fragments. I tumbled in the darkness and saw…Ludwig. How long have I been here?* She heard a man's gravelly voice but didn't understand the words. Then she felt the splash of cool water hitting her.

"Dydre! Wake up, Dydre!" Clay said. His voice throbbed in her ears.

"Clay…why?" she said, the effects of the drug still affecting her speech. Through glazed eyes she managed to see two men in the room with Clay and she didn't like the odds. As best she could, Dydre mentally prepared for what was coming and she hoped to withstand his punishment long enough to find some way to escape.

"Dydre, don't play innocent with me. You know why you're here."

"Wake her up!" Clay said to one of the men.

The man grabbed her by the hair, pulling her head up, and slapped her twice across her face.

"Dydre, you shortchanged me. You stole from me. After all I have done for you."

"Get it over with, Clay. You're going to kill me, so do it!"

"Not so quick, my dear. First you'll pay. Then I get my money back. I may or may not kill you."

Clay nodded to the man who again stepped in front of her, punching her in the face several times then the abdomen before Clay signaled him to stop.

"You made me very angry, Dydre."

"This makes you feel better?" she said behind numb and swollen lips. "Just get on with it!"

"We're going to have a nice little time in here for a while. Then David may want to visit you."

"You bastard!"

"Probably I am," he said. "But you're learning the lesson. Do you know what this is, Dydre?" He held his hand in front of her.

Dydre looked in silence at the black, oblong, plastic box that was curved at the end, then stared him in the eyes.

"That's right—a stun gun. You'll see, it's a very effective little tool."

Dydre's eyes widened, but she said nothing. Determined not to show fear, she maintained her stare into his eyes.

"A five-second shock of four hundred thousand volts does wonders." Clay smiled as he bragged on the instrument, twisting his hand and inspecting it like a pistol.

"You sadistic bastard!" she said with clinched teeth. "If you're going to use it, get on with it! Your taunting bores me."

"This little thing…kind of short-circuits your nervous system. It interrupts the tiny neurological impulses that travel through the body to control and direct muscle movement. Your body will cease to function properly. You'll be dazed, your muscles will go into spasms, and you'll be instantly disoriented. Nasty little thing really. I want you to evaluate it."

Dydre struggled to free her hands but the bindings, too strong and too tight, only dug into her wrists. She braced herself for the inevitable.

"Oh! I forgot to mention, you'll feel like you fell out of a two-story window. You may even pass out. But don't worry—the effects aren't permanent. You'll be incapacitated for only about fifteen or twenty minutes."

Clay reached out and zapped her on the shoulder.

The pain filled her body, causing her to groan and jerk, then grunt and moan again. Her head spun and her eyes wouldn't focus. Somewhere in all the confusion she knew she was convulsing and thrashing. Unable to tell if she was conscious, dazed or dead, she lost all concept of time. Saliva ran from her grimacing mouth. Finally, her body slumped in darkness.

"She'll be out for a while," Clay said. "Let's go. We'll visit her again in the morning." He stepped out of the room followed by the two men. The last man out shut the door and closed the hasp that was welded to the metal frame. Then he inserted a lock and snapped it closed.

Anthony tailed Dydre to the meeting with Ludwig, spotting the Mercedes and two men in the shadows as he eased to a stop. Not knowing where they fit in, he stayed at a distance where he could observe the house and men. The entire situation unfolded in front of him, from her abduction and drugging to the point where a third man emerged from the house and got into the Mercedes. "Shit!" he said to himself. "This may end it all here. Not good. Where are they taking you, Red?"

At a safe distance behind, he followed the Mercedes to a vacant building in the industrial area off Werkhofstrasse and Bürgenstrasse. At first Anthony thought Ludwig was helping her and she paid him off, but when he saw Ludwig with the men who drugged her, he figured it had to be a double cross. The odds didn't look promising. *Who are these men? Where are they taking her?* He wanted answers. She was the connection to the Ranger devices. He needed the woman alive and he had to keep himself alive in the process.

When the Mercedes turned into the compound, Anthony glided into a parking spot just past the entrance near another parked car. Hugging the buildings and shrubs, he made his way along an L-shaped brick building. He then crossed a driveway and moved past another brick building shaped like a backwards L. Reaching its corner, he peeked around and saw the car parked next to another Mercedes in front of a building about forty meters across the pavement from him. One man stood outside by the door. *There's the sentry*, he thought. *It's too far across open ground to make it without being seen. Dammit!* He turned around and moved alongside the same building with the idea that he would circle around and come in behind the sentry.

I hope there isn't a diligent night watchman making his security rounds, he thought. Anthony moved as fast as he dared. For all he knew, all of the property belonged to whoever was in the Mercedes, which meant he could run into one of the owner's men at any moment. If he did meet someone, it would slow him down and might cause him to lose Dydre. Anthony heard a door squeak open from the building on his left, and squatted behind a trash bin. A woman emerged followed by a man. The two stopped and embraced. *The night shift has some perks*, Anthony thought. The man patted the woman's butt as she turned and walked to a car at the end of the building. Without waiting to watch her drive off, the man went back inside.

Confident he hadn't been seen, Anthony moved on as the woman drove off. He reached the dark corner of the building and saw the back of the building where the sentry stood. A small shed was about halfway between the two structures. Anthony checked to ensure the area was clear, then darted to the back of the shed about fifteen meters away. He moved slowly around the corner to the front of the shed. Again, he checked the surroundings before dashing the ten meters to the next building. He proceeded to the front corner and located the sentry. *I've got one but how many are inside?* he thought. He backed up and went around the back of the building to find a window or an entrance so he could see inside. Halfway along the wall he came upon a door, but it was locked. Moving on he found a window, but it too was locked tight. He peered through the dirty glass but could see nothing inside. Eventually, he came to the corner of the building and found two more windows and a rollup metal door, none of which was any help. He continued on until he reached the front corner.

He studied the man standing guard and tried to determine how he was armed. When the man opened his blazer to retrieve a pack of cigarettes, Anthony saw a shoulder holster. As the man smoked the cigarette, then flipped the butt onto the pavement, Anthony thought, *Hired thug. I'll have to deal with him but not much of a problem.* At that moment the door opened and three men emerged. The Fat Man spoke to one of the men, then the other. The three men left and the sentry remained.

As soon as the car disappeared around the corner, he lit another cigarette and stepped off the landing. *Good,* Anthony thought. *Bored already. Just keep moving around.* The man aimlessly made a circle, then meandered close to Anthony's position. Just as the sentry turned his back, Anthony whacked him on the head with his pistol. The man crumpled to the ground with a groan.

Anthony felt the man's pockets, took out the car keys, then opened the car's trunk and stuffed the brawny man inside. He pulled out the man's pistol before he shut the lid. Dropping the magazine out of the pistol, he then flipped the gun and magazine inside the car. *What's behind the door? The Lady or the tiger? It'd better be the lady!*

32

Anthony slowly opened the door to the warehouse and looked in to see if anyone else was inside. The lights were on but the room was vacant. A padlocked door across from him and three other doors without padlocks lined the hall. With a wary eye, he approached the doors. *The ones without the padlock first. No one can come out of the door with the padlock.*

He grasped the knob of the first door and briefly studied it before giving it a slow twist. The door opened onto a dark, empty room. He moved to the next door, and twisted its knob. Another empty room. At the third door, he once more applied a slow twist to the knob and opened the door. This room contained a dilapidated old truck; several truck parts on the floor; and various tools; including a pry bar and a hydraulic floor jack. *So far, no tiger,* he thought.

In front of the last door, the padlocked one, a light emerged beneath it. *Must be the lady. I didn't see her come out with the men. Is anyone else in there with her?* Anthony returned to the other room to get the pry bar and placed its pointed end into the shackle of the lock without making a sound. He checked his pistol with his hand, then yanked down hard on the bar, and popped the shackle out of the lock. He withdrew his pistol and shoved the door open.

The room was bare except for the redheaded woman, slumped forward in a chair in the center of the room with her hands bound behind her and her legs tied to the legs of the chair. There was no other exit. Anthony moved toward Dydre and saw red marks on her shoulder as he stood in front of her, but could not tell if she was alive. "They worked you over, didn't they?" he said, gently lifting her head and feeling the warmth of her skin.

Dydre moaned and opened her eyes but they wouldn't focus. She tried to speak but the sounds were unintelligible. Her mind was still not working correctly. She blinked several times and forced herself to concentrate. "Who…Anthony?"

"Yes, it's Anthony. They sure did a number on you. Wake up. I'm going to get you out of here. Do you understand me?"

"Yeah, stun gun. No such thing as coincidences," she said, her voice labored. "I should've known."

"Stun gun. That explains a lot. I'm going to untie you."

"I guess you're going to have your way with me now. Clay's man, aren't you?"

"Wake up!" he said. "I'm going to get you out of here."

"Who are you?" she asked.

"I'm someone who wants you alive. Now hold still." He withdrew his knife and cut the bindings on her hands and her feet.

Her body ached and was still uncooperative. The freeing of her arms and legs brought some relief but her head pounded. "You don't work for Clay, do you?"

"No. We're getting out of here. Do you think you can stand or do I need to carry you?"

"Hold on a minute. How'd you find me? You followed me!"

"That's right. Sorry I couldn't get in here sooner. The odds were against me."

"I know the feeling." Dydre saw the Heckler and Koch with attached seven and a half inch suppressor in his hand. "You don't really work for an IT company, do you?"

"No, now stand up. We've got to get out of here."

He's not Arabic and they wouldn't hire an American to do their dirty work, she thought. "Who the hell are you and what's going on?"

188

"I said I'm someone who wants you alive. I'll explain later. Let's go!"

Dydre started to stand and collapsed, her body still not ready to cooperate. Anthony stood her up, draped her over his shoulder, then carried her out.

In his hotel room he laid her on the bed, gave her three aspirins, and then switched on the radio to soft music. He cleaned her face with a cool wash cloth and covered her with a light blanket. Within a few minutes she was asleep. *She's damn good and one hell of a fighter,* he thought. *Mr. Kneeling died from snake venom. But how? I'd better be careful.* He slipped on a pair of rubber exam gloves then gently searched her—her pockets, cuffs, collar, and anyplace where she could hide something. He discovered her car keys, a stiletto, and a tube of liquid with a roller ball on the end. Thinking the clear, oily substance was lip gloss, he removed the cap, sniffed it, then dabbed a tissue with the substance in the tube and placed the sample into a small plastic bag along with the gloves. He photographed the items before he returned them to where he found them. She was still out when he finished.

Anthony, believing she would continue to sleep for a while, placed a chair in front of the door to take advantage of the opportunity to rest as well—not knowing when he might have the next chance. "Sleep it off," he said as he looked back at her. "I want you to have a clear head when we talk." He sat in the chair, propped his feet on the coffee table, and held his pistol in his lap.

After adjusting to a more comfortable position, he called the special operations cell in the Pentagon. "I've got her, she's asleep now," he said softly into the mobile phone. "They worked her over pretty good. She'll probably sleep the rest of the night. I have some photos and a sample for you. I'll send them by Federal Express in the morning."

"Good, I'll let the Old Man know," the man's voice replied. "Mary Ellen found out that she had a son. She's trying to find out where he is now."

"That's something. It could be to our advantage. Anything new on the senator or the other guy?"

"We've got pretty good evidence on the senator. He's made a number of calls to Zsigmond and we're not sure yet if he's a middle man or the top guy. More to come on him. Mary Ellen is compiling quite a list on the other one, I'll get it to you when she finishes."

"How about the devices, anything on them?"

"There's a lot of chatter and reference to them keeps popping up in the signal traffic. We think they're still in the Balkans but no definite location yet. The terrorists are promising something big and that NATO will fall. Mary Ellen is working closely with the CIA. They believe the terrorists are getting ready to attack NATO's computer network with the devices and try to bring it down."

"Can they do that?"

"The best guess—if the devices work as Reynolds claimed, they just need to get to any military unit, tap into their network and take over, disrupt, or bring it down altogether. By the time NATO realizes what's happening, it'll be too late."

"Shit!"

"Yeah, pretty much. The woman is key. We really need her help in getting those devices. The Old Man has an idea and wants me to float it by you."

"What's he thinking?"

"We can't destroy the devices unless we can locate them. To locate them we need someone inside. You and the woman go to Bosnia and fix the rest of the devices. We'll know then where they are. They'll be watching you. You won't be able to plant any bugs or trackers."

"That's a bit risky and will depend on the woman."

"The Old Man is aware of the risk, but he thinks you might be able to pull it off. Think it over and get back to me."

"Okay, I'll see what I can do." Anthony ended the call and relaxed in the chair. *She can't get by me without waking me,* he thought as he looked around to the door, then switched off the light.

33

The morning sun found its way into the room around the drawn curtain. When a beam of light pierced a slight opening in the center of the curtain and moved onto Dydre's face, she stirred. Opening her eyes slowly and smelling coffee, she moved her head out of the light. Without rolling over, she listened, then cautiously looked around the room. *Where am I? What happened? I was dreaming....* Her memory of the previous night blurred into bits and pieces. Unable to discern what was real and what was a dream kicked her mind into high gear, and she sensed someone else was in the room. With her eyes open wide, she rolled over slowly.

"Good morning," Anthony said. Do you feel better this morning?"

She sprang out of bed and faced him in a defensive position. He stood between her and the door. *Who, what—,* she thought. The sudden jolt of going from the pain and disorientation she last remembered to waking up in a hotel room was overpowering. As she tried to make sense of her situation, she felt the pain of her bruised eye.

"You can relax. You're safe," he said, his voice reassuring.

She noted his relaxed manner as he sat in the chair. Then she sat on the edge of the bed and gently touched her eye.

"Yes, you've got a black eye," he said. He scooped up a handful of ice from the ice bucket and placed it in a towel. "Here, put this on it." Stretching out his arm, he offered her the towel with ice.

"You...you got me out of the warehouse, didn't you?"

"Yes. Then I brought you back here to my hotel room."

"I remember now. Clay had one of his men beat me up. Then Clay zapped me with a stun gun." She rubbed her shoulder in the spot that Clay had targeted. "Why?"

"Like I said last night, I want you alive."

"Who are you?" She stood and backed to the wall like a cornered animal ready to fight.

"Relax! I'm not going to hurt you. I need your help." He extended his arm offering her a cup of coffee.

"Who are you? Who do you work for?" She took the coffee. "That pistol tells me you're someone special. I've never seen one like it."

"I guess not. It's a .45 caliber, Heckler and Koch, Mark 23."

"You're not CIA. Who—"

"I'm someone that wants you alive and I need your help."

"German? Israeli? Who? And what do you need my help for? You're not giving me any answers."

"You supplied a group of Arab terrorists with some Ranger devices. I want those devices back or destroyed. I need your help to do it."

"Sorry, I'm not your girl."

"Yes, you are. You can help me or I can turn you over to the authorities. The CIA would love to get their hands on you. The FBI wants to talk to you about the death of Steve Albritten and perhaps Reynolds's murder. My guess is there are several other unexplained deaths they could pin on you, and no telling what else. In any event they'll have you so deep behind bars you'll never get out."

Albritten, Reynolds? How does he know about Reynolds? she thought. "The paper said Albritten died in a car wreck. You can't pin that on me."

"That was the papers. We know he was poisoned."

"I didn't kill Reynolds. Someone else did." She felt for the tube in her pocket.

"Maybe, but you'll spend a lot of time with the police. They'll get you on trafficking in arms and supplying terrorists." He paused and looked her in the eyes. "Your call. I'd hate to see a beautiful woman like you get stuck in some maximum security prison someplace. The CIA has secret prisons all over the world. They're no cakewalk either. They'll shuffle you from hellhole to hellhole for years."

"What happens if I cooperate with you?"

"That's being debated now but I guarantee your life will be a lot better cooperating than not."

"You don't offer much, do you?"

"No, not until I see how well you do. If we're successful, and you help us get the top guy and bring down his organization, you may get put in a witness protection program."

"I need to think." *Clay will kill David and he'll have all of his thugs around the world looking for me. I don't have a chance no matter which way I go,* she thought.

"Think about my offer. In the meantime, how about some breakfast?" Anthony called to have breakfast brought to the room.

Twenty minutes later, room service delivered the order.

"Clay Zsigmond, the man who had me worked over last night, will be furious that I got away from him," Dydre said as she ate a piece of wheat toast. "He'll have an army of men out looking for me."

"He wants you pretty bad, does he? What did you do to him, double-cross him?" Anthony said, taking a bite of boiled eggs.

"Something like that. I tried to get out from under his control. He's crazy and won't give up."

"I'll take care of him. So, are you going to help me?"

"I don't know, I....don't know what to do. I'm dead no matter what."

"Your chances are better with me than against me."

"You'll never get close enough to the Arabs to locate the devices let alone destroy them."

"With your help I think I can."

"They're pissed at me now. I was trying to fix their devices until Reynolds was shot. I told them I'd be there today to fix them. They probably think I skipped out on them and they'll be after me as well. Clay's no doubt fuelled their fire."

"Now you're the one not answering. Are you going to help me? At least you have a pretty good chance with me."

Dydre looked at him as she took a bite of her boiled eggs. *I'll just use him and play along until I can get away from him,* she thought. "I might but I want to make a deal with you."

"A deal? What kind of deal?"

"I have another problem."

"What is it?"

"Clay Zsigmond has my son, David. He's going to kill him if the police charge in. I can get David out but will need help. If you help me get him out and to a safe place, I'll help you get the devices."

"The police can handle getting him out as we go for the devices," he said. "They're good at that sort of thing, and better equipped."

"No! We do this my way or I don't help you. We get David first. When he's safe we go for the devices. Otherwise, no deal."

"Hmm…Now it's my turn to think about it," Anthony replied.

The two continued to eat in silence. When Anthony was finished, he said, "Okay, I'll help you. But if you renege on any part of our deal or cross me, I'll turn you over to the authorities—that is, if I don't kill you."

Dydre just nodded her head. *David first, then take advantage of the first opportunity to get away from him and disappear,* she thought. "What do you have in mind?"

"You were in the process of fixing the devices when Reynolds was killed, right?"

"That's right. How do you know that?"

"Where's the disk Reynolds made with the fix on it? I know you have it."

"In my room."

"Let's go get it," Anthony said as he stood and motioned her to the door.

She sat on the bed, in Anthony's room, as he pulled the secure radio from his bag and contacted the operations cell in the Pentagon. "The woman agreed and I have the fix for the devices, over."

"Roger, upload the fix to me here," the voice said. "Have the woman set up the meeting for tomorrow. Go to Trieste, Italy, and meet with Günter Schenck. He runs a computer shop there. He'll have everything you need and will brief you on what you are to do. It'll take about six hours to drive to Trieste. One more thing, Günter was the one she had verify the devices worked. She'll know he's our man, so don't lose her or we'll lose Günter."

"Hold on, I'm modifying things," he replied. "She worked for Clay Zsigmond and he's the top dog. Hold off on going after him. Zsigmond has her son and I agreed to help her get him to safety first. Otherwise, she said it's no deal."

"Newport won't like it."

"I figured as much but didn't have much choice. It shouldn't delay us very long, maybe twelve to twenty-four hours. I'll be in touch, over."

"Good luck, out."

34

Thursday, June 1, 1995
Frankfurt, Germany

Zsigmond sat at his desk and rolled the ash from the end of his Montecristo. Just as he took a sip of Scotch, the phone rang. Anticipating news from the man that was leading the search for Dydre, Clay shoved the cigar into his mouth and lifted the receiver. "Hello!" he said in a harsh tone.

"Clay, this is Senator Griffith."

"Who? Oh, Senator. I hope you have some good news for me."

"A Delta team is being sent to Bosnia. You wanted to know right away."

"What's going on? Why are they going to Bosnia?"

"I don't know. The Pentagon is holding back a lot of information on this. All I know is that a Delta team is deploying. Stalling is more like it."

"I don't like it. That's a little too close," he puffed his cigar. "You have no idea what their mission is?"

"No. Like I said, they haven't given out anything on it. But rumors have it that it's very sensitive and a number of people are worried about it. Clay, I've got to lay low for a while."

"Senator, we've had this conversation before. You have aspirations for the White House. Let me remind you what would happen to your chances if some compromising photos were to wind up at the *Washington Post*. You'll do as you're told!"

The senator hesitated before speaking. "I'll see what I can do."

"All right. Get back to me as soon as you find out something, anything, about that mission." And with those parting remarks, Clay hung up the phone.

Lucerne, Switzerland

Dydre cleared the coffee table, laid down a pad of paper and pencil, then sat in a chair to one side. "Have a seat," she said. "Here's what we're going to do." Dydre started sketching the layout of David's school, the roads in and out and a general description of the surrounding neighborhood. "Clay will have alerted his men and they'll be expecting me to make a try for David tomorrow night. I think the best time for us to move will be in the dead of night after things have quieted down and everyone is asleep. The nuns like me and know that Clay keeps David from me. But he gives the school a lot of money every year." She looked up at Anthony.

"Are you saying the nuns are loyal to Clay?" He asked.

"The mother superior is the one I worry about the most, but she'll be asleep."

"Where's her room in relation to David's?"

"Here's her room." She pointed to the room on the sketch. "Here's David's room on the opposite end of the building on the second floor."

"What security do they have?"

"Sister Rosa's room is on David's floor, at the top of the stairs. She takes care of the children if any of them need anything during the night. She goes to bed late and is a very light sleeper."

"What'll she do if she sees us?"

"I think she will help me. I don't believe she'll sound an alarm."

"You think?"

"Don't worry. Sister Rosa doesn't like what Clay is doing with David. There'll be a couple of Clay's men outside and probably, at that hour, only one awake in the hall near David's room. He'll have a backup or two in a room that is across the hall and down a little ways, maybe ten feet."

"Is there a burglar alarm, motion sensors, or anything like that?"

"There's a fire alarm but no motion sensors or burglar alarm."

She continued to review the details with Anthony for the next hour. His questions probed into every aspect of the school and area. As he took in her answers, he memorized every aspect of the place.

"There's one more thing," she said. "I went to Ludwig Stäbler's house to hire him to help me. As it turned out, Clay offered him more money and I walked into his trap."

"And you told him of your plan?"

"Pretty much," she nodded.

"We've got to locate and get past the men outside; get into the locked building and to David's floor unnoticed; get past the guard by his door; get David out without frightening him or being seen, and back out past the guards outside. Oh, and Ludwig Stäbler knows of your plan…and he works for Clay. So Clay and all of his men know when and how you are going to snatch your son, correct?"

"That's about the size of it."

"Lady, there are a lot of places where things can go wrong, particularly at the starting line. I think our chances are nil at best. You were too fixated on your son and not thinking clearly when you planned this. You've just handed me a hand grenade with the pin pulled. It can't be done. The police can handle it. We'll go for the devices."

"No! We get David or no deal."

"This is a suicide mission. We don't have the resources—"

"David first or no deal!" She stared at him.

"Let me think a minute," he said as he paced.

Dydre watched him and began contemplating her next move if he refused her. Finally, Anthony said, "Well, maybe we might have a chance. I'm guessing they still think that's how you will try to grab him and you're trying to recruit more help. They probably don't expect you until tomorrow night or later." He paused to study her. "We've got to keep it simple—minimize where things can go wrong and act quickly. I think I've got a better idea." Then he proceeded to lay out his plan and contrast it with hers. He constructed a rudimentary model of the area using things he had in the room, placing a small book, pieces of paper, paperclips, pencils, eraser, and whatever else he could find to represent the buildings, trees, and other obstacles. Quizzing her time and again to remember minute details of the campus and surrounding area, he labeled each item and placed it in relation to David's dormitory. Anthony then pointed to each of his props to explain what would happen and when. Then he had Dydre reiterate the plan, using the model, until she completed it seamlessly.

"All right, you've got it. We'll go tonight. Do you have any questions?"

"And you think this will work?" she asked.

"Yes, I do but timing is the key. It's our best chance, and only chance."

"It just seems…so risky and too simple."

"It is simple and quick, but it will work."

"I hope you're right. I'll just have this one chance."

"We've got to get you something to cover up that black eye and bruises plus several other items."

"Dermablend will do the trick. I need to pick up some toiletries and a few things anyway."

"The next problem is David," Anthony continued. "We get him out of the school, and then we need to put him someplace safe. We can't take him with us. Remember our deal?"

He's making it tough, she thought. *His plan doesn't provide any opportunity to get away from him.* Nodding, she said, "I remember. Let me think a minute."

"We need to get out of the city as soon as we can after we get David," he said. "Clay will have his men watching the train station and airport. The roads will be our best bet to get out, but he'll have people trying to spot us driving out of the city."

"I have a live-in housekeeper who could take care of him. It'll take us about four hours to get to my house in Italy. Clay doesn't know about my house."

"We can't afford that much time. We're going to return here to the hotel with David. When the local traffic picks up in the morning, we'll leave and blend in with it. It'll be very difficult to spot us in the traffic and, my guess is, Clay will be expecting you to leave Lucerne immediately."

"You want me to have her come here and pick him up?"

"Milan is two and a half hours away. Have her meet us at the train station and we'll give David to her. Then we can fly to Bosnia out of Malpensa Airport."

Dydre sat back in the chair and relaxed as if she was thinking of the plan to get David. *That's a relief,* she thought. *I didn't want to divulge where my house was located.* "I'll have to call my housekeeper right away. She doesn't have much time. She'll have to take the train this evening. There isn't one early enough in the morning."

"That's fine. Just tell her to meet us at the train station and be on time," he said. "We've got several things to do before tonight. You call your housekeeper and make the arrangements with her. Then set up the meeting in Bosnia for tomorrow with the Arabs. I've got a call to make as well. Let's get going."

Anthony, using the secure radio, contacted the Pentagon. "We're on for tonight, over."

"Roger, the Old Man is nervous."

"I figured he would be. After we get the boy, we're driving to Milan. We'll drop him off at the train station with Dydre's housekeeper, and then we'll drive over to Malpensa Airport. Have Mary Ellen get two seats on the morning flight to Bosnia and coordinate for my clearance to take my weapon. We should be at the train station by 8:30."

"The Old Man has a Delta team on standby. They'll be in position and be watching for you. Once you've fixed the last device, get out of there. We want to nail them before they have time to scatter. Günter has a couple of things for you and he'll exchange laptops. He'll go over everything with you. The Old Man wants you to have help, if you need it. More to follow later. I'll have someone follow the housekeeper."

"Have Schenck meet us at Malpensa with everything I need." Anthony looked up and saw Dydre's eyes open wide with surprise at hearing Schenck's name.

"He'll pick you up in the vicinity of the ticket counter. Anything else?"

"Keep your fingers crossed. I'll give you an update when I get back to the hotel tonight, over."

"Roger, good luck! Out."

"Günter Schenck?" Dydre said, forcing the name. "He works for the same people you do?"

"That's right."

"The Germans, Israelis, or American—"

"I told you before that I want you alive and I need your help. Does it matter who I work for as long as I keep you alive and help you get your son back?"

"No, but—"

"Then that's all that matters. When we meet Schenck at Malpensa Airport, play your part. We are meeting a business associate. Got it?"

"I got it. I know what to do." She felt cold and stared into his eyes. *Günter Schenck*, she thought. *That explains a lot. It's going to be a little more difficult than I thought. The Arab fanatics…I've got to think this through. It might work.*

35

SCIF Conference Room
The Pentagon

"The woman is cooperating with Mangiano and they're executing tonight," Newport said. "Alice, where's Senator Griffith?"

"At his residence in Alexandria. We've got him under surveillance."

"Okay. Execute the warrant for his arrest," Newport said. "Do it by the book. I don't want him out of jail in thirty minutes. Make sure there're no slipups and keep me posted."

"Yes, sir!" Alice said. "I'll have the slimy bastard bagged and in the crossbar hotel before he knows what happened. Captain Jordan is no slouch and he knows what's at stake. I'll brief all of them before we go."

"Mary Ellen, stay on your toes. Let me know the first sign of trouble. I want Mangiano pulled if the slightest thing goes wrong."

"Yes, sir!" Mary Ellen replied. "I've got good communications with the Delta commander and the watch officer here at the Pentagon. Also, I'm monitoring all sources for anything unusual or spike in chatter."

Alice sprang out of the car and dashed to the front door of Senator Griffith's house. She and Jordan, followed by a team of officers, reached the door at the same instant. Two uniformed officers darted to the rear of the house while two others stood guard in front. Alice rang the doorbell.

Griffith opened the door and before he could speak, Alice barged in with Jordan right behind her.

"What's the meaning of this?" the senator said when he saw the woman holding her FBI identification. "Do you know who I am?"

"Senator James Griffith?" Alice asked, more of a statement than question.

"That's right!"

"Senator Griffith, we have a warrant for your arrest and to search your house. We can do this the easy way or hard way. Sir, I suggest we do it the easy way."

"This is absurd!" Griffith said. "Arrest for what?"

"Espionage and divulging classified information to a foreign entity to start with," Alice replied.

"I'm a United States senator and that's bullshit. Get out of my house. Call my lawyer and discuss it with him!"

"Senator, shut the fuck up!" Alice said. "I'll do the talking. I'm FBI Special Agent Alice Johnson and—"

"How dare you barge in here like this!" Griffith said. "I'll have your badge faster than you can spit! I'm calling the attorney general."

"Senator, when the time comes, you can call whomever you wish. For now, shut your damn mouth and stand right here."

"You can't talk to me that way."

"We'll discuss formalities later," Alice said. "This is Captain Jordan, Alexandria Police." Alice motioned for the officers to commence searching the house, then read the senator his Miranda rights.

Griffith's complexion turned pale and his hands began to tremble. He stood motionless.

"Senator, are you all right?" Captain Jordan asked. "Maybe you should sit down."

"I, I...maybe. No, I'm...I think I need a drink of water and some aspirin."

"We'll get you some water." Captain Jordan motioned to an officer to get the water.

"I'll do it." Griffith stood. His demeanor was calm but his body seemed to slump as he walked to the kitchen ignoring everyone.

Jordan looked to the officer, then gestured with his hand for him to escort the once powerful man.

Griffith, with a trembling hand, took a glass from the cabinet and stood motionless as if disoriented.

"Senator, are you all right?" the young officer asked.

"What...oh, yes. Aspirin, in the pantry," Griffith mumbled as he turned and shuffled to the pantry. The officer kept a close watch on the senator as he opened the pantry door and stepped just inside. His large frame filled the door, his back to the officer. Reaching to the shelf, grasping a .38 Special revolver, Griffith stuck the gun in his mouth and squeezed the trigger.

The officer saw what was about to happen and shouted, "No!" But he was too late.

The .38 took out a large portion of the back of the senator's head, killing him instantly. His body collapsed backwards and blood poured from his mouth, forming a rapidly expanding dark pool. Alice, followed by Captain Jordan, arrived in the kitchen almost immediately. "Goddammit!" Alice said. "I wanted him alive."

36

1:09 a.m.
Friday, June 2
Lucerne, Switzerland

As they drove around the school, Anthony and Dydre tried to locate the men who guarded David and get a firsthand view of the area. The campus layout featured main buildings that formed a rectangle with a courtyard in the center; a soccer field was on the south side of the campus. "The last building on the south side, by the soccer field is David's dormitory," Dydre said. "The mother superior's room is on the west side of that building."

"That's good," he said. "That end of the building is dark and the adjacent building conceals the area in close to the building."

"There are only two ways to get into the campus—the north end at the main entrance and through the soccer field. But there are a couple of fences to get past going through the soccer field."

Anthony studied the layout as the car passed by the school. At this hour in the morning, he wouldn't chance circling the campus more than twice. Although he didn't see Clay's men, he knew they would be guarding the two possible entrances. A second pass behind the school revealed a faint glowing ember from a cigarette. The smoker stood in the alcove of a small building at the north end of the soccer field near David's dormitory. "There's the guard at the rear of the campus. Are you ready?"

Dydre checked her wig and makeup. "I'm ready."

Anthony parked the car on the west side of the campus next to a small building that blocked the view from where he saw the guard smoking a cigarette. He got out of the car. Dydre waited inside until it was her turn as sequenced by Anthony's plan. Dressed in dark coveralls, he stayed close to the side of the building where the car was parked. When he reached the building's north side, he looked for the guard he previously spotted. The campus was dark and quiet. Occasionally, the sound of a car broke the tranquility and the slight odor of cigarette smoke lingered in the still air. *Cigarette man was here but how long ago?* he thought. The absence of any significant breeze allowed the smell to remain longer before dissipating. When his eyes adjusted to the ambient light; he slowly searched for the man but didn't see him. He darted to the west end of the dormitory building and looked up to the darkened window of the mother superior's room. It was open at the bottom about six inches for fresh air. *Perfect,* he thought. A large garbage dumpster and several trash cans sat close to the end of the building. He removed the lids of two full trash cans, and then positioned them near the first-story window of the mother superior.

Another quick look of the area still showed no sign of anyone roaming about. He opened the dumpster to expose a three-quarters-full bin of trash, bags, and other miscellaneous bits of rubbish. He tore open a corner of a trash bag and lit the paper. Once certain it was burning, he shoved it farther back into the bin and positioned another bag next to it so it, too, would catch fire quickly. Turning to the trash cans, he lit the paper in one can and then the other. The smoke billowed upward and drifted into the open window. Looking back at the dumpster, he saw the glow from the burning bags inside intensify. *It won't be long now,* he thought. If it worked, he had only a few minutes before the next sequence of events. Anthony raced back to the car.

He stood beside the car and removed his coveralls. Now dressed in a plain, dark cotton shirt and pants, he would resemble the neighbors as they came out of their houses to watch the fire brigade in action. At that moment he heard the fire alarm sound. He tousled his hair to make it look like he had just tumbled out of bed. Then he turned to Dydre. "Are you ready?"

Dydre nodded and got out of the car.

"The children should start pouring out of the building at any moment," he said. "As soon as you see the guard move to the building, head to the edge of the soccer field. Remember, don't go onto the field until there's a crowd of students."

"I know," she said as she adjusted her robe.

Anthony looked her over. "You did a good job on your costume. You look like a little old lady that just got out of bed in a hurry. You'll have no problems with all the commotion." He handed her a small pair of bolt cutters. "These are to cut the locks on the gates. You do know how to use them, don't you?"

"I've used them a time or two."

"Remember to close the gate when you go through."

The lights to the soccer field popped on, illuminating the field, and the children started to spill out of the dormitory. Groups of children led by an older woman, presumably one of the nuns dressed just as Dydre, took them onto the lighted field. The orderly procession formed into platoons of little people as they assembled on their spots, just as they had rehearsed many times before.

Dydre moved to the side of the building, peered around the corner, and saw a guard on the north end of the soccer field. Another one walked alongside one of the groups of children. She passed her eyes over them, then looked down and picked up a smooth stone approximately two inches in diameter and an inch thick. *That's perfect,* she thought as she dropped the stone into her robe pocket. She looked back and saw the guard at the edge of the soccer field dart into the dormitory. She turned to tell Anthony but he had already disappeared into the darkness.

As she hurried toward the first gate, Dydre heard the sirens of approaching fire trucks. At the gate, she placed the jaws of the bolt cutter on the shank of the lock and squeezed the handles. The powerful jaws bit through the steel and the lock dropped to the ground. Observing that half of the shank remained, she used her free hand to remove it and dropped it beside the post. She opened the gate and stepped through, closing it behind her. At the second gate, she repeated the process, then discarded the bolt cutters along the fence several feet from where she stood. Waiting in the darkness until a group of students formed on her side of the field; she could smell the burning rubbish that permeated the cool, night air as the smoke began to hover overhead. Finally, she stepped out, unnoticed, onto the field to the rear of the children.

Everyone's attention focused on the big fire truck followed by another as they entered the campus with their blue lights flashing. The orderly formation of the little platoons soon lost their discipline as the children became engrossed in the actions of the firemen setting up their trucks, pulling out hoses, and assessing the situation. Talking, pointing, laughter, and even cheers ensued. Several nuns went from one group of children to the next, checking and double-checking that all of the children were accounted for. It was all the nuns could do to keep the excited children away from the working firemen. As with any sudden emergency situation, regardless of how well everyone is trained, a brief period of chaos reigned; just as Anthony had expected.

Numerous neighbors from the surrounding homes filled the sides of the perimeter fence, while others made their way through the unlocked gate and onto the field. Excitement and curiosity swelled. Anthony mingled in with the crowd, keeping Dydre in sight as he pretended to be one of the onlookers. He saw two men he suspected as Zsigmond's hired guns rush into David's dormitory. *It won't take them long to figure out this was just a ruse, and they'll sound their alarm to hunt for Dydre and the boy,* he thought. *Come on, Dydre. Find him. You don't have much time.* Within minutes the same two men bolted out of the door followed by two more men, the last one talking into a radio. Anthony sauntered toward Dydre.

She progressed from group to group, searching for Sister Rosa. The combination of the early hour and the encroaching neighbors made it difficult for her to locate the nun. Sister Rosa was her best chance to locate David, but all the women were dressed the same—pajamas and robe. Eventually, Dydre spotted the nun's red, disheveled hair; and moved as quickly toward her as she dared. Then she saw a guard at the far end of the nun's group. Dydre stopped behind Sister Rosa. Her eyes darted from child to child as she skimmed over the children, looking for David. She resisted the urge to shout out his name. One such slip would alert the guard and blow her rescue attempt. *David, where are you?* she thought. When her eyes landed on him at the edge of the group, kneeling and talking with one of the other boys, she struggled not to run to him. Instead, she watched the guard out of the corner of her eye, her adrenaline intensifying as she maneuvered slowly toward her son. "David, it's Mommy," she whispered as she knelt beside him.

David looked at her but didn't speak.

"It's me," she said. "I had to wear this disguise to get you out of here."

"It sounded like you. But what…why…I didn't recognize you."

"I know, honey," she said, reaching into her pocket, withdrawing the stone. "Remember the story of the dragons? This is a dragon stone. It will protect you and help you to be brave. Can you be brave like the little boy that fell into the cave between the two dragons?"

"Sure, I'll be brave," he replied. "I won't be like old Stempflin."

"Good. Now hold on to the dragon stone and do just as I say, no matter what. You must be brave. We're leaving and will never be apart again. Are you ready?"

"I'm ready."

Dydre stood for a moment, then casually led him through the group. Just as she neared the next loosely formed platoon of little people, she felt a tug on her arm.

"Where are you going with that boy?" Sister Rosa said. "Who are you?"

"Sister Rosa, it's me, Dydre."

"Why—"

"I'm taking David. This is the only way I could get him out of here."

"I know, my child. God be with you. Please let me hear from you."

"Thank you. I will."

A movement about ten feet beyond the nun caught Dydre's eye, and she looked up to see the guard shove children to the side as he rushed toward her. To her right she saw Anthony approaching her and nodding his head as a signal to get to the car. She looked back to the dormitory, where she saw three men running toward the children, now a gaggle caused by the commotion of the man who ran and shoved the children, obviously looking for her and David. A fourth man trailed and talked into a radio. The bitter taste of adrenaline filled her mouth and she fought the urge to run. She looked down at David and said, "Hold on to my hand tight." Approaching the gate, she took two more steps, then felt something poke her in the back—the barrel of a pistol.

"Nice try," the man said. "Dydre, isn't it?"

She froze and tried to figure out what to do next. She couldn't chance David being shot.

"Let's take a little walk back to the dormitory," he said. "You just made me a lot of money."

"Don't spend it too fast there, bucko," Anthony said as he jammed his Mark 23 into the man's back. "Do just as I say or I'll take out your kidney." He nudged the pistol into the man's back. "Have you got that?"

The man nodded.

"Hand her your pistol."

Dydre took the gun and contemplated keeping it until she read the expression on Anthony's face. She dropped out the magazine, pitched it to the left, and then tossed the pistol to the right.

"Dydre, get going. I'll catch up." Turning to the man, Anthony poked him with his pistol and said, "Let's go." He steered him through the first gate and turned left, disappearing into the darkness.

Dydre closed the gate behind them, retrieved the shank she had placed by the post, and inserted it into the hole where the lock previously hung. Picking up the bolt cutters, she jammed it into the gate preventing it from easily being opened.

"Come on, David," she said. "We've got to hurry." Grasping his hand, she pulled him along. Dydre looked over her shoulder for Anthony then back to her front, searching the area for any threats. *I might have time to hot-wire the car,* she thought. "Hurry, David!"

David tripped and fell, dropping Dydre's hand. "David, are you all right?" she asked, turning to see him on the ground. He nodded as she pulled him up.

"Wait," he said. "My dragon stone." He stooped and picked it up. As soon as he stood, Dydre took his free hand and tugged him on.

37

Anthony escorted the man about fifteen yards into the darkness, pulled a plastic wire tie from his pocket, and looped it around the man's crossed wrists behind his back. With another plastic tie, he secured the man in a crouching position to the fence post. He connected two more plastic ties, then slid them over the man's head and across his mouth. "Sorry, dude, I don't have a nice little gag for you. Your buddies will find you soon enough." Anthony cinched the plastic snug enough to cause the man's mouth to gape open. Satisfied, he sprinted to the gate and shut it behind him. He stopped to put the shank back into the gate latch, hoping it would slow a pursuer just long enough for them to get away. He reached the car just as Dydre put David into the backseat and closed the door.

"David, put your seat belt on and get down," she said, then looked up at Anthony.

Sliding behind the wheel as Dydre got into the passenger side, Anthony started the engine and dropped the transmission lever into drive. A hard stomp on the accelerator raced the engine and the car sped away, turning right at the first intersection past the school then left at the following intersection. "Watch for them," he said.

"There they are—"

Anthony spun the wheel as another car came at them from the right. Pushing the gas pedal to the floor, he turned left again. Zigzagging right then left, he never drove more than a few blocks in any one direction before he executed another turn. Tires screeched and the car swayed from side to side. The two chasing cars were right on his bumper. A shot rang out followed by another and shattered the passenger side rearview mirror.

"Damn!" Anthony said. He handed Dydre his Heckler and Koch. "See if you can get them to back off."

Grasping the pistol, Dydre stuck her arm out of the window and fired. The car swerved and slowed. She fired again, and again. The trailing car veered hard to the left and flipped over. The second car's tires screeched as it tried to avoid the first car, but it was too close. It crashed into the rear fender of the upturned car and spun it around. The accident caused the second car to lose ground as Anthony sped on in his meandering course.

"You're losing them!"

"I'm going to make a couple of quick turns and hopefully I'll shake 'em." Anthony spun the wheel and the car swayed as it swung around the corner. He then straightened it and sped to the next intersection. Again, he turned the wheel hard over, and the car swayed in the opposite direction as it made the corner. Just as the car was coming out of the corner, he stomped on the gas pedal. The speeding car approached another intersection, and again he worked the wheel. "See anything?"

"I don't see them," Dydre said, then looked back at David. "Still nothing. I think you lost them."

"For the time being," Anthony replied. "I'll cut over to the highway. See if you can figure out where we are." He reached over and took his pistol from her.

Dydre looked up at him and knew what he was thinking. Turning her attention back to the map, she used each passing street sign to check their location. Within a few minutes she said, "I've got us on the map. In three blocks turn right. There'll be an entrance to the highway about two blocks after you turn."

"Got it."

"David, are you okay?"

"Yes, I'm okay." He squeezed the stone.

After driving in a circling and twisting path to keep from being followed, they wended their way to the hotel. Once they arrived, Anthony ushered them into his room not only for their collective safety but also to see to it that Dydre didn't renege on her agreement to take him to the Arabs in Bosnia.

"Try and get some sleep," Anthony said as he locked the door.

Dydre led David to the bed opposite the door and helped him onto it. When he was comfortable, she curled up beside him and laid her arm across his chest. She watched Anthony prop a chair against the door. He cradled his pistol in his lap as he sat down, then switched off the light. *He knows,* she thought. *He's good, no mistakes and it's going to be a challenge to get away from him. I can't get past him without waking him.* Closing her eyes, she tried to determine how to get away from him. *It won't be tonight.* Without realizing it, she drifted into a sound sleep.

38

Dydre woke at the sound of Anthony's voice and looked at the clock.

"That's right, six brötchen with butter and jam, three bottles of juice, and one milk," he said into the phone.

"Can we have some coffee to go with that?" Dydre asked.

Anthony looked to her and replied, "Good morning. I think we can do that. We need to leave in the next fifteen or twenty minutes. You and David better get moving." Anthony turned back to the phone and said, "Can you fix two large coffees for me as well?" He paused to listen, then replied, "Thank you."

Dydre kissed David's cheek. "Time to wake up, David," she whispered. Gently shaking him, she whispered again, "Time to get up. We'll have a brötchen and juice in the car."

David rubbed his eyes and nodded. Dydre helped him up.

Within fifteen minutes Anthony led them out of the room, stopping at the desk to pick up the breakfast he ordered, then to the car. They headed onto the expressway. The morning traffic, which was building in intensity, allowed them to blend in—and with any luck, enough to make them undetectable.

"Anthony, there's a helicopter coming up fast behind us," Dydre said as she looked out the back window.

"It could be a traffic helicopter, but keep an eye on it and let me know what it does," he replied as he glanced in the mirror.

"Still coming on strong."

Anthony examined their route but saw nothing unusual or threatening. Repeatedly, he checked the rearview mirror to identify anyone who might be following them. Then the helicopter roared passed overhead without showing any sign of interest in them, and continued its low, fast course down the highway. "Stay alert," he said.

"I don't think that was a traffic helicopter, but they were sure in a hurry," she said.

"It could be nothing but stay alert."

He looked into the rearview mirror and said, "Get down. Two cars—one right and one left—gaining fast."

"David, get down on the floor and don't get up until I tell you. Do you still have your stone?"

"Yes, I have it." David fished the stone out of his pocket, and held it in his hand as he knelt on the floor.

"I'm getting down, too, David. I'll tell you when to get up." Dydre wiggled down to the floorboard. "What are they doing?"

"Hold on." Anthony maintained his pace with traffic, mimicking a commuter on his way to work. He watched in the rearview mirror as the two cars pulled up alongside of him. Out of the corner of his eyes he saw the men in each vehicle match his speed, check him out, then speed on. "That was probably some of Clay's thugs," he said. "They're obviously looking for the three of us. Keep down for just a bit. Let them get a little farther up ahead."

"Clay doesn't give up easily. He plays hardball," Dydre said.

"Okay, you can get up now."

They drove on for about ten more minutes, then Anthony said, "Heads up. The helicopter is coming back." He pointed it out as it approached over the oncoming traffic. "The cars will be back as well. Get ready to duck down."

Searching the oncoming traffic, Dydre said, "There they are." She pointed to the two cars moving around in the traffic. "David, lie down on the seat. I'll tell you when you can get up." David obeyed her instructions, closing his little fingers around the stone in his hand.

"They're gone. You can get up now," Anthony said.

Their tension subsided with the passing of the cars, but Anthony kept an ever-vigilant eye as he drove on. Reaching the outskirts of the city without event, he sighed, with relief at not having to deal with Clay's men. "Chances are they won't be looking for us this far south," Anthony said.

"I just hope the rest of the trip is uneventful," Dydre said.

It was 8:19 when Anthony turned into the parking lot of the Milan train station. The trio entered the station, both Anthony and Dydre scanning the crowd to see if they recognized any of Clay's men or anyone interested in them. As a couple, they proceeded to the ticket counter, staying in a mass of people as much as possible. Then Dydre leaned toward Anthony and said in a low voice, "There's Magda, my housekeeper, the blond-headed woman carrying the overnight bag."

"Do you recognize anyone around her?"

"No, it looks clear."

"Okay, take David to her. I'll stay back and keep watch. Make it quick."

"I know."

"Dydre, remember our deal."

"Don't worry. I'll keep my end of the bargain." *At least for now,* she thought.

Dydre walked to the slender woman as Anthony watched her every move.

"Ciao, signora! Here's the overnight bag you wanted," Magda said as she approached.

"Ciao, Magda!" She took the overnight bag and continued, "Take David and go straight to the train. Be careful and don't let anyone follow you. If you think anyone is following you, don't go home. Call me if there are any problems."

"I will. What's going on? I don't like the looks of that man over there watching us. Will you be all right?"

"No questions for now. He helped me get David and now I'm going to help him. Don't talk to anyone and stay out of sight. I'll be back in a couple of days."

"Ciao, signora."

"Ciao, Magda."

"Okay, let's go," Dydre said as she approached Anthony.

"You did very well," he replied as he looked over Dydre's shoulder and saw Magda with David in tow disappear into the crowd. He reached over, taking the overnight bag from her.

She released the bag and the couple walked out of the station like any other traveler.

They walked directly to the car and got in. Anthony sat the overnight bag on his lap, glanced around for anyone who might be tailing them, then unzipped the bag.

"It's just the things I need for Bosnia," she said.

"I know. But I'll keep the pistol."

"How do you know I have a pistol?"

"Because that's what I'd do." He pulled the pistol out of the bag and held it low to examine it. "Walther P5. Not bad. Now to the airport."

After picking up their tickets at the Lufthansa ticket counter, Anthony and Dydre walked toward the security checkpoint. Within a few steps beyond the corner of the counter, Dydre whispered to Anthony, "The man walking towards us with gray, scraggly hair and mustache is Günter Schenck."

Anthony gave a slight nod and examined the surrounding area for any sign of trouble. The man she identified as Schenck looked to be in his late forties. A newspaper stuck out of the left coat pocket of his threadbare tweed coat. As he reached Anthony, Schenck shifted the satchel he carried to his left hand, then extended his right in greeting.

"Morgen, Anthony." He grasped Anthony's hand as if meeting a business acquaintance.

Anthony smiled. "Hello, Günter! It's good to see you."

"Morgen, Günter." Dydre extended her hand but could barely hold her contempt.

"Ja, a pleasure to see you again, my dear."

Dydre smiled but said nothing. *I bet!* she thought.

"Let's get a coffee," he said as he placed his hand on Anthony's back.

Günter guided them into a restaurant where they sat against the wall, facing the entrance of the restaurant. He withdrew the newspaper from his pocket and laid it on the table. They casually ordered coffee as the waitress approached. As soon as she stepped away, Günter withdrew from his satchel two pieces of paper stapled together, and handed them to Anthony. "Read this and we'll go over it. You must memorize this in detail." He then pulled a laptop computer and cable out of the satchel. "This is for you. The patch is already on the hard drive, and this is a cable you will use to connect the laptop to the devices. As soon as you see the first Ranger, push the F2 key. That activates a tracking device in the computer, and we'll have the location of not only you but the Rangers. You understand, ja?"

"I've got it. Go on."

"On the second page of the paper, you will see a diagram where to hook the cable and the sequence to apply the fix. You understand, ja?"

"I've got it. It seems simple enough."

As the waitress approached, Anthony turned the paper facedown on the table, and the three fell silent. As soon as she left, Günter picked up where he had left off. "We'll rehearse now to make sure you understand, ja?"

"Okay, from the top," Anthony said.

PATRICK PARKER

Dydre watched Günter coach Anthony through the sequence, all the while thinking how difficult it was going to be. *This is risky. One misstep and they'll start shooting. The Arabs are skittish and may shoot us on sight anyway.*

"Dydre," Anthony said, looking into her eyes. "You've got to convince them I'm Reynolds. Do they know him or who he is?"

"They don't know him, just his name and that he invented the devices."

"You've got to make it good and believable. It'll be up to you to keep us from being discovered. Can you do it?"

"It won't be easy but I can do it. You just make sure you know how to patch the Rangers."

"Memorize the sequence and you will be fine," Günter said as he withdrew another stapled paper from his satchel. "This is some background on IT Security Solutions, Inc. and CEO George Reynolds. Be very familiar with this as they may test you."

Anthony read through the paper, then laid it down. "Next?"

Günter sipped his coffee. "After you have loaded the fix, reboot the device by turning it off then back on. When the green light on the front glows steady, you're all set, ja. That's it."

"That's pretty simple," Anthony said.

"You're fixing them and walking out?" Dydre asked.

"That's about it and that's exactly what we want them to think," Anthony said.

"They aren't going to let you just waltz in, fiddle with the devices, then let you walk out," Dydre said.

"Ja! Ja, you're right." Günter said. "They currently don't work and they want them to, ja?"

"That's right," she said.

"You must convince them you're there to fix them. Each device will work perfectly after Anthony installs the fix. They will be happy and will relax a little."

"But I thought you wanted to destroy them," she said.

"Ja! Ja, they will work four times after the fix is installed. Your Arab friends will want to see them work and verify they are fixed, ja? After the fourth attempt to turn on a device, a program inside the code Anthony loaded activates, destroying all the code, not just shut it down as Reynolds did. That way if we can't recover them, they're useless. The Arabs need to see that they work or you'll never walk out. When the Arabs see that they work, you must get out of there while they're happy. As a last resort, they can be destroyed by typing 666 and then hitting Enter." Günter looked at both of them. "You understand, ja?"

They both nodded.

"Fix each Ranger and show them that it works. Then turn it off," Günter said. Producing a small tube of a liquid substance, he added, "Smear this over the soles of your shoes before you meet with them, then let it dry."

"Okay. But why?" Anthony asked.

"As you walk, it will leave a trail that can be seen with an ultraviolet light and special glasses. We can track you if necessary. Put this pen in your pocket." Günter handed him a ballpoint pen. "It has a tracking device in it and works just like a normal pen. Use it when you are with them and, if possible, leave the pen with them. I made these labels for you. They will give you an excuse to use the pen and it will look natural. Just write the date on the label and attach it to the device before you fix it. Do this for each device. Tell them it is a reference for the last patch."

Anthony placed the pen in his shirt pocket and the labels with the laptop.

"And just in case, here's another tool"—Günter held out a coin—"that will help us keep tabs on your location. Just slip this into your pocket and keep it with you. Unless you have any questions, I must be off."

"Thank you," Anthony said as they stood.

The three shook hands. Günter picked up the newspaper, stuffed it back into his pocket, and said, "Auf Wiedersehen!"

"Auf Wiedersehen," they replied.

Dydre, followed by Anthony then Günter, negotiated the chairs and other tables as they headed out of the restaurant. Displaying the appearance of business acquaintances, the trio parted company.

Frankfurt, Germany

"What do you mean you can't find them?" Clay said into the phone, his face florid. "You have all the resources and men all over the city."

"We'll find her," the man's voice said in the phone.

"Who was the man that helped her? Do you have any leads on him?"

"So far nothing. We don't have that good of a description of him. He's clean."

"You call yourselves professional. You're just a bunch of buffoons," Clay said, striking his desk with his fist clinched. "I'm paying you for results, not excuses. Find them!" He slammed the phone down, then stood and picked up the smoldering Montecristo Gran Corona from the ashtray. With a trembling hand, he shoved it in his mouth. Leaning over to the credenza, he poured a snifter of brandy and took a sip. He paced the room, alternating puffs of the cigar and sips of brandy. Finally, calm enough to think, he dialed a number in Bosnia.

On the second ring a man's voice said, "Yes…"

"This is Clay Zsigmond. I need to speak with Osama."

"I will tell the Master you wish to speak with him. He will call you."

"I will be waiting for his call."

The cigar was about half-consumed when his call was returned. "My messenger has turned on me. She is a traitor," Clay said into the phone.

"A traitor?" the voice replied.

"Yes, she stole from me and you. She took money from me and sold you devices that don't work. She may even try to get more money from you to replace or fix them."

"I see. This is most serious."

"I'm looking for her but if you should find her first, aside from avenging what she has done to you, I'm prepared to pay you one million US dollars for her death." Clay continued for several more minutes, ensuring Osama bin Laden would take care of Dydre. "I'll call you when I find her," Clay said.

"That will be most appreciated," the voice said. The phone line went dead.

Clay continued to pace and puff, his disposition becoming increasingly sour. A large ash from the cigar dropped onto his shirt. He flicked it to the floor, took another sip of brandy, and then dialed Senator Griffith's number. The phone rang and rang without being answered. Frustrated, he slammed the phone down. After a moment, he called his driver. "Franz, get the car ready. We're going to Lucerne."

39

Ilidža, Bosnia-Herzegovina

"Park and we'll walk from here," Dydre said. "My pistol, please." She held out her hand.

"Too risky. We leave the weapons in the car. We're supposed to be friendly, remember? If they find a weapon on us, it'll cause them to get defensive and start asking a lot of questions."

"I know these crazies—"

"We go unarmed and follow the plan. In and out."

"This is my funeral too, you know."

"Do your part and there won't be a funeral...for us anyway. Let's go."

Walking along the littered street, they encountered numerous abandoned cars—some intact and others burned-out shells. They quickly checked each one. The smell of smoke and burning rubbish filled the late afternoon air. Although the streets showed no sign of life, they both sensed watchful eyes scrutinizing their every move. The sound of gravel crunching beneath their feet seemed thunderous in the eerie silence.

Approaching an intersection, they stayed close to the side of the building. Anthony shifted the laptop computer to his other hand and peered around the corner before proceeding down yet another empty street. About halfway down the block they were met by two Arab men with AK-47s.

"You are Sam?" one of the men asked through heavily stained, bad teeth.

"I am," Dydre replied.

"Put your hands on the wall."

"Look, camel breath, we came to meet with Jamaal."

Anthony shot a disapproving look at Dydre, then said, "We are not armed. We came as friends."

Bad Teeth motioned for the other Arab, a boy of not more than sixteen, to search them, then said, "Jamaal said you would object. But the last time you were here, you killed two brothers. If you move, I will shoot him. Then we will do as we wish with you, and you'll finally beg us to kill you."

"I told you, we are not armed," Anthony said. "Take us to Jamaal now or we leave. If we leave, Jamaal and the Master will be not be pleased with you."

"If he does not search you, Jamaal will not be pleased," Bad Teeth replied. He nodded to the other Arab, and then took the laptop from Anthony.

The boy held his Kalashnikov in his left hand and ran his right hand over Anthony. Bad Teeth watched, pointing his assault rifle at them.

As soon as he finished with Anthony, he stepped to Dydre and began feeling across her back, down her waist, then around to her breasts. Stopping suddenly, he looked at Bad Teeth and said, "The woman wears—"

"It is something that fat women wear!" Dydre said. "The goats you sleep with don't wear such things." She knew she was on thin ice but wanted to keep him off guard. If he realized she was wearing a disguise and padding, the meeting would go dramatically downhill. "Finish your search of me. We must go see Jamaal. I want you to know that I am *unclean*."

Arab Boy paused. Dydre looked over her shoulder at him and knew by his hesitation that her bluff worked. Brainwashed by the strict fundamentalist teachings of Islamic law that he had received since birth—the forbidden touching of a woman during her menstrual cycle—he was suffering from an internal conflict that was almost too much for him.

"Evening prayers are soon," Dydre said. "Will you find water in time to wash?"

"Silence!" Bad Teeth said. "We will see Jamaal."

The two Arabs escorted Anthony and Dydre along a meandering course through the cluttered streets and alleys, then through a bombed-out building and out another. Turning into another alley, they proceeded to the back of a building and turned the corner. They stopped in front of a door and Bad Teeth knocked.

Once inside the building, Arab Boy led them into a room, the air thick with a dirty, musty smell and body odor, with Bad Teeth following behind. Light streamed through broken shutters on the windows and illuminated a bare wooden table with chairs on either side. Dust particles danced about the room while trash and several broken pieces of furniture littered the floor. A closed door, presumably, led to the front of the building. Large cracks ran through the brick walls—damage from the bombings. Figures stood as sentries in the shadows of the two forward corners, their Kalashnikovs pointing in the direction of the visitors.

Another man entered from a draped doorway to the right and looked at Bad Teeth. Bad Teeth nodded. "You have come to fix the Rangers, yes?"

"Jamaal, I come as a friend. I said I would bring Reynolds, the man that built the Rangers. This is George Reynolds."

"Clayborne Zsigmond told the Master that you are a traitor. You stole from him and you sold us devices that do not work. He has offered us $1 million to kill you."

"Shit!" Anthony said under his breath. Their chances of getting out alive, already practically nonexistent, were going downhill fast. *No mistakes and play it to the max,* he thought. *What's she going to do?*

"I want nothing from you," Dydre said. "I brought Reynolds to you in good faith. If anyone is a traitor, it is Reynolds. Kill him."

Anthony shot a look of surprise at Dydre. "If you kill me, Jamaal, you will not get the Rangers fixed," Anthony said. "The money you spent will be for nothing. I've brought my laptop to fix them." He pointed to the laptop Bad Teeth was still holding.

"Put the computer on the table," Jamaal said. "Why do the Rangers not work?"

"There was a coding error," Anthony said. "It's not an unusual problem. We discovered the error shortly after they were shipped. Sam contacted us about that time and before we could contact you. I was trying to fix them when Zsigmond's man tried to kill us. That's why I couldn't finish."

"Jamaal, I'm not sure I can get your money back from Clay Zsigmond. He is the traitor if anyone is. If you shoot Reynolds, I will take several of your men to find him, and you can take revenge on him. Maybe we can get your money back."

"If you kill me the Rangers cannot be fixed," Anthony said. "The Rangers are worth more than anything else. More than ten thousand rifles, even more than a nuclear bomb."

"I am here in good faith and as a friend," Dydre said. "Kill him and let's move on. I'll help you go after Clay Zsigmond."

"Can we get more Rangers from Reynolds's company?" Jamaal asked.

"I don't think so," Dydre said. "The American government has the company under strict surveillance. Their agents are scrutinizing all orders, watching the company and everything that enters or leaves the place. Nothing goes out of the country."

"She's right," Anthony said. "I came here to fix your devices. I have the only code to repair them and I can get you more Rangers. Allow me to fix one of them to show you I am truthful."

Jamaal, with his lips pursed, stared at the man before responding. "Sit. I will be back." Bad Teeth and Arab Boy ushered the visitors to the two chairs, then took standing positions in front of them. "Shoot them both if they try anything," Jamaal said as he left the room.

About fifteen minutes later, he returned followed by a short, slim Arab man carrying a Ranger in his hand. The man placed the device on the table in front of Anthony. "Fix the Ranger or you will die," Jamaal said.

Anthony looked at Jamaal, the men guarding them, and then Dydre. He wanted to speak but didn't. Opening the laptop he set the labels to the side and booted up the machine. Next he retrieved the pen from his pocket, entered the date on the label, and then affixed it to the Ranger. When he pushed the top of the pen to expose the tip, the tiny tracking device started sending out an electronic signal of their location. As Anthony connected the cables to the device, Jamaal leaned over and placed his right hand on the computer while his left steadied his Kalashnikov. "Make sure you fix it and nothing else. I will be watching you."

"I said I came to fix the Rangers. You will see in a few minutes. Let me work."

The room went quiet except for the sound of Anthony tapping the keys on the laptop. As soon as the computer came to life, he slid his hand across the keys, depressing the F2 key with the ring finger of his left hand—an inconspicuous move that could very well save his life. Without hesitation, he then began the sequence Günter told him to memorize and worked methodically through each step. Dydre and Jamaal watched his every move. Several minutes later, Anthony disconnected the cable and pressed the button to shut down the device so it could be restarted, thus allowing Günter's handiwork to take effect. Looking up at Jamaal who stared at the blinking lights on the small box, Anthony maintained a demeanor of confidence.

Not really superstitious but lacking confidence in Anthony's ability, Dydre crossed her fingers as she held her hands in her lap and took a nonchalant glance around the room. *I'll only have a split second to react if the device doesn't work after he tries to fix it,* she thought. She quickly examined how each man stood holding his weapon and her best course of action. *Jamaal first. Shove him into Bad Teeth...the sentries might not shoot for fear of harming Jamaal. Then take his AK-47, fire, and out the door. Not a goddamned prayer!* Slowly she moved into a position and readied herself to spring into action at the right moment.

"This one is fixed," Anthony said as he pushed the Ranger across the table toward Jamaal.

Jamaal picked up the device and depressed the button to switch it off. Keeping his eyes on Dydre and Anthony, he depressed the On button to boot the device again. As soon as the green light glowed steady, he looked at Anthony. He depressed the Off button again. Looking back at Anthony, he switched it back on again.

"Are you going to just play with it all night, or are we going to fix the rest of them?" Dydre asked, fearful that he may restart it again.

Jamaal looked from one to the other then back to the device. The green light glowed again. "I will be back," he said. He nodded to Bad Teeth, and then to the slim Arab man who had brought the Ranger in. The Arab man picked up the device, cradling it in his arm as though it was a gold bar, and followed Jamaal out.

Twenty minutes later Jamaal stepped through the draped doorway and paused just inside. Expressionless, he stepped to the table followed by another Arab man. "The Master is pleased with your loyalty." He motioned to the Arab man to place another one of the devices on the table. "Continue." He slid the Ranger closer to Anthony. "I am watching."

"I know," Anthony replied. "Just let me fix them so we can get out of here. Where are the rest of them? There were four total."

"Do not worry yourself where the other ones are," Jamaal said with a straight face. "I will bring them to you. Three need to be fixed, not four."

"I need to fix all of them," Anthony replied. "The error is still in the first one. At some point it will malfunction as well. Also, I am placing a new build of software on the devices that makes them more efficient and detects more vulnerabilities than the previous build. If you don't keep the devices upgraded, they will soon become obsolete."

"Fix the Ranger," Jamaal said, pointing to the one on the table.

Anthony slid the device close to him and connected it to the laptop. Silence filled the room again as everyone watched him methodically go through the sequence of applying the patch again. *A different man brings in a Ranger to be fixed*, Anthony thought as he worked through the procedure. *One man is responsible for one Ranger—probably an honor to be entrusted with such a powerful device. When Reynolds was on the phone before he was shot, he had talked to one of the Arab men to make the patch. If the man on the phone hears my voice, he'll know I'm not Reynolds. Most likely he's still holding the device.*

When Anthony finished, he switched off and then rebooted the Ranger. He slid the device across the table to Jamaal and stared into his eyes. Jamaal switched the device off and on twice, just as he had done before. When the green light glowed steady, he switched it off and said, "I will return."

"Okay, General MacArthur," Dydre said. "Let's get on with the show. Bring the other two out so he can fix them." She knew the longer they stayed with Jamaal and his men, the more likely they would be discovered. This was the first time she depended on the skill of someone else for her survival. *So far, Anthony has been flawless in his performance but can he continue? Can he pull it off if they start asking him questions?*

Jamaal continued his practice of entering the room and pausing before making his way to the table. It was a way to torment them a little, to allow their fear to rise before he approached. Each absence lasted about twenty minutes. Each return brought a new man, another device, and the same order to fix it—all of which was followed by Jamaal's double rebooting of the device. His rebooting each device twice began to annoy Anthony.

When Jamaal left with the third Ranger patched, Anthony studied the sentries standing in the corners. *They're getting lax. Good!* he thought. *But they have the advantage with the AK-47s.* He slid his chair back to wait.

Jamaal returned with the fourth and final device. Anthony, again, slid the Ranger close to him and began his work. *Time is about up*, he thought. *Are we going to walk or do we fight?* When he finished this time, he didn't push the device toward Jamaal. Instead, he rebooted the Ranger twice, looking up at Jamaal each time it activated. When it shut down the final time, Anthony flipped the device onto the table and sat back in his chair as if daring Jamaal to reboot it again.

"Done!" he said, with a deadpan expression. "Do we keep playing this game or what?"

Jamaal looked at Anthony, then picked up the device. He started to press the On button then stopped. "You have kept your word. The Master is pleased." He smiled. "May Allah be with you." He turned and walked out of the room with the two sentries following him.

Bad Teeth motioned for them to stand. "We will go now."

Arab Boy went to the door first and looked out before exiting the building. Seeing no one, he motioned for the three to follow. Then he led them back along their meandering route to where they had picked up Dydre and Anthony. Just as they reached the block where they met, an explosion rocked the building they just left. Then there was another explosion followed by automatic weapons fire. Chaos ensued as the area erupted in violence, explosions, and more gun fire. Anthony knocked Dydre to the ground with the first blast. The explosions disoriented the two Arabs, who flinched and then looked back to see the remnants of their building emerge from the smoke and dust, with debris falling like rain.

Anthony reached out and jerked Arab Boy's feet out from underneath him. The confused boy went down, landing with his arms open, the Kalashnikov in his right hand. Before the startled man could react, Anthony lunged for the weapon. His strength and skill far superior to Arab Boy's, he wrestled the automatic rifle from the struggling boy. Gripping the AK-47, he fired a short burst. The bullets ripped through the Arab's chest from lower right to upper left. Then Anthony spun around to take out Bad Teeth, only to see him on the ground.

When Anthony made his play for Arab Boy, Dydre had sprung to her feet and attacked Bad Teeth, kneeing him first in the crotch. As his body bent forward from her blow, she brought up the heel of her hand and caught Bad Teeth on the end of the nose, driving that cartilage, like a spear, into his brain.

Anthony looked up as he heard the familiar sound of the Spectre gunship. "Come on!" he shouted. "It's time we get the hell out of here." Grasping her hand, he pulled her along without waiting for a reply.

"That was close," Dydre said.

He pointed to the gunship. "Günter's tracking signal in the computer worked as promised. That was 105 millimeter rounds slamming into the building. They were watching for us."

The intensity of the automatic weapons firing began to subside as they ran along the street back to the car. The explosions stopped but the smell of burnt propellant and smoke lingered in the air. As they passed a building entrance a military man in combat gear began jogging alongside of them. The only identification on his uniform was the small American flag on his shoulder. "Are you all right?" he asked.

"We're okay," Anthony replied.

"We've got four Ranger devices, which were scattered around the area in four different locations," he said. "Each time your messenger boy left your location with a man and a device and dropped them off at the safe house where the man came from, we recovered the device. So four locations, four devices—and we picked each one of the Arabs up like turkeys."

"Thanks for the information. Has the Old Man been notified yet?"

"The commander is talking with him now. I'm to give you whatever support you need. Do you want to go out with us?"

"What's the intel on the area and way out of here?"

"It's clear. They scattered when we lit the place up."

"We'll drive out," Anthony replied. "It'll be more direct, faster. We're good to go. Thanks for the help."

The Delta team member dropped away from Anthony and Dydre but stayed behind them until they reached the car. They wasted no time in leaving the area. The sun was setting fast and as the darkness returned, so would the terrorists.

"Now what?" Dydre asked as the car sped away.

"What do you mean?" Anthony replied.

"I have David and you have the Rangers back."

"The first thing is we get out of here. I need you to go with me to be debriefed. From there, I don't know yet. I still have to talk to the boss."

"I'll go but I want to see David first."

40

Bressanone, Italy
Saturday, June 3, 1995

Dydre opened the large, carved-wood door and brought Anthony into her house. Her shoes clicked on the marble floor as she entered expecting David and Magda to greet her. But the only greeting she received came from the fragrance of fresh flowers—the house was silent. "Magda! David!" she called out. Turning to Anthony, she said, "That's odd. Something—"

"Welcome home, Dydre," Clay said as he and another man entered from another room.

"Clay…what…how…?"

The door closed behind her and Anthony. Looking around, they saw Ludwig Stäbler standing, pointing an automatic pistol at them.

Clay lit a cigar, puffed it several times and wiped his glistening face with his handkerchief. "Dydre, I've known about this house for a long time." He glared at her. "When you disappeared in Lucerne, I knew where you would go. You should know by now you can't keep anything from me. But the thing I don't know yet is who your friend is and why he's helping you. That will come."

"Where's David…and Magda? What have you done with them?"

Clay puffed the Montecristo Gran Corona. "They're fine, for now." He motioned to Ludwig and the other man. The two men escorted Dydre and Anthony into the living room, seating them, then duct-taped their arms and legs to the chairs.

"Just kill us and get it over with," Dydre said.

"Oh, not so quick, my dear," Clay replied. "I want to get to know your friend first. Then we'll enjoy each other's company for a bit. After a while, you'll want to tell me things."

Anthony, having seen these men's earlier work on Dydre, knew what to expect. *Clay's probably not armed and won't be a problem, but the other two are,* he thought. *They'll make a mistake, but when?*

"I introduced you to this before, didn't I?" Clay held up the stun gun he used on her in Switzerland. "Let's play with it again." He touched Dydre on the shoulder. Then he turned to Anthony and touched his shoulder.

Waking to his aching muscles, Anthony realized he was on the floor, facing the wall but still bound to the chair. He felt saliva dribbling from his mouth. *I probably threshed around and they just left me alone,* he thought. *My aching head! I must have banged it a couple of times on the floor. My nose hurts.* He turned his head to look around the room. *Where's Dydre? They've separated us. That figures. How long was I out? They'll be back in here soon.* Wiggling, he tried to free himself but it was no use. He froze when he heard the door open. Then he closed his eyes and pretended to be asleep.

As footsteps approached, he tried to prepare himself for what he thought was his turn at an interrogation from Clay's men. But his mind felt clouded, his body sluggish.

"Anthony," a man's voice said, low and close to his ear. "Anthony, wake up. Are you all right?"

"What...who? I'm okay."

The man cut the tape from Anthony's arms and legs. "Come on, we've got to get out of here," he said in a low voice.

Anthony rubbed his face and looked at the man, trying to clear his mind. He shook his head and looked once more at the man. "Hector, what're you doing here?"

"The boss sent me here to follow the housekeeper. He wanted to keep the number of people in the investigation as low as possible. So he sent me. I was watching the house when you and the woman arrived."

"Okay, help me up." Anthony raised his arm and grabbed hold of Hector, unsure of his stance as he stood.

"What happened? Are you sure you're all right?"

"I'm fine. It'll just take me a minute. They got us by surprise when we walked in—a stun gun."

"Oooh! I wasn't sure what happened. By the time I got to the window to see what was happening, you were on the floor and they were taking the woman out of the room. We've got to get the *sheet* out of here!"

"First things first. Do you have a gun?"

"No."

"Great!" Anthony said, his sarcasm heavy. "We'll just have to make do. Come on. We've got to get the woman and her son. There are four men—Clay and three of his hired guns."

"Six. There's two outside," Hector added.

At that moment Anthony held up his hand. "Listen!" The faint tapping of shoes on the marble floor could be heard on the other side of the closed door. "Someone is coming!"

Shoving Hector to the hinged side of the door, the two men stood in silence. As the door opened, concealing them on the back side, a man began to enter. The moment he cleared the door, Anthony lunged for him and Hector closed the door. He hit him twice in rapid succession and flipped him to the floor. As soon as he was down, Anthony rolled him onto his stomach, bringing both of the man's arms up behind him and holding them securely in place. He removed the 9mm automatic from the man's shoulder holster, and then checked him for other weapons. "Hector, get that roll of tape and bring it over here."

Hector grabbed the duct tape from the coffee table and handed it to him.

"Here, take the pistol and keep him covered," Anthony said, handing Hector the pistol.

Anthony taped the man's hands securely behind his back, taped his legs together, and put another wrap around his mouth to keep him quiet. Drawing the man's legs up from behind, he secured them to his hands. Then he dragged the man behind the couch to prevent him from being seen from the door. He took the pistol from Hector and said to the man, "Just lie there and be quiet. Otherwise, I'll shoot you. Do you understand?"

Wide-eyed, the man nodded.

"Come on, Hector. We've got to get Dydre and the boy," Anthony said, reaching for the door.

"I'm right behind you."

Anthony peered into the adjoining room as he slowly opened the door. Just as he was about step out, he caught a glimpse of a man entering from the front door. Jerking back inside, knocking Hector backward, Anthony closed the door and placed his finger to his lips in a gesture of silence. He then signaled with his hand that a man from outside was entering. Both men moved to the hinged side of the door, waiting for the man to come in. Anthony held his pistol high and watched the door slowly open.

A woman's voice cried out in agony. The door stopped. Muffled sounds, then a thud came from another room. The door began to move again. A barrel emerged, then fingers around the pistol grip. When the wrist was inside the door, Anthony chopped his hand down as hard as he could, striking the man's wrist with the butt of his pistol. The gun flipped out of the man's hand onto the floor. Anthony grabbed the man with his left hand as he bent forward from the crashing blow, and jerked the man toward him. Then thrusting up with his right and knocking the man's head back, Anthony immediately brought his hand down hard and crashed his pistol onto his head. The now-disarmed man collapsed. Anthony slid him out of the way, stepped back to the door, then opened it again. Bam! Bam, bam! Shots rang out and wood shards exploded from the door.

Sweat streaked down Clay's red face. He retrieved his handkerchief from his rear pocket and shook it open. Wiping his face and hands, he paused when he saw the blood on the handkerchief. A slight smirk appeared on his face. "Pick her up!" he said, motioning for Ludwig to lift Dydre off the floor.

Ludwig propped her up, but her head hung limp. Clay grasped her disheveled hair with his fat fingers and pulled her head up. "One more time, you little bitch! Where's my money?" His gravelly voice echoed in the room.

"I... told you...before..." Her lip was split and numb, her right eye swollen. "I don't have it...gave it to Reynolds. Get it over with, Clay...or are you...getting excited?"

Her response infuriated him more. Clay looked to Ludwig and said, "Get the boy." Then turning back to Dydre, he continued, "You'll talk when David gets in here. I'll break a few of his little fingers. You'll tell me."

Ludwig winced at Clay's words. Even a ruthless mercenary had a limit on how low he would go. And torturing a small boy in front of his mother to get her to talk was well below that threshold.

Through swollen eyes, Dydre looked hard at Clay. She mumbled something. Then with the fierceness and savagery of a wounded lion, she sprang on him with all her might. Her sudden burst caught Clay by surprise, as well as Ludwig.

Clay fell back and Ludwig jumped to free Clay from the lioness's attack. She was going after Clay's face with her hands, her legs kicking and kneeing. Every ounce of her strength went into her attack. Tumbling backward as Ludwig freed Clay, she hit the floor but immediately regained her footing and prepared to spring again at Clay. Just as the wounded cat lunged, Ludwig touched her shoulder with the stun gun. Her body crumpled to the floor, convulsing.

Hearing the shots, Ludwig reached for his pistol. Clay nodded toward the door.

41

Anthony and Hector flattened themselves against the wall on either side of door. The second outside guard, who had seen Anthony attack the first guard, entered the house and fired when he saw the door open. Anthony, on the left side of the door, could see slightly into the adjoining room through the partially opened door, but he could not see the guard that fired. *He's on my side of the door,* Anthony thought. *But where're the others?*

Anthony motioned to Hector to go out the window and distract the man. Hector nodded. Concealed by the opened door, he moved toward the window and climbed out.

Hector stayed close to the side of the house as he crept in a crouched position toward the front door, keeping his eyes wide open for any surprises. Unarmed and inexperienced, he never considered what he would do if he encountered someone. When he was close to the door, he picked up a handful of pebbles and pitched them onto the glass sidelights.

The pebbles struck the glass and diverted the attention of the man inside for an instant. Anthony didn't hesitate. He flipped the door open, lunged forward, and fired twice. The deadly shots caught the man under the chin and in the chest. He was dead when he hit the floor.

Another shot rang out, stinging Anthony in his left arm. Instinctively, he dove behind an overstuffed chair. But he was vulnerable and he knew it.

Ludwig, leading, motioned for the other man to move to his left so as to trap Anthony in crossfire. "One shot, just one shot is all I need," Ludwig said in a low voice. "You're good but I'm better."

Anthony saw a faint shadow on the floor to his right, moving. *I thought so. Not today.* The shadow arced around and Anthony predicted where the shooter was standing, *One quick shot*, he thought. *Roll out, shoot, roll back.* As the shadow inched across the floor, Anthony listened for any sound that would reveal either man's true location. Snug behind the chair, he was ready to fire. The shadow continued like the incoming tide. Still no sounds. Anthony sensed the man was close, very close. At that moment the glass window shattered and a large rock tumbled across the floor. Rolling out, Anthony fired, striking the man in the chest. Then he shifted his position and fired again just as another shot rang out. Ludwig's shot, a few inches high, hit the wall behind Anthony. Ludwig's body fell to the floor and silence filled the room once again.

As Anthony readjusted his position, he saw the front door begin to open. He took aim on the door and waited. Not knowing who was on the other side, he was ready to fire as soon as he identified the target. When Hector peeked around the door in a hunkered position, Anthony relaxed and exhaled. The faint waxing of the Carabinieri sirens found its way into the room. He motioned for Hector to stop and remain at the door. Anthony approached the man closest to him and kicked the pistol out of reach. He stooped and felt for a pulse, then looked up at Hector and shook his head. Next, he moved to Ludwig and kicked his pistol clear. He was alive but unconscious. *Now where's the Fat Man?*

His pistol ready, Anthony stepped past Ludwig and proceeded toward the door. He hugged the wall as he moved, not knowing what to expect in the next room. After a deep breath, he took a quick look inside and saw Dydre's crumpled, inanimate body on the floor. He ducked back behind the cover of the wall, and then peeked around the corner again. Taking in a different quadrant of the room this time, he saw the Fat Man slumped in an overstuffed chair. Anthony entered the room and searched for any other shooters or hazards before checking Dydre. She was out cold. He felt his heart jump when he saw the Fat Man slowly look up at him, drooling from the corner of his mouth; his Montecristo Gran Corona smoldering on the floor in front of him. Blood stained the right shoulder of his shirt where a stray round had found its mark.

"You going to shoot me?" he asked, his face displaying defeat.

"It crossed my mind."

"How much do you want? I'll pay you—"

"Don't push it. I prefer you alive," Anthony said. "Just sit there and be quiet."

The sound of the Carabinieri sirens indicated their imminent arrival. Anthony turned back to check Dydre for wounds or broken bones. Her torn blouse revealed the red marks on her shoulder from Clay's stun gun. "You sure had a time of it, didn't you?" he said as he scooped her up and laid her on the couch. Hector entered, leading a Carabinieri major.

"Hector, where's the boy and Magda?" Anthony asked, looking up at him.

"Outside with the Carabinieri. They're fine," Hector said. "This is Maggiore de Carlo."

"Glad you could make it," Anthony said as he stood.

"At your service, sir!" he replied with a sharp salute and click of his heels.

"Take that one and call an ambulance for her," Anthony said, pointing first to Clay then to Dydre. "The one by the door is still alive too."

As the paramedics attended to Dydre, Anthony contacted the special operations cell to report that he had Dydre Rowyn and Clayborne Zsigmond. "The woman was worked over again by Zsigmond and his goons," he said. "She's unconscious. Zsigmond has a wound to the shoulder and is a bit incoherent right now. Maggiore de Carlo, Carabinieri, is in charge here. He is going to put a guard on the woman's room at the hospital."

"Very good," Assistant Secretary Newport said. "Mary Ellen has mined quite a bit of information on Zsigmond and she's not through yet. He's got an extensive network—no telling where it will lead us. I'm sure he'll lawyer up pretty quick and it will be tough to get much out of him. I still think our best bet is the woman. Let's see if we can get her to cooperate. Do what you need to get her to talk."

"Will do. Maggiore de Carlo is going to provide whatever help I need. I'll go to the hospital and stay with her. When she wakes up, I'll see what I can get. I don't think she'll be too difficult."

"BND wants to talk with Zsigmond," Newport said. "I'd like for us to talk to him before the Germans. I'm trying to get them to hold off, but they are being very persistent. See if you can get de Carlo to stall them."

"Will do."

The next morning, Dydre slowly opened her swollen, bloodshot eyes. Her head was sluggish and her body ached. The last thing she remembered was attacking Clay. It took a moment for her to realize she was in a hospital. Her eyes began to focus as she explored the room. She saw the fresh flowers. And then the face of Anthony. A smile spread across her face. "What...where am I?" she said, the drugs impairing her speech.

"The Bressanone Hospital." Anthony stepped closer and sat in the chair beside the bed.

"David...where's David!"

"He's fine. He's with your housekeeper. How do you feel?"

"Like a truck ran over me."

"Zsigmond played pretty rough."

"Your arm," she said, seeing the bandage around his left arm.

"Ludwig Stäbler. He was good but not good enough."

"Ludwig, oh yeah. Did you kill the bastard?"

"He's in ICU. Don't know if he'll make it."

"Clay—did you kill him?"

"No, the Carabinieri have him. You're safe now. Just get some rest. Then we can talk. I'll be here."

Dydre took Anthony's hand and gave it a gentle squeeze. "Thank you."

Bending over, Anthony kissed her on the cheek. "Get some rest."

"Who—"

"We'll talk later," Anthony said, his voice only a whisper.

Epilogue

A Week Later
Safe House
Potomac Falls, Virginia

A black Lincoln limousine turned onto the long asphalt drive and pulled up in front of the stately house on the Potomac River just outside of Washington, DC. As the car came to a stop, Anthony saw FBI Special Agent Alice Johnson walking toward the limousine. He shifted his attention back to Dydre and grasped her hand, then placed a small stone in her palm. "David told me to give you this. It will give you courage," he said.

She smiled as she closed her hand around the stone and thought of her son. David had accompanied her to the US as part of her agreement to give her testimony and cooperate, and it was time for her to be with him after all she had been through. While she was being interviewed, Anthony had made arrangements for someone to take care of him each day.

Anthony got out of the left side, as Alice opened the right rear door and said, "Let's go." Alice fought to suppress her disdain.

Dydre looked up at her with a piercing stare before getting out of the car. She walked next to Anthony.

Alice escorted them to a spacious and well-appointed dining room with large windows overlooking the grounds and the river beyond. Two cameras hung unobtrusively from the high ceiling. "There's water on the table, and if you would like coffee, I can have some brought in." she said, motioning to the large walnut conference table topped with a silver tray, pitcher, and six glasses. Four notepads with pens were on the table in front of each chair. Alice, stepping back, took her place by the door next to Hector.

A man of Greek descent, with neatly trimmed dark hair, entered the room carrying a brown, leather briefcase just as Assistant Secretary Newport walked to Dydre and extended his hand, "I'm Roger Newport and this is Alex Rokos," he said, gesturing toward the man. "You understand why you are here?"

"Yes," Dydre replied.

The formalities and introductions complete, Newport pointed toward the chairs and said, "Please be seated." He pressed a button on the small control box next to him to record the meeting, both video and voice. Rokos, a senior intelligence officer at the CIA, was well-built and physically fit. He sat down next to Newport and placed a file next to his notepad.

"Thank you for coming in," Rokos said. "I hope you are feeling much better now."

"Yes, thank you. I really didn't have much choice, did I?" Dydre noted that although he spoke in a cordial tone, his words sounded somewhat guarded.

"It's my understanding that you will cooperate with us in exchange for our protection. Is that correct?" Rokos asked, keeping his eyes trained on Dydre.

"Yes," she replied, looking first at Rokos then Newport. *Divulge little and gain a lot,* she thought. *This is down to survival.*

Over the next several days, Newport and Rokos interviewed Dydre, comparing her testimony with what BND extracted from Zsigmond when he was questioned. Her testimony would seal Zsigmond's fate. Discovery and verification of other activities was needed to ensure intelligence leaks in DOD were stopped. The days were long and, at times, intense.

Rokos was smooth. Slow at first, asking easy questions to verify her cooperation, he periodically interjected questions he already knew the answers to in order to confirm the truthfulness of Dydre's answers. His questioning seemed to meander from topic to topic, and some questions seemed harmless while others were more relevant—all leading her to questions or points yet to be discussed. Then he would hit her with a very pointed question. Many times, during the interview, he asked the same questions again but in different ways and then compared Dydre's answers for consistency. He evaluated not only what she said and how she said it but her mannerisms as well. By late afternoon the first day, the intensity of the questions increased as they became more specific and direct. Dydre occasionally objected to a question, but Rokos didn't allow her the luxury to opt out. It was all or nothing.

Early on in the interrogation, Dydre, more fearful of Zsigmond than these two men, began to have second thoughts about telling all she knew. Her challenge was trumped when Rokos opened the folder next to his notepad and retrieved an eight-by-ten copy of a photograph that identified Dydre. He slid it in front of her.

"Where did you get this?" she asked, looking at it with an expression of surprise.

"Tell us about the photo."

Dydre looked into his cold, dark eyes and shifted in her seat. "That's me with my head circled in red. How did you get this photo?" Always careful to avoid having her picture taken, she was unaware that any had been taken at that meeting.

This first piece of documented evidence unsettled her. She didn't know what evidence they had or where they were bluffing. Above all, she had no sense of what her fate was going to be. Rokos constantly kept her off guard, continuing his questions with no sign of any emotion.

"It was at a meeting with warlord Mohamed Farrah Aidid. That's him." Dydre pointed to one of the men. "It was in June of 1993 at his compound in Mogadishu."

Rokos's eyes commanded her to continue.

"Clay's got a big network." She leaned back and folded her arms across her chest.

"As you have been told, if you cooperate with us, we'll protect you," Newport said, holding his gaze on her.

"If I don't?" she said, with raised eyebrows. She knew Clay would kill her if he could.

"You'll spend the rest of your days in a federal prison, maximum security," Rokos said. "You won't see your son again. BND found a very interesting dossier on you in Zsigmond's safe when they searched his house." He reached into his briefcase and withdrew a leather-bound black journal. Looking directly into her brown eyes, he dropped it on the table in front of her. The color faded from her face at the mention of the dossier, and her posture slumped. She attempted to speak but stumbled on the words. It was the same dossier Zsigmond used and incessantly held over her head to keep her in line, reminding her of events, dates, places, and people. The book alone was enough to put her away for several lifetimes.

"You bastard! I'm dead either way. So why should I help you anymore?"

"Because it's the right thing to do," Newport said. "What if the death of your son's father was because of someone like you?" Newport's eyes seemed to drill into her soul.

"You fucking bastards!" Dydre's voice filled the room. She stood and walked around the table. Her face was flush and her fists clinched.

Alice and Hector exchanged a knowing look with each other, and moved in front of the door to preempt any attempt by Dydre to bolt. She took note of their action and returned to her chair with a glare toward Newport.

"If you cooperate, this dossier will get buried and never see the light of day again." Newport went on to remind her once again that she and David would be given protection and new identities in exchange for her full cooperation, which included testifying against Zsgmond at his trial.

She dropped her eyes and contemplated what he said. *David*, she thought. *He needs his mother. It's what I've always wanted. I'm so close.* She looked up at Anthony who gave her a slight nod.

"Clay was very good at what he did," she said. "He supplied weapons, intelligence, and mercenaries—all around the world. He worked with major defense contractors in the US, Canada, Germany, France, anyone who could pay his price. Based on intelligence and issues, he acted accordingly. He provided what others couldn't or wouldn't. That was his business. He was a war merchant. He exploited every opportunity to create a conflict or expand it. Then he would supply the arms and mercenaries necessary for that conflict."

When Rokos asked about the intelligence, she replied, "Most of it came from the US government, but he also had contacts in Canada, Germany, and France. There was always an arrogant politician willing to take Clay's money in exchange for information."

She explained that Zsigmond targeted the political stars. "The more powerful and senior a politician, the easier it was," she said. "Zsigmond was their ATM machine, contributing money to their reelection. In the beginning, there were no strings attached but as they returned to the trough, he started asking for small, insignificant favors. As they asked for more money, he discovered their weaknesses, got dirt on them and then used blackmail to keep them in line. Senator James Griffith was one such politician. Zsigmond also supported Griffith's vices of Cuban cigars, high-class prostitutes, and booze."

Agreeing to provide a list of Zsigmond's political contacts, Dydre glanced at Newport, then scribbled on her notepad a list of names from Canada, Germany, and France. Senator Griffith was the only one she knew of from the US.

The names she provided would initiate investigations and facilitate subsequent arrests in those countries.

When Rokos asked her about Zsigmond's involvement with warlord Mohamed Farrah Aidid, she told them that David McNair arranged the meeting. She confirmed that Zsigmond supplied him with mercenaries, weapons, ammunition, satellite imagery, intelligence, plans, and timing of the US invasion. All the information came from Senator Griffith and Steve Albritten.

Dydre answered their questions about Zsigmond, giving a brief synopsis of his background going back more than twenty years as an arms broker. "Clay was licensed and approved as a consultant, supplier of arms, trainers, and services to the countries he worked in. Just like other companies in this particular market. After Johanna's death, he didn't care which side he supplied. All he cared about was money and power.

"I was vulnerable and naïve. He used me. I finally realized I was in so deep with him that I would be the fall guy if I crossed him or if things went wrong. He would simply kill me and David."

Late in the third day both Newport and Rokos were satisfied with her cooperation and the information she supplied.

Newport withdrew a sheet of paper from a folder beneath his notepad, and signed a prepared letter to Dydre stating that she was being recommended for the Federal Witness Security Program. He slid the paper in front of her and summarized its contents.

She leaned back in her chair during his summary. Exhausted and emotionally drained, she began to think about her new life. Newport's final words, informing her that Anthony would continue to escort her until the US Marshals Service transferred her to a secure location, barely registered. She nodded acknowledgment of his caveat.

As the limo drove out the long asphalt drive, Dydre's thoughts went immediately to David. *It will be just as I have imagined, David and me, together, mother and son. No Clay, no fanatics, no mercenaries, no killing. Just me and David.* Anthony began to speak, but she was so lost in her own private world that she made no attempt to respond.

Also by Patrick Parker

Treasures of the Fourth Reich

A Titian, a Bruegel, and a panel from the Amber Room—vanished during WWII—come to life again.

A string of deaths drags Dix Connor and his art expert wife into a suspense-filled game of cat & mouse with a clandestine organization dating back to WWII.

It was one of the greatest crimes of the century.... Grand museums and families lost countless valuables and works of art to Nazi lootings in what has been called "the rape of Europa." Parker's story begins just outside the Bavarian salt mines as the American and Russian armies are closing in. Amid the chaos, SS officers scramble to hide ill-gotten treasures that will finance the "Fourth Reich." Only a precious journal detailing an inventory of treasure caches around the Tirol holds a clue.

Forty plus years later, the hunt for Europe's lost art falls to a husband and wife team who become entangled in this web of stolen treasures. Dix and Maria Connor face down a secret and deadly network trafficking in Titians, Bruegels and remnants of Peter the Great's magnificent Amber Room. From northeast Italy to Brussels, these amateur detectives risk everything to right the wrongs of history. Crisscross Europe's past and present in this thinking man's action novel.

The lust for loot crosses paths with history's ghosts in this high-octane thriller.

Get your copy here: http://amzn.to/1vNKzu6

Acknowledgments

I want to thank my wife and best friend, Carole, for her confidence and support. You have been my best critic and provided invaluable input.

Donna Andrews and her Reston writers group. You are a great group and helped me to bring my story to life. Through the many writings, critiques, edits and rewrites, thank you. I appreciate your candor, support and confidence.

Bob Sabasteanski, a big thank you for your critique, suggestions and attention to detail. My go to guy for a reality check and a weapons expert. Thank you.

To Patricia Peters, a superb editor, who is terrific! You very quickly understood what the story was about and took it to the next level. Your attention to detail kept me straight.

Stefanie Stevenson, you took the story to a graphic form with a fantastic cover. I appreciate the counsel you gave me. It has been a real pleasure to work with you on this project. Thank you.

About Patrick Parker

Patrick accepted the challenge from his wife and wrote *Treasures of the Fourth Reich*. He and his family lived in Italy for five years of his Army career and traveled extensively during his off duty time. Many hours were spent visiting museums, castles, cathedrals, churches and historical sites in Europe. The history of the Nazi lootings became the catalyst for his first novel. He met a fascinating art dealer in Panama just prior to the invasion and who helped form the basis for his character Maria in that story.

After retiring from the Army, Patrick worked in the defense industry for fifteen years. While pursuing his writing, he developed the concept of *War Merchant*, which is taken from his corporate experience and coupled with his military background. After retiring a second time, *War Merchant* came to life.

Patrick, now settled in Texas, enjoys writing and is well into his next suspense filled novel.

For questions and comments click:
Facebook: http://on.fb.me/1pnfAoM
Google+: http://bit.ly/1y8cCI5
Amazon Author's Page: http://amzn.to/1izsnBH

Did you like *War Merchant*?
Please take few minutes to let everyone know by posting a review. This link will take you to the reviews page http://amzn.to/1tUlqxd. People get to know what you are reading and I will be forever grateful to you.

Best Regards,

Patrick Parker

Made in the USA
Las Vegas, NV
02 February 2023

66740161R00152